KU-077-493

For Anna and Max

MURDER AT
BLETCHLEY PARK

By Christina Koning

MURDER AT BLETCHLEY PARK

CHRISTINA KONING

Allison & Busby Limited
11 Wardour Mews
London W1F 8AN
allisonandbusby.com
First published in Great Britain by Allison & Busby in 2023.

Copyright © 2023 by CHRISTINA KONING

The moral right of the author is hereby asserted in accordance with the
Copyright, Designs and Patents Act 1988.

All characters and events in this publication,
other than those clearly in the public domain,
are fictitious and any resemblance to actual persons,
living or dead, is purely coincidental.

All rights reserved. No part of this publication may be reproduced,
stored in a retrieval system, or transmitted, in any form or by
any means without the prior written permission of the publisher,
nor be otherwise circulated in any form of binding or cover.
other than that in which it is published and without a similar
condition being imposed on the subsequent buyer.
A CIP catalogue record for this book is available from
the British Library.

First Edition

ISBN 978-0-7490-3058-2

Typeset in 11/16 pt Sabon LT Pro by Typo•glyphix.

MIX
Paper | Supporting
responsible forestry
FSC® C171272

By choosing this product, you help take care of the world's forests.
Learn more: www.fsc.org

Printed and bound by
CPI Group (UK) Ltd, Croydon, CR0 4YY

Chapter One

Cambridge was utterly silent and, he knew, as dark as it was quiet – the one condition, which was the blackout, bringing about the other. Not that the darkness made much difference to Frederick Rowlands. But it had certainly cast a spell upon the streets of this university town, as it had upon those of the capital, from which he had travelled earlier that day. There, the blackout had the effect of making sounds seem louder, as they did in thick fog, so that the roar of a motorbus or the clip-clopping of a rag-and-bone man's horse seemed to come at you unmuffled by other sounds, such as the tramp of feet, or the murmur of a rush-hour crowd. Because, after three months of continuous night-time bombing, London's streets were starting to get the deserted feel Rowlands recalled from the last war. It wasn't quite the feeling that a curfew had been imposed (it hadn't – or not officially), more that, if you didn't have anywhere particular to go, you oughtn't to be out. New sounds had also been added to the more familiar ones of traffic and people's voices. The icy tinkle of broken glass, being swept up after a night's raid; the sudden crash, as a building collapsed. The smell of the city had changed, too: now a smoky fog composed of brick dust and smashed plaster hung in the air, sometimes overlaid with fouler smells, of broken drains, and dank cellars full of rotting things, now exposed to view.

'I think we must be nearly there,' said his companion, breaking into these thoughts. Margaret sounded as if she didn't quite believe this, however. After she'd met his train at the station, the two of them had agreed that it would be quicker to walk into the town centre, rather than to wait for a bus, which was likely to be crowded with home-going workers at this time of day. So, having turned out of Station Road, they'd set off down Hills Road and thence along Regent Street and St Andrew's Street – not in itself a great distance, but it was funny how much further it seemed in the dark, said Rowlands's daughter, adding, with a little laugh, that it was a good thing he'd only brought an overnight bag.

They turned at last along Downing Street, and reached the turning into Free School Lane.

'It's just down here to the left,' said Rowlands. 'If memory serves.' Which, in his case, it usually did – memory having to stand in for the sense of sight. Not that it would be of much help in this pitch blackness, he supposed, if one *could* see. Through the darkness to their left, he knew, loomed the magnificent late Perpendicular Gothic edifice of King's College Chapel – built by a succession of Tudor kings and eventually completed by the notorious wife-killer, for the glory of his immortal soul. Rowlands's visual memories of the chapel, and indeed of Cambridge as a whole, went back to before the last war, when he'd come here as a representative of the publishing firm for which he'd worked at the time. He remembered wandering around the great building, marvelling at the splendours of its sixteenth-century fan-vaulting and Flemish stained glass, in the half-hour before his meeting at Heffers Bookshop in Petty Cury.

'Here we are,' he said, as they reached the junction with Bene't Street. 'I remember the cobblestones.' These belonged to the courtyard of the Eagle – that well-known Cambridge hostelry, beloved of many generations of undergraduates. It was several years since Rowlands had last visited it, in the company of his old friend, the artist Percy Loveless. When last heard of, Loveless was in Canada – stranded there for the duration – having arrived in that country just before the outbreak of hostilities, in order to carry out a portrait commission. 'This place is as cold as the ninth circle of Hell,' he had written, with uncharacteristic gloom. 'If anywhere could make me long for the dreary reaches of Notting Hill, then Toronto in midwinter is that place . . .'

Even if the feel of cobblestones underfoot hadn't alerted Rowlands to the fact that they'd reached their destination, the sound of voices would have done so: it was only just past opening time, and yet the pub was already filling up with its regular clientele of rowdy students, glad to have finished with lectures for the day, as well as some older men – whether dons or college porters wasn't always easy to determine – also taking a break from their labours.

'What'll you have?' said Rowlands to his daughter as they reached the bar. 'A nice glass of sherry?'

'Daddy!'

'Isn't that what you university types usually drink?' he said innocently.

'No, thanks,' was the reply. 'I'll have half a bitter, please.'

'Right you are.' He gave the order, and exchanged a few pleasantries with the barmaid – a friendly soul, hailed by all and sundry as Doris. 'Busy tonight,' said Rowlands, for something to say, as the young woman filled their glasses at the taps.

'Oh, it'll be busier still tonight, with all the RAF boys coming in,' she replied, in the soft accent of the region.

'I say, Doris my love, hurry up and get us some beers, will you?' said a bold young man, standing behind Rowlands.

'You mind your manners,' said Doris, then to Rowlands: 'That'll be one-and-ninepence, sir, if you please.'

Rowlands paid her, and then he and Margaret carried their glasses over to a table in the corner of the back bar, which was quieter than the rest of the pub.

'So,' he said, having taken an appreciative draught of his pint. 'What's all this about your giving up your studies?'

Margaret didn't say anything for a moment. Her father got the impression she was choosing her words carefully. 'I've told you – I'm simply deferring my research until the war's over. Lots of people are doing it.'

'I suppose you'll be telling me next that you want to join up?' he said.

Again, there was a slight hesitation before she replied, 'Not exactly.'

'Then what *are* you intending to do?' He kept his voice

level, but really it was exasperating – his brilliant daughter, who'd delighted them all by winning a scholarship to Cambridge to study mathematics, and then had achieved further distinction after graduation by being offered a junior research fellowship, was now proposing to give it all up, to do . . . what? He took another pull of his beer.

'I . . . I can't tell you,' said Margaret.

'But surely,' he persisted, 'research was what you wanted to do? Or have you changed your mind?'

'No . . . it's not that. I still want to do it – more than anything else in the world. It's just that I'm going to have to defer it until the war's over . . . Oh, don't ask me to explain!' she cried suddenly, sounding so miserable that Rowlands instantly resolved to drop his inquisitorial tone.

'It's all right,' he said. 'Let's talk about something else . . . How's that young man of yours, these days?'

'No, that's not fair,' she said, lowering her voice – although as far as Rowlands could tell, there was nobody sitting close enough to overhear. 'You *deserve* an explanation. At least,' she added, 'as far as I can give one. I've been offered a job. In . . . in a government department. But that's all I can say, I'm afraid.'

'All very hush-hush, eh?' said her father. '"Careless talk costs lives" and so forth?'

'Yes.'

'Then you needn't say another thing. I'll tell your mother she's not to ask you any more questions, either.'

'Thanks, Daddy.' The relief in her voice was all too apparent. 'And he's *not* my "young man", as you call him,' she added, in a lighter tone. 'We're just friends. Why, Jonty's almost like a brother.'

11

Rowlands wondered if Jonathan Simkins, the son of family friends, felt the same. Wisely, he said nothing.

'As a matter of fact, he's joining the RAF,' Margaret went on. 'His engineering course at Durham has finished, anyway, and so he's decided to waste no more time.'

'Very public-spirited of him,' said Rowlands, although his heart sank at the thought of all these young men and women who were so eager to join the war effort. Memories of his own youth, and the way he and his Pals had rushed to join up in 1914, to fight for what they believed was a noble cause, could not but cast a long shadow. He shrugged away the thought. 'So I take it,' he said, picking up the thread of an earlier conversation, 'that you'd rather your mother and I didn't come and meet you at the end of term?'

'Yes,' said Margaret. 'That is . . . I won't be coming home when I leave college. The . . . the job I've mentioned requires me to start straight away. I'll be going into diggings.'

'I see.' He wondered if Edith would. He foresaw that he would have his work cut out, explaining all this to her, when he got back to London the following day. It had been his wife's suggestion that the two of them should go and collect their daughter from Cambridge at the end of the Michaelmas term that had set the whole thing off. A neighbour, with a son at Downing, had offered to take them in his Austin, and to bring them back, with the two young people and their luggage, the following day. They would share the petrol costs, of course. This agreeable plan had brought forth an agitated telephone call from Margaret, in response to her mother's letter, in which she (Margaret) had said that it wouldn't be any use, their coming to St Gertrude's, because she wasn't going to be at college more than another week; nor would she be returning after the Christmas holidays.

This had been followed – at Edith's insistence – by a telephone conversation between Rowlands and Miss Phillips, the mistress of St Gertrude's, which had left him, if anything, more mystified than he was before. They had been informed by their daughter (he said) that she would be leaving university – apparently for good – in a few days' time. He wondered what the reason for this might be. Was the college dissatisfied with her work? In which case, shouldn't the matter be discussed, to see if it might be resolved? At which point, he was interrupted by the unexpected sound of the mistress's laughter.

'No, no,' she said. 'It's nothing like that, I assure you. You and Mrs Rowlands can set your minds at rest, where Margaret is concerned. In fact,' Beryl Phillips went on, 'we at St Gertrude's are delighted with Margaret's work. She's become a real asset to the college.'

'Then why on earth . . . ?' he began, but again, she silenced him.

'I'm afraid I can't discuss this on the telephone, Mr Rowlands. Perhaps you'd care to come and talk things over in person? Let me see . . .' She must have consulted a diary. 'I have some time available tomorrow . . . or later in the week, if you prefer?' They'd fixed an appointment for the following morning. In order to be in good time for this (given the erratic nature of the trains at present) and so that he could see his daughter beforehand, Rowlands had elected to travel up on the previous evening, and to

13

spend the night in one of the college guest rooms. Which was how he came to be sitting over a pint of Ruddles in the Eagle's back bar, and feeling only a little the wiser as to how his daughter would be spending her time in the months that were to follow.

'We should drink up,' she said, in the faintly anxious tone that seemed to have become habitual. 'If we want to get the bus back in time for Hall.'

Rowlands took another sip of his beer. He remembered those dinners at St Gertrude's from the last time – now five years ago – he'd been staying at the college, during what had turned out to be a murder investigation. The memory, like everything else associated with that troubling episode, wasn't an especially pleasant one – not least where the food was concerned. Female academics, unlike their male counterparts, had to put up with distinctly unexciting fare.

'I rather thought,' he said quickly, 'that we'd have dinner out. I don't very often get the chance to treat my favourite junior research fellow.' Although it occurred to him as he said it that, as of next week, he could no longer consider her as such.

To his relief, she didn't seem to notice his slip. 'That'd be awfully nice,' she said. 'If it wouldn't be too expensive, we could try the Varsity. I've heard they sometimes have roast chicken.'

The rest of the evening passed pleasantly enough. They managed to get a table at the establishment Margaret had mentioned – which was a bit of luck, she said, since otherwise the choice was between steak and kidney pudding at the Baron of Beef, or shepherd's pie at the British Empire restaurant in Petty Cury, neither of which would have matched the culinary delights on offer here. Roast chicken, as it happened, was 'off', but steak was available – a rare treat, in the first year of the war. With it, there was mashed potato and green peas (tinned), with half a bottle of Burgundy to wash it down. At her father's insistence, Margaret had the pudding – a treacle sponge she pronounced 'almost as good as Mother's', while he himself had the cheese, and a brandy to follow. The meal, although unexceptional to his mind, was far superior to the one they'd have had in Hall – 'Watery stew, with prunes and custard for afters,' said Margaret, with a shudder. No more was said about her plans for the immediate future, which, Rowlands sensed, came as a relief to her; Edith, he knew, wouldn't have let it go quite so readily.

Instead, they talked of other things: the driving lessons Edith was taking ('Although how we'll be able to run a car, let alone afford the petrol for it, is anybody's guess,' said her husband); how Anne was getting on in Oxford, where the Slade had established temporary quarters at the Ruskin School of Drawing and Fine Art; and Joan's prowess in the school hockey team: 'Nice to have *one* sporty child, at least,' said Rowlands, savouring his brandy. Although she contributed her fair share to this conversation, Rowlands couldn't help feeling that his eldest daughter's thoughts were elsewhere. 'Promise me one thing, Meg,' he said, when he'd paid the bill and summoned a taxi to take them out to St Gertrude's. 'That if there's anything worrying you about this new arrangement of yours, you'll let me know.'

'I can't . . .'

'I know, I know. You're not supposed to talk about it.

But you can at least let your mother and me know you're all right. A postcard when you get there will do.'

'All right,' she said, after a moment. 'I'll try.'

Next morning, after breakfast, Rowlands strolled in the grounds of the college, to smoke a cigarette and think over what to say to his wife about the situation. Margaret said she had some things to see to – library books to return, and notes to leave for her supervisors. So Rowlands had time to kill before his meeting with the mistress at half past ten. Fortunately, the St Gertrude's grounds were extensive, and the weather (in late November) too cold to tempt the undergraduates outside – always supposing that any of them had leisure to stroll about the woods and meadows surrounding the college, and were not presently engrossed in study. At this thought, he felt a pang of sadness at the choice his daughter had made. What exactly that choice entailed he couldn't be sure, although his (albeit limited) encounters with the secret service in past years gave him an inkling of what Margaret's future work might involve.

He was so absorbed in these reflections that it took him a moment to realise that somebody was trying to attract his attention, by vigorously tapping on one of the first-floor windows beneath which his perambulations had brought him. A moment later, the window in question was flung up, and that somebody stuck her head out. 'Hi! Fred! Fred Rowlands! I thought it must be you.'

'Hello, Maud.'

'Come up to my office, will you? No, on second thoughts, wait there. I'll come and get you.' As he waited, stamping his feet to keep himself warm, Rowlands groaned inwardly. Fond as he was of Maud Rickards, she was the last person he'd wanted to run into on this particular visit. Quite how much she knew of his reasons for being here – or of his daughter's predicament – he could only surmise. One thing was certain: he didn't feel like discussing it with her – not least because she was Edith's oldest friend. If he was going to find it difficult to persuade his wife to be discreet on this matter of Margaret's new role, it would become doubly so if Maud added fuel to the fire.

But, not for the first time, it appeared that he had misjudged her. 'Do come in out of the cold,' she said. 'I wonder that you can stand it. Such a raw morning! I've a nice fire in my office, you'll be glad to know. You've time for a cup of coffee before your meeting with the mistress.'

So she knew about that, then? thought Rowlands. Well, that was hardly surprising. As college bursar, it was Miss Rickards's business to know everything about the running of the college – including, no doubt, the fact that one of its brightest research students was shortly to leave, to take up an unspecified post at an unnamed destination. Yes, Maud Rickards must have known all this, but you wouldn't have guessed it, as, having ushered him into her room ('Take the armchair next to the fire – it's the most comfortable . . .'), she busied herself with brewing a fresh pot of her famously good coffee.

'How's Edith?' she asked, setting out cups and saucers on a tray and placing this, with the stainless-steel percolator that was her pride and joy, on the low table in front of the fire.

'She's very well,' he replied – at which Maud laughed.

'Silly question. Edie's always well. And how's Anne? Enjoying Oxford?'

'Very much, from what she says in her letters,' replied Rowlands.

'That's good,' said the bursar vaguely. 'Although I still think it's a pity that she didn't try for St Gertrude's. She could always have carried on with her drawing in her spare time.'

To which Rowlands diplomatically said nothing, although this was far from being Anne's own view of the situation. Ever since the visit to Paris she had made, aged sixteen, and what it had revealed to her of the bohemian life, she had been determined to become a painter – or, failing that, a best-selling novelist. Academic life played no part in this vision.

The conversation turned to other things – Miss Rickards's walking tour of the Scottish Highlands the previous July ('It was supposed to have been Italy, but I don't suppose I'll be visiting *that* country again for a while.') and the conversion of the new St Dunstan's building at Ovingdean, opened only two years before, into a hospital and training centre for newly blinded casualties of the war.

'So where are you going to put the existing residents?' enquired Miss Rickards, refilling her own cup and that of her guest. 'It must be rather hard on the long-term men, to have to turn out so soon after moving into that nice new accommodation.'

'Oh, we'll find places for them, never fear,' he said. 'There's a building at Church Stretton we're in the process of adapting. And most of our chaps understand perfectly well that priority has to be given to the new cases. Why, some of 'em have got sons in the forces, and so . . .' He didn't need to finish the sentence.

'Quite,' said Maud Rickards drily. 'I think everyone knows that sacrifices have to be made.'

This oblique reference to what was uppermost in Rowlands's mind – his daughter's decision to leave St Gertrude's – was all that was said on the subject, until, a few minutes before eleven, he made a move to go.

'I'll walk as far as the mistress's office with you,' said the bursar. 'I know it isn't the first time you've been here, but finding one's way in college can be confusing.' Rowlands, recalling the seemingly endless corridors that were a feature of the place, was grateful for her offer. She gave him her arm.

'It'll be all right,' she said – and he guessed it wasn't only the forthcoming interview to which she referred. 'You'll see.'

The mistress's rooms were to be found at the end of a corridor on the first floor of the old wing. Rowlands and his companion were a few paces away, when the door opened, and someone came out – perhaps 'swept out' was a better description, thought Rowlands, feeling the brush of the man's voluminous doctor's gown, as the latter passed him.

'Good morning to you!' sang out this individual, to which Miss Rickards returned a suitably cordial reply. Footsteps tapped briskly away along the corridor.

'Now, what's the famous Aubrey Blake doing here, I wonder?' said the bursar, *sotto voce*. 'He doesn't often venture out of Trinity – let alone as far as St Gertrude's.'

'Blake?' said Rowlands. 'I don't think I . . .'

'Oh, you won't have heard of him!' said Maud Rickards. 'Although he fancies himself a bit of a star in his own field. Modern languages. His *real* interest is in art history, but of course we don't consider that a subject here. I gather his lectures on French painting are much admired by the aesthetic element in Cambridge. All young men, of course,' she added with a sniff. 'I can't imagine what brings him to *this* college . . . Well, here we are,' she went on, as they reached the mistress's door. 'Good to see you, Fred. Give my love to Edie, won't you?'

'I will,' he said, waiting until she had walked away before announcing his presence with a soft double-knock.

'Mr Rowlands. How very nice to see you again!' said the mistress, as she opened the door of her office – if that was the right word for what he recalled from previous visits to be a large and well-appointed sitting room. 'Do come in.' She guided him to a chair opposite her own in front of the fire. 'Can I offer you something? A cup of coffee, perhaps?' He explained that he had just come from Miss Rickards's room. 'Ah, so you'll have had some of her splendid Italian brew? In which case, how about a cigarette? I've Turkish or Virginian.' He accepted one of the latter, and she lit it for him, and then lit one for herself. 'I hope you and Mrs Rowlands are keeping well?' she said, when this little ceremony had been performed. 'It was so nice to see you both at the graduation ceremony in June. Although,' she added apologetically, 'one of the disadvantages of this job is that one never does get to talk to people for very long.'

'No,' he said. The meeting to which she referred had occurred during his last visit to St Gertrude's – one of the few occasions he'd been to the college, in fact, since that previous, ill-fated, time five years before, when he and Edith had come as guests of Maud Rickards to an end-of-term garden party. Of course, at that time, Margaret hadn't yet applied to the college; it had been the mistress herself who'd suggested that Rowlands's eldest daughter, then only fifteen, should apply for a scholarship when the time came. With the school's encouragement, she had done just that. And just look where all that hard work had ended up, sighed Rowlands.

As if she guessed something of what was passing through his mind, Miss Phillips said, 'You wanted to talk to me about Margaret?'

'Yes. That is . . .' He hesitated. 'I gather from talking to my daughter earlier that I'm not supposed to ask questions about . . . well, whatever it is she's made up her mind to do.'

'She's told you that much, has she?'

'And no more than that,' he said. 'In fact, I can honestly say that I'm almost as much in the dark as I was before . . . which is saying something,' he added with a smile.

If she got the joke, it wasn't obvious from the gravity with which she replied. 'One thing I *can* tell you is that your Margaret is a very clever young woman. As I mentioned when we spoke on the telephone, she's set to become one of our most outstanding alumnae. We've high hopes that she'll eventually come back to us.'

'"Eventually" being the key word,' he said.

'Well, yes . . .' He couldn't see the shrug with which Beryl Phillips accompanied the words, but it was implicit in her tone. 'This war,' she said, 'has thrown everything out of kilter.'

'Wars do,' he replied. 'And I know you can't tell me any more about what Margaret will be doing. Although I think the very fact that it's such a secret tells its own story.'

'It's work of national importance on which she'll be engaged,' said Miss Phillips. 'You – and your wife – have a right to know that much.'

'Thank you,' he said. 'It's rather what I thought.'

So that, it seemed, was that. Rowlands took his leave of his daughter ('At any rate, we'll be seeing you at Christmas, won't we?' – 'I don't know, Daddy. I hope so.') and got his taxi to the station. In spite of Miss Phillips's words of reassurance, it was with a heavy heart that he left the university town. What depressed him wasn't just the thought of how he'd explain things to Edith, as the fact that he now had a pretty good idea of the kind of world to which their daughter would now belong. The little experience he'd had of the secret service had been acquired through his relations with one member of it in particular: the woman who called herself Iris Barnes, and with whose path his had crossed on several occasions since their first meeting in London more than ten years before. From her, he had learnt as much, if not more, than he wanted to know about the workings of the world of espionage.

He wondered now, as he stood in the corridor of the packed train, whether it might make sense to try to get in touch with Miss Barnes again, then realised that he had no idea how to do this. Besides which, he thought wryly, Margaret would never forgive him if he went behind her back to find out what exactly it was that constituted the 'work of national importance' on which she'd be engaged.

As the train rattled over the points outside Bishop's Stortford, he puzzled it out: what in Heaven's name could the spies want with his gentle Margaret? She was only twenty-one – and hardly cast in the same worldly-wise mould as Iris Barnes. The latter, to Rowlands's certain knowledge, was fluent in several languages, as well as being a dab hand with a .38, whereas Meg . . . 'One of our most outstanding alumnae,' Miss Phillips had called her. So was *that* the reason she'd been chosen for this particular kind of work? He found it hard to imagine how a superior knowledge of mathematics might be an asset to the war effort.

Chapter Two

Liverpool Street station was a teeming hive of human activity of every variety, from the military (the station was the departure point for RAF and army bases in Cambridgeshire and Norfolk) to the domestic. As he got off the train, a large woman with a clipboard barged into him (he felt the impact of both woman and clipboard), evidently too preoccupied with her task of marshalling a band of evacuees to notice a blind man – even one provided, as he was, with a white-painted walking stick.

'Come along, children!' she bawled. 'Form up in a line – that's right! Now quick march! You don't want us to miss our train, do you?' At once a chorus of wails started up – these emanated as much from the mothers who had come to see their infants off, as from the infants themselves, it seemed. Smiling and apologising, Rowlands made his way as best he could through this clamorous throng, and reached the ticket barrier at last.

Most people, it was true, got out of his way once they

saw the stick. It had been Edith who'd insisted he should start using it; up until a few months ago, he'd managed without. Then, on a visit to friends in Ireland the previous year, he'd borrowed an ordinary walking-stick from his host, to help him over rough countryside. The habit had stuck. Since the early days of his blindness, Rowlands always hated being perceived as 'different', but Edith had persuaded him in the end to put these feelings aside. 'It isn't fair to other people,' she'd said. '*I* know you can manage without a stick – but how do *they* know that? And it'll stop you walking into things when I'm not there to guide you.' All of which was true enough – he'd come a cropper more times than he cared to admit, by simply acting as if he wasn't blind.

So, holding the stick a little way in front of him, he moved through the crowd in the main concourse, and got himself to the head of the steps that led to the Underground.

'Give you a hand, mate?' said a cheery voice next to him; the next moment, he felt his arm gripped just above the elbow, and the uniformed man (the peculiar smell of khaki serge was one Rowlands recalled from his own army days) piloted him down the stairs, talking all the way. 'On your way home, are you? That's the ticket. I'm off to see the wife myself. Two days' leave, and then we're for it. Won't tell us where we've been posted, o' course . . .' His companion insisted on seeing Rowlands all the way down the escalator and onto the Metropolitan line platform before taking himself off ('I'm going in the other direction. Cheery-bye, old son').

The Underground train was packed, as usual, even though it wasn't yet the rush hour, and Rowlands stood most of the way, refusing the offer of a seat from another considerate member of the public, and only accepting the offer of someone else's arm when alighting at Baker Street because he didn't want to offend the chap. With what remained to him of sight (he could tell light from dark, and make out shapes of things), and with his excellent hearing, he'd been used to getting around without asking for help more than was absolutely necessary. Now, with the stick as his 'badge', he often found help thrust upon him.

It was a relief to leave behind Marylebone Road and its roar of traffic – buses, taxis and heavy goods vehicles, mainly. It struck him that the number of private cars on the road had declined in recent months – the result of petrol rationing, no doubt. Regent's Park, too, was quieter than usual, owing to the inclement weather. As he left the Outer Circle for the gravel path that would lead him, by a circuitous route, to the building he and his fellow St Dunstaners referred to as The Lodge, he reflected on what he had learnt that day. One thing was certain: he couldn't discuss the matter, even with his nearest and dearest. That was the thing about the secret world – it imposed its silence upon all who came into contact with it. This fact was put to the test rather sooner than Rowlands had expected. He had just arrived in his office, and sent Miss Symonds for lunch, when the phone rang.

'Ah, you're back. Good,' said a familiar voice. 'I was wondering if I might pick your brains about something.'

'Hello, Major. Yes, of course, I'll come over straight away.'

'My wife wondered if you'd had lunch? Only she says

you're welcome to join us, if not. Just pot-luck, you know.'

'Thanks. Please tell her I'd like that very much,' said Rowlands, and rang off. A few minutes later, he was crossing the wide lawn that lay between his office – located in the mansion's former stable-block – and the main building, once a private residence, which was now St Dunstan's HQ. The larger part of this had been converted during the last war for residential use; the main rooms – library, ballroom, sitting and dining rooms – being reserved for communal activities. Now that most of the long-term residents had been moved out of London for their own safety, there remained a core of thirty or so – mostly employed in and about the grounds and workshops. As he passed, Wilf Thackeray, one of the gardeners, called out a greeting, which Rowlands returned, adding a cheery, 'Cold enough for you?'

'It is that, Mr Rowlands. Not that I mind a bit of cold. It's the damp as gets to you.'

In the cosy dining room of the Frasers' flat ('Quite a squeeze to get eight around this table, but three or four's just right,' said Lady Fraser), Rowlands felt himself relax for the first time that day. The 'pot-luck' turned out to be a very good mutton stew; remembering Margaret's disdain for the 'watery stew' on offer at St Gertrude's the night before made Rowlands smile. *This* lunch, modest as it was, was doubtless considerably better than the standard fare of a women's college operating on a wartime budget. Although of course, he reminded himself, Margaret would soon no longer be in a position to complain about this or any other aspect of college life. At this unwelcome thought, Rowlands must have frowned, for Iris Fraser, always sensitive to the moods of others, said, 'Haven't seen you in ages, Fred. Edith's well, I hope – and the girls?'

'All well, thanks.'

'Ian tells me you've been up to Cambridge to see Margaret.'

'Yes.' At once Rowlands felt uncomfortable, not knowing how much he could or should divulge about the reason for his visit. 'She . . . she's decided to defer her studies for the time being and get a job,' he said. He supposed it would do as a form of words to cover the situation.

'Only what I'd have expected of her,' said Lady Fraser. 'So many young people are wanting to do their bit for the war effort.'

'Very commendable,' agreed her husband. Neither of them asked what the 'job' entailed. The conversation moved on to other things. 'This is really a matter for the next committee meeting,' said the major. 'But I wanted your opinion, Fred . . .' It was already apparent, he went on to say, that this was going to be a different kind of war from the one in which they had both served, over twenty years before. *That* had been predominantly a war of armies in the field, facing each other across a militarised landscape of trenches and redoubts. The injuries suffered – including those to the face and eyes – had been consistent with this. *Now* the theatre of war had become much wider, encompassing not only the battlefield, but civilian terrain. 'We feel . . . that is, I feel . . . that St Dunstan's needs to open its doors to a broader clientele,' said Sir Ian. 'We've always been an organisation that catered mainly to servicemen.'

'And servicewomen,' put in Iris Fraser.

'And servicewomen, too, of course. Now we think . . . *I* think . . . we ought to offer our assistance to the wider community – the police and fire services, civil defence, the women's services, naturally . . .'

'I agree,' said Rowlands.

'Good. Thought you might,' said the major. 'We'll still remain principally a service for soldiers, sailors and airmen . . . and their female counterparts,' he added hastily. 'But if this war becomes total, as I fear it might, then . . .' He let the sentence tail off. They were all silent a moment. Both men, and Iris Fraser, in her days as a VAD, had seen enough of what war could do to be able to envisage what 'total war' might mean.

'On a lighter note,' went on Ian Fraser, 'I've been asked to give a talk on Getting About in the Dark, for the benefit of people coping with the blackout. Apparently, rather a lot of Londoners have been having accidents – falling down area steps and walking into lamp posts – through not being able to see where they're going. Extraordinary!' All three laughed. 'Any suggestions as to what I might recommend, as safety procedures to follow during the blackout?'

'Well, counting steps between one's starting point and destination, for a start,' said Rowlands. 'It's how I learnt to get about London by myself in the early days.'

'Holding on to banisters,' put in Lady Fraser. 'Or a friendly arm, if offered.'

'Leaning back slightly when walking,' went on Rowlands. 'Watching out for the edges of things . . .'

'Doors, especially,' said the major. 'Good Lord! The black eyes I gave myself at first, before I got used to *that* rule.'

'Using one's *other* senses as much as possible,' said Rowlands. 'Hearing, mainly – but also touch, and sense of smell.'

'Excellent,' said Fraser. 'Iris, you'll make a note of all these for me, won't you? Funny, isn't it?' he added. 'The blackout's made us all equal in that respect, hasn't it? Now *we're* the ones helping the sighted, instead of the other way around.'

After his pleasant lunch with the Frasers, the rest of the afternoon passed quickly enough for Rowlands. As well as the extra paperwork generated by the adaptation of the Ovingdean centre into a hospital (a new wing, complete with operating theatre, was presently being constructed) there was also the day-to-day administrative work to do with running a large organisation. Since the outbreak of war, it had become clear that changes would have to be made to that organisation's output. St Dunstan's men whose skills had been directed, say, towards the weaving of baskets and the manufacture of doormats might now be conscripted into the making of camouflage nets. And so Rowlands dictated letters to the said departments and to the War Office about the nets, and signed those Miss Symonds typed up – although if push came to shove, and his admirably efficient secretary decided she'd be more usefully employed in one of the services, he'd be perfectly capable of typing his own letters. It was one of the first skills he'd been taught when he arrived at St Dunstan's in 1917. But for the moment, he was grateful for those nimble fingers of hers, which flew over the keys of her machine with impressive speed. Yes, he'd be sorry to lose her, if it came to that. It occurred to him as he signed the last letter of the day, ready for Miss Symonds to stamp and address it, that he didn't really know her very well. She'd only been with him six months – the previous incumbent, Miss Collins, having left to get married the week before her bridegroom was posted overseas. He wondered if perhaps this girl – *Jean, wasn't it?* – had a young man in the services, too; it was something he ought to find out, he thought.

Edith, although evidently glad to see him back from Cambridge, was strangely reticent about the matter that had taken him there. Rowlands assumed that it was the presence of the other members of the household – his mother-in-law, Helen, and his youngest daughter, Joan – that prevented her from speaking. When they were alone together after supper, Helen having retired to her room to write letters, and Joan occupied with homework, he braced himself for what was coming. Which turned out to be surprisingly little.

'Maud telephoned,' said Edith. She was busy knitting something – a sock, he guessed, since there had been an appeal at church for local women to contribute in this way towards the war effort. Socks for Sailors . . . or maybe it was Socks for Soldiers? Her needles clicked. 'She said I wasn't to pester you . . . at least, that was the gist of what she said. "Don't ask him any questions he won't be able to answer," was how she put it. I suppose it was questions about Margaret she meant. Just what is going on, Fred? Has Margaret done something wrong?'

'Emphatically not. Miss Phillips was quite clear about that. In fact, she let me know in no uncertain terms that we can be very proud of Margaret.'

'Then what . . .'

'We're not to know what this new job of hers entails – and we mustn't ask,' he said. 'One thing the mistress *did* say was that it's important work – important for the country.'

'Fred, she's twenty-one. What can somebody of her age possibly contribute?'

'Her brains,' he said. 'At least, that's the conclusion I've come to. And it sounds as if this will be an office job of some sort, so she won't be joining one of the women's services.'

'Well, that's a relief, I suppose,' said Edith. 'Which reminds me . . . I had a letter from Daphne Simkins this morning, to say that both the twins are joining up. Rory's plumped for the navy, because that was John's service, but Jonathan's still hesitating between that and the RAF.'

'Yes, Margaret said.'

'How *is* she?' said her mother. 'I mean, how did she seem?'

'She seemed all right.' He shook his head. 'No, not all right. Anxious. But I think it's mainly because she's been told that she mustn't talk about any of this – the job, or what she'll be doing, or even where they're sending her.'

'A bit cloak-and-dagger, isn't it?' said Edith, clicking her needles. 'But she seemed otherwise all right, you think?'

'Oh yes. You know our Margaret. An old head on young shoulders.'

'Perhaps it's just as well, if she's to cope with all of this. Did the mistress say what's to happen about her research? It seems such a waste to have to give it up, after all her hard work.'

'The mistress,' said Rowlands, 'seemed confident that Margaret can look forward to a distinguished academic career, when the time comes.'

'Ah, and when will that be, I wonder?' said his wife sadly.

A postcard arrived a few days later. 'Post-marked Bletchley,' said Edith, turning it over. 'Where's that exactly? Somewhere in the Midlands, isn't it?'

'Buckinghamshire. What does she say?'

'Not much. One can't, on a postcard.' Although Margaret's letters had always tended to be brief and to-the-point, unlike the more fulsome productions of her sister Anne, which sometimes ran to pages of description. '"*Dearest Mother and Father,*"' read Edith aloud. '"*I hope you are well, and that Granny and Joanie are well, too. I have settled in nicely and am quite comfortable in my new 'digs'. Letter to follow . . .*" Well, that's something, at least.'

'What?'

'She says the lodgings are comfortable.'

'Mm. Does she give an address?'

'That'll be in the letter, I expect.' Which it was, the next day. 'She doesn't say very much about it – the place she's staying,' said Edith, having skimmed the two closely written sheets of this missive. 'Only that she's sharing with another girl . . . Pamela Wingate. Her people live abroad, Margaret says . . . Stranded there by the war, of course.'

Rowlands wasn't particularly interested in Pamela Wingate. 'How's Margaret?'

Edith turned over a page. 'She's well, as far as I can

make out. You know Margaret. She never says much about herself.'

'No,' he said. 'I suppose,' he added after a moment, 'she'd tell us if there were anything wrong?'

'I expect so,' was the reply. 'Anyway, there isn't.'

'Isn't what?'

'Anything wrong. It's nice that she's got this other girl for company. They have to take turns for baths. I remember *that* from my days in the VAD,' said Edith, as if the memory were a happy one. 'Shillings in the meter. She asks if I'll send her warm nightdress, and the bed-socks Mother knitted for her last Christmas.'

From which Rowlands deduced that, wherever it was that his daughter was currently lodging, the heating was far from adequate.

The weather continued to be cold. In the first week of December, it snowed. Trudging along in the icy slush of Marylebone Road, Rowlands thought that this would doubtless mean an increase in the number of accidents for those already struggling with blackout conditions. More twisted ankles, black eyes and broken legs . . . He wondered if the major had thought to add another suggestion to his list of hints for getting about in the blackout: 'Wear rubber-soled shoes – or better still, stay at home' was advice more people ought to take to heart. Underlying the daily struggle to get by in this grimmest of seasons was the news of the war, as it was being played out across the world. The news from Greece in the past few days had been encouraging, with Mussolini's forces suffering defeat after defeat. British and colonial troops had invaded North Africa, and successes against the enemy were being reported daily. At home, the news was less heartening: bombing raids on Coventry, Liverpool, Southampton, Birmingham and Bristol added to the misery being endured by the capital.

For Rowlands, all that mattered was that his loved ones were all right. His job was to keep them safe. Failing to do so, through some unforeseen circumstance – enemy action or otherwise – didn't bear thinking about. And so, although he couldn't stop himself worrying about them collectively and individually, he did his best to suppress these feelings. At least they'd all be together at Christmas. Anne's term had already finished, and she'd arrived home a few days before, full of the joys of Oxford, and what her painting tutor had said about her work. Then a letter came from his eldest daughter, saying she'd be coming home on Christmas Eve. Forty-eight hours' leave. 'That's good news,' said Rowlands.

'Yes,' said his wife. 'Oh! She's bringing that girl with her.'

'What girl?'

'*That* girl. You know . . .' She read aloud: '"*I've asked Pamela to stay. I hope that's all right, Mummy? She doesn't have anywhere else to go, and she oughtn't to be on her own at Christmas. I thought she and I could share my old room, if Anne doesn't mind going in with Joanie.*" Just as well I've ordered a goose from the butcher's,' said Edith. 'I had to queue for an hour to get it. Let's hope it'll stretch to feeding seven.'

* * *

It was a fifteen-minute walk from Kingston railway station to the Rowlandses' house in Grove Crescent; last night's fall of snow would make it a longer one. Rowlands offered to go and meet Margaret and Pamela's train, which was due at four-fifteen, but Edith overruled that. 'Mr Harris said he'll drive us.' Harris was the neighbour – a retired civil servant – who'd offered to drive them up to Cambridge; he'd also been teaching Edith to drive. 'Actually,' she added. '*I'm* going to drive. I need the practice.'

'But it'll be dark by then. And the roads'll be icing up.'

'All the more reason to fetch the girls by car.' The vehicle, a four year-old Austin 7, had room for four passengers – including of course Harris, who would be there in his role as driving instructor – and so Rowlands had agreed to stay home, in order to make things ready for the arrivals. After Edith and their neighbour had set off, at what her husband had to admit was a suitably cautious speed, he occupied himself by building up the fire in the sitting room. When he had a nice blaze going, he set the guard in front of it, and thought what else he might do by way of welcoming his daughter home. Tea. Those girls'd be chilled to the bone after their journey. He went to the kitchen to see about it, and found that his middle daughter, and his mother-in-law, were ahead of him.

'I won't make the toast until they arrive,' said Anne, stacking plates and cups on a tray. 'It'll be nice to see old Megs again. It's been ages.'

'What time do we expect them?' asked Helen.

'A quarter to five, at the latest.' But it was gone half past by the time they heard the Austin pull up outside Number 44. 'What took you so long?' he couldn't stop himself from saying as he opened the door.

Edith, calling her thanks to Harris, who was just driving off, paid no attention to this.

'Our train was late, Daddy,' said Margaret, coming up to kiss him.

'Yes. Beastly journey,' said another voice. 'Train was absolutely packed. Standing room only.'

'Daddy, this is my friend Pamela.'

Rowlands felt embarrassed by his momentary loss of temper. 'How do you do?' he said. 'Come in, won't you?' Then, to Margaret, 'Your grandmother's just making some tea.'

'Oh, good. It seems hours and hours since we had our sandwiches in the train.' Then, as her sister appeared, 'Hello, Anne. What've you done to your hair?'

'Cut it,' was the reply.

'Hmph. It suits you – I think. Pam, this is my sister.'

'Hello,' said the girl.

'Margaret, why don't you show Pamela where to wash her hands?' said Edith. 'I've put you both in your old room, as you asked.'

'All right, Mummy. Come on, Pam.'

As the two girls went upstairs, leaving their bags, at Rowlands's request, for him to bring up later, the voice of the newcomer floated down the stairs: 'I think your parents are *charming* . . .'

'Glad we've passed the test,' murmured Edith, as, having hung up her coat, she preceded her husband into the sitting room. 'No thanks to *you*, Fred. Did you have to make such a fuss? We were only twenty minutes late.'

'Three-quarters of an hour.'

'Well, that's nothing these days. Trains are routinely delayed. It's wartime, in case you'd forgotten – *and* it's Christmas Eve.'

'I know,' he said. 'I'm sorry. It's just that with the roads so icy – not to mention the blackout . . .'

'You of all people should know that one takes extra care in the blackout,' said Edith severely. 'And I'm a very careful driver. Mr Harris was only saying . . . Ah, here are the girls, now!'

Because their voices could be heard on the stairs – Margaret's and Joan's, with the languid tones of Pamela Wingate sounding above them all. 'So this is your kid sister? I'm Pamela – but you can call me Pam.'

'I'm not a kid, I'm thirteen,' said Joan, then, coming into the room, 'Ooh, is that Christmas cake?'

'She seems a nice girl,' said Edith, that night in bed – to which Rowlands responded with a non-committal grunt. 'A bit fond of the sound of her own voice, of course, but that's just nerves. Hard for her, being dropped into the middle of a strange family at Christmastime, and with her own family so far away.'

They had certainly heard a good deal about Pamela's family over tea. Her father was in the Diplomatic Corps.

'Not the faintest idea what he actually *does*,' said his daughter with a laugh. 'Probably runs half the country, for all I know.' The country in question being Kenya, where her people had a large estate.

'It's a day's ride to get around it,' said Pamela. 'Do you ride, Maggie?' Margaret said that she did not. 'Pity,' was the reply. 'I was thinking it'd be rather fun to hire a couple of horses on our next weekend off. Charlotte was telling me – you know Charlotte, don't you? The one who's just got engaged to that flight lieutenant – that there's quite a decent riding stables at Stony Stratford . . . Thank you, Mrs Rowlands. I'd love another cup of tea . . . and one of those delicious mince-pies.'

There had been no mention of how the girls had been spending their time in between 'weekends off' – nor did anybody ask them about this. Anne and Joan had been instructed by their mother not to bother their sister with questions. 'I thought Margaret was looking rather washed-out,' said Edith now. 'And she's too thin.'

'Yes,' he agreed sleepily. 'We'd better feed her up as much as possible, while she's here.'

In this endeavour, he had to admit that Edith excelled herself on Christmas Day. The goose was done to a turn, with sufficient quantities of roast potatoes, parsnips and Brussels sprouts, to make a bird intended for six people stretch to feed one more. Rowlands took care to slip an extra potato or two onto his eldest daughter's plate – not neglecting that of her friend, who, as their guest, was entitled to the lion's share. It occurred to him that this phrase might have a more literal meaning for this young daughter of Africa.

'I suppose you'll have seen lions – in the wild, I mean?' he said, interrupting an account of what sounded like a very grand reception at Government House.

'Rather. Shot 'em, too,' was the reply. 'Well, one, actually. Man-eater. You can't have that sort roaming around. They get a taste for it, you know. Human flesh.'

'Fancy,' murmured Helen Edwards, arrested in the act

of bringing in the coffee (they had by this time passed the Christmas pudding stage). 'You young people lead such a *varied* life. In my day, the nearest we got to a lion was the zoo. Sleepy old things they were, too.' His mother-in-law's gently sceptical tone reflected Rowlands's own attitude towards Miss Wingate's storytelling. If that's what it was. Certainly, as the day wore on, the embassy parties got grander and the adventures wilder.

'You must miss Kenya very much,' said Joan, evidently beguiled by these colourful tales. 'Nothing ever happens here.'

Chapter Three

It was late in the afternoon of Christmas Day that Rowlands, having left his wife and daughters preparing a high tea that nobody would feel much inclined to eat, went outside for a smoke. It had stopped snowing, but the air was decidedly crisp, and so after lighting up, he decided to make for the shed, where an old Lloyd Loom chair that Edith had banished from the house offered a comfortable seat. Here, he sat back to enjoy the taste of his Churchman's, and to think over the events of that second wartime Christmas. On the face of it, it hadn't been so very unlike the Christmases of the two peacetime decades that had preceded it – a period that would now be described as being 'between the wars', he supposed. How they'd all taken that peaceful interval for granted! In his sermon that morning, the vicar had chosen as his text Matthew 5:44: 'Love your enemies, bless them that curse you, do good to them that hate you, and pray for them that despitefully use you, and persecute you . . .'

There had been rebellious mutterings by some members of the congregation, as they left the church. '*Not* a very Christmassy message,' Rowlands overheard one woman say tartly.

'Love your enemy! I should say not!' replied her spouse. 'Catch me loving a Jerry!'

Rowlands, who had happened to find himself in Berlin at the time of Hitler's accession to power in 1933, knew there would be many Germans as horrified as he was by what their country had become under such a regime. Many more were even now suffering under its brutalities. And yet here was this complacent oaf, pontificating about the importance of 'knowing your enemy . . .' It was hard not to feel overwhelmed by anger – and despair. Having fought in the last war, Rowlands was all too aware of the horrors that ensued from failing to regard others as human beings. Hitler had begun it, of course, with his persecution of the Jews. But he saw no reason why they should lower themselves to Hitler's level. The creaking of the shed door alerted him to the fact that he was no longer alone.

'Hello,' he said. 'Which one of you is it?' Usually he'd have had no difficulty distinguishing Margaret's brisk step from Anne's more languid gait, nor Joan, his youngest's, headlong dash from the more sedate approach of both her sisters. But today's snow had muffled all sounds, so it was only when she spoke that he knew it was his eldest daughter.

'It's me, Daddy. Mummy said I was to tell you tea'll be ready in five minutes.'

'Good. Then we've five minutes before we need go in.'

He got to his feet. 'Sit down, Meg.' She did so. Rowlands perched himself on the edge of his workbench. 'So tell me,' he said. 'How are you getting on?' Then, before she could reply, 'Oh, I know you can't say much. I just want to know that you're all right.'

'I'm fine,' said Margaret. 'In fact . . .' She gave a tremulous laugh. 'I'm really rather enjoying the work. It's . . . interesting.'

'That's good to know. And your billet's comfortable, I hope?'

'Not very.' This time her laugh was whole-hearted. 'Mrs B – that's our landlady – has done her best to make us feel at home. But with only one bath a week allowed, and coal being rationed the way it is, so that the house is always freezing, it's hardly The Ritz,' she added – a phrase Rowlands guessed wasn't one she'd come up with herself. It sounded more like the sort of thing Pamela Wingate might have said.

'That reminds me of when I was in France during the last war,' he said. 'Some of the chaps in our unit thought it was a good joke to nail up boards over the entrance to the dugouts that said 'The Ritz', or 'The Savoy', or 'Buckingham Palace'. Which, if you'd seen what those dugouts were like, would've struck you as pretty funny.'

'Oh, it's not as bad as *that*,' said Margaret, with, mercifully, no idea what that particular hell had been like. 'I say, I couldn't have a cigarette, could I?'

'Help yourself,' he replied, handing her the pack. 'Although your mother won't be very pleased to know you've taken up the habit.'

'She doesn't have to know, does she?'

'I suppose not.' It wasn't like Margaret to be secretive. Still, she was a grown woman, he thought. It wasn't his business to interfere.

'Pamela smokes,' she said suddenly, as if she guessed what he was thinking. 'All the girls do. It helps pass the time.'

And calms the nerves, he thought, remembering his own days on active service – which, he supposed, was what this was.

'She seems a good sort,' he said, for something to say.

'Oh, she is!' said Margaret. 'She was ever so kind to me when I first arrived at BP . . .' She broke off. 'I shouldn't have mentioned that,' she said unhappily.

Rowlands smiled. 'Mentioned what?' he said.

The Rowlands family and their guest were invited to Richmond for Boxing Day: Edith's brother, Ralph, had sent the Daimler to collect them. With eight of them to fit in, including the driver, it'd be a squeeze, but it was only a few miles, after all. 'What a charming house!' cried Miss Wingate as the car pulled into the drive. It was certainly a large place, Rowlands knew, although of its features – which were those of the Old English style that had been so popular forty years ago, with a steeply pitched roof, diamond-paned windows and a baronial front door – he had only the haziest idea.

'Come in, come in,' said Ralph Edwards, coming out of the house onto the low brick terrace that ran in front of the building. 'Don't stand in the cold . . . Diana! They're here!'

This brought Mrs Edwards from the sitting room, where, she confessed, she'd been 'dying of boredom', whiling away the time between breakfast and luncheon with a game of clock patience.

'Hello, Mother, how are you keeping?' she said to her mother-in-law, kissing Helen.

'*Lovely* to see you, too, Edith, dear. It's been simply *ages* . . . Frightful weather, what?' Before her marriage, Diana had been renowned for her prowess on the links; she still retained an Amazonian heartiness. 'Peter's been *longing* to see his cousins, haven't you, Peterkin?' This to her son, a stolid fifteen-year-old, who muttered something unintelligible and fled upstairs. 'Oh dear!' said his mother, laughing immoderately. 'He's so terribly *shy*, poor boy.'

With Ralph's assistance, the party divested itself of its coats, and trooped into the room so recently vacated by Mrs Edwards. Still talking nineteen to the dozen, she drew her guests towards the fire – which, Rowlands had to admit, was chucking out a wonderful heat. No coal rationing for the Edwardses, it seemed.

'And how are my favourite nieces?' cried Diana. 'Anne, you get prettier and prettier. Having fun in Oxford, are you? Joanie, you're getting so *tall*! How's Cambridge, Margaret? Oh, I was forgetting – you're not *at* Cambridge any more. Working in an office these days, aren't you? *Frightfully* grown-up!'

'This is my friend Pamela,' said Margaret. 'She works in my office, too.'

'So kind of you to invite me, Mrs Edwards,' said Pamela, rising to the occasion. 'And what a charming house! It reminds me so much of my family's place in Sussex.' There was a slight catch in her voice as she went on, 'Of course, it's all shut up, now.'

'Pamela's people are in Kenya for the duration,' explained Edith. A brief silence followed this remark.

'Well, it's jolly nice you're here, that's all,' said Diana. 'Ralph and I have been pigging it on our own, with the servants away. Of course, one realises that they want to visit their families at Christmas, but even so . . .'

Over lunch – 'Bit of a scratch affair, I'm afraid,' said Diana. 'Just cold ham and beef, and leftover turkey from yesterday, but with Cook away, what can you do?' – further details were solicited by the Edwardses about their young guest's family circumstances.

'Your father's an ambassador, I hear?' said Ralph, who loved an important job almost as much as he loved a lord.

'Oh, nothing so grand,' was the reply. 'Merely a district commissioner – whatever that means.' It struck Rowlands that she'd said something else yesterday . . . but maybe he was wrong. He hadn't really been paying attention.

Ralph seemed satisfied with this account, however. 'Charming girl,' he said, when the young folk had taken themselves off to another part of the house (Pamela having begged to be shown around; she loved 'picturesque' old places like this, she said). 'Her father sounds like quite a big pot. I wonder if old Chevening knows him?' This was the chairman of the bank for which Ralph worked. '*He* was out in Africa, for a time . . . or was it India? No matter. These Foreign Office types always stick together. I might sound him out about this Wingate cove. Wouldn't do any harm to have someone who could put in a good word for Peter, when he comes to do his Civil Service exams, after Oxford.'

The conversation continued in a desultory fashion,

with talk of the war vetoed by Diana as 'too, too depressing', and other topics in short supply. Since the Rowlandses did not employ a cook or a parlourmaid, Mrs Edwards's favourite subject – the unreliability of servants – had to be confined to a further lament at the absence of Cook until that evening ('We had to give her yesterday afternoon off *as well* . . .'). Ralph's preferred subjects, which were his golf handicap, and the number of miles per gallon he (or rather his chauffeur) could get out of the Daimler, were of similarly limited interest to his guests, neither of whom played golf, and who did not own a car. Edith's driving lessons were briefly discussed: 'Let me know when it'd suit you, and I'll run over and take you out for a spin,' said her brother. 'That's if I can get the extra petrol. Dashed annoying, all these restrictions.'

It was something of a relief when Margaret came in to say that she and Pam had better be going soon, if they were to catch the four o'clock train from Euston. 'I'll get Carter to drive you to the station,' said Ralph. Evidently the chauffeur wasn't having a day off. 'So nice to meet you, Miss Wingate – or may I call you Pamela? Do give my regards to your father when you next write. I believe we might have an acquaintance in common. My chairman, you know – Lord Chevening.'

Pamela said that she'd certainly mention it to Daddy. A pretty speech of thanks to her hostess followed. Kisses were exchanged between the various family members. 'I'll come and see you off,' said Rowlands, who felt that he'd spent little enough of the past forty-eight hours with his daughter. But this was not to be. For just then, there came the sound of a car turning in to the drive, and the scrunch of wheels on gravel as it drew up in front of the house.

'Who can *that* be?' said Diana. 'We're not expecting anybody, are we, dear?'

Before he could reply, there came a delighted cry from Pamela Wingate, 'Well, look who's here! I never thought they'd make it.'

'They' turned out to be two young men – friends of hers, it emerged. 'This is Hugh Montfitchet. *Lieutenant* Montfitchet, I should say.'

'How d'you do,' said the young naval officer, vaguely addressing the assembled company. 'Awf'lly sorry for blowing in like this.'

'And *this* is Gilbert Burton – Gil to his friends.'

'*Charmed*, I'm sure,' drawled this individual. He refused Diana's offer of a cup of tea ('Never touch the stuff. Poison to me.') but didn't need much encouragement from Ralph to join him in a whisky ('One for the road, then – why not? Here's mud in your eye . . .'). It was he who was the driver of the vehicle currently parked outside the Edwardses' door – 'Latest model Alvis. Pretty, isn't she?' – although it transpired that the car actually belonged to his friend. 'He lets me borrow it if I ask him nicely, don't you, Monty?' – to which Montfitchet's only reply was an embarrassed laugh. The fact that the young man now cheerfully swigging whisky sometimes borrowed his friend's car was a matter of indifference to Rowlands – until it became apparent that the two young men were intending to drive his daughter and her friend back to Bletchley. 'With the roads clear like this, it shouldn't take more than a couple of hours – an hour and a half, if I put my foot down,' said Burton.

Perhaps the alarm Rowlands felt at this confident assertion showed in his face, for Margaret came over and slipped her arm through his. 'It'll be all right, Daddy,' she said. 'And it'll be so nice not to have to travel on that stuffy old train . . . and in the blackout, too.' With which it was hard to disagree.

Last farewells were exchanged and overnight bags gathered up, and then the four young people clambered into the waiting vehicle. A cheerful toot of the horn, and they were off, leaving at least one member of the family party more than a little envious.

'What fun!' said Diana wistfully. 'I remember when *you* used to drive something a lot more sporty, darling. So much more *dashing* than that dreary old Daimler.'

'Yes, well, I happen to think the Daimler's a very reliable car,' said her husband. But he didn't contest the point. 'Well,' he went on, as the Rowlandses, too, made ready to leave. 'Your Margaret's certainly got herself a very smart set of friends. Montfitchet . . . Montfitchet . . . I know the name. Lord Montfitchet's boy, isn't he?'

'I couldn't tell you,' said Rowlands, feeling that, as far as he was concerned, this Christmas had gone on quite long enough.

December moved into January, with no let-up in the weather conditions. Snow, which had seemed delightfully seasonal at Christmas, now became a nuisance, freezing pipes and creating hazards for pedestrians and drivers alike. Shortages of fuel made the situation worse. Rowlands had taken to keeping his coat on in the office, and had told Jean Symonds she might do the same. Since it was dark at four o'clock, the blackout came earlier and earlier. Never had the Winter War – a term coined to describe Finland's heroic resistance to Soviet Russia the year before – seemed more apposite to what they themselves were going through. Food rationing added to the misery. Meat, butter and sugar had been scarce for months, but it was now becoming almost impossible to get hold of eggs, said Edith. As for tinned fruit . . . you could forget about that.

'Then it's a good thing we've still got a supply of apples in the cellar,' said her husband, who was proud of his fruit trees. His vegetable garden, too, had proved a welcome source of produce over the winter months. But there was a limit to one's appetite for turnips and cabbages, said Edith.

At work, too, there were difficulties getting hold of essential supplies, Rowlands found. Not all the men whose livelihoods depended on St Dunstan's keeping them supplied with the materials for making household items could be retrained as factory workers, although some were – blind men being particularly skilled in work that required sensitivity of touch. Fitting delicate instruments into aircraft panels and examining parts for minute faults were just some of the tasks at which blind operators were adept, in the factories where they had been deployed. Other jobs of a less specialised kind could be undertaken by St Dunstan's men, releasing sighted workers for the armed forces. A machine shop was set up at the new premises at Church Stretton, to train men to work lathes, drills and presses. One thing many of these newly fledged factory workers complained of was the noise the machines made, which drowned out the aural clues to what was going on around them that most relied on. This was something they'd have to get used to, along with all the other changes to a hard-won normality.

Letters came at intervals from both their elder daughters. Anne was back in Oxford, sharing rooms with another art student, and Margaret had returned to work. Her letters studiously avoiding any mention of this, talking only of inconsequential matters. There had been a New Year's Eve dance, one said, to which Margaret and some of the other girls had gone; there'd been 'real champagne' at midnight. Another mentioned a 'revue' being got up by 'some of the theatrical types', in which she was to have a small part. 'I'll need a Hawaiian costume,' she wrote. 'Any idea where I can find a grass skirt?'

January moved into February. It was noticeable that the mentions of Pamela Wingate, so frequent in the early days, were fewer – a fact that Edith remarked upon, after reading Margaret's last letter aloud to her husband one evening.

'She doesn't seem to be going about with that girl Pamela quite as much as she used to. Wonder if they've had a falling-out?'

'Perhaps Meg's found other friends,' said Rowlands, who wasn't particularly sorry to hear of this development. It wasn't only that his daughter and Miss Wingate belonged to different social sets – such things needn't matter if there was a real rapport, as he had reason to know . . . But there'd been something about the young woman – Pamela – that hadn't quite rung true. He couldn't have said exactly what it was; it was just a feeling he'd had.

The reason for the friendship's apparent cooling-off emerged in a subsequent letter that had talked about very little at considerable length. The film – *Suspicion*, a new

Hitchcock thriller – she and Marjorie (evidently a new friend) had gone to see at the local picture-house. A tea-party they'd had in the office to celebrate another girl's birthday ('We all put our butter and sugar rations together to make a cake.'). The difficulty she'd had finding wool to darn her stockings. Then came the postscript: 'Guess what! Pamela Wingate's engaged! The lucky chap's Hugh Montfitchet, whom you'll remember meeting on Boxing Day. Pam's been showing off her ring – with the most enormous diamond. Wonder if I'll get an invitation to the wedding?'

'Which only goes to show,' said Edith, folding up the letter, 'that they're not such great friends as they used to be – otherwise Margaret would be in no doubt that she'd be invited.' Her sniff perfectly expressed her feelings on the matter. 'I always *did* think that young woman was rather full of herself.' That letter, with its (marginally) interesting piece of news, had arrived a week ago. Since then, there had been no further missives, even though Edith had written back straight away, asking when the wedding was to be, and if Margaret had yet received an invitation. 'Because really, after we made the girl so welcome, it would simply be bad manners not to invite Margaret,' she said. Rowlands wisely refrained from comment. Still, he wondered why there'd been no weekly letter from his usually punctilious daughter. She must be busy, he told himself. No doubt she'd write again when she had time.

The news, towards the end of February, was all of British and Australian successes in North Africa – although Rommel was a worry. The Afrika Korps had had its share of successes, too. So that when Rowlands got home from work, the first thing he did was to switch on the wireless.

'You might take your coat off first,' said Edith, following him into the sitting room.

'Sorry. It's just that I don't want to miss the news headlines.'

'And you're back late *again*,' she said, ignoring this. 'That's the third time this week. How I'm supposed to provide a decent hot meal for you, when I've no idea what time you'll be in, I *don't* know.'

'I'm sorry. A large order came in just as I was leaving. Mats for anti-aircraft guns.'

'Yes, yes, I realise you can't just drop everything, but—'

'Shh,' he said, holding up his hand. 'I want to listen to this.'

'*The arrival of General Rommel as the new commander of Axis forces in the Western Desert marks a decisive shift in the way the North African campaign has so far been conducted . . .*'

The telephone rang. 'I'll go,' said Edith, in a resigned tone.

'*After the decisive victories by Allied armies at Tobruk and Benghazi . . .*'

'Kingston 435 . . . Oh, hello! This *is* a surprise . . . Is everything all right?' A brief silence followed, as whoever it was at the other end of the line spoke, then, 'When did you say she left . . . two days ago? But that *isn't* very long . . . Perhaps she went to visit friends . . .' Another silence, during which Rowlands found himself rapidly losing interest in the Allied victories and German counter-attack. 'All right. I'll get your father . . .' But he was already at his wife's side. 'Fred, it's Margaret. She wants to talk to you.'

He took the receiver from Edith's hand. 'Hello, Meg. What's up?'

'Oh, Daddy,' she said. 'I'm so worried. It's Pamela. She's disappeared – two days ago. Mummy thinks she might be visiting friends. But she never mentioned putting in for leave . . . and besides, it's the middle of the week, and . . . and she wouldn't just go *off* like that, without telling anyone . . .' Her voice cracked. 'What if something awful's happened to her?'

'I'm sure there's a perfectly reasonable explanation,' he said. 'So you last saw her – when?'

'Tuesday afternoon . . . about four o'clock, when we finished work. We were both on the early shift, and we usually went back to our digs together . . . Only she said she had something she had to do, and not to wait for her.'

'When did you first miss her?'

'Oh, not until much later, when she didn't come back. Although . . .' She broke off, then went on, 'She didn't always . . . come back to Mrs B's, I mean. Sometimes she stayed overnight with . . . with a friend. So I didn't really think anything of it until I got into work on Wednesday and found she hadn't turned up for the eight o'clock shift. None of the other girls seemed to know where she was, and so . . . well, I started to worry a bit. It's not like Pam to leave people in the lurch. Then when she *still* didn't appear this afternoon – we'd both been moved to lates – I thought there must be something wrong.'

'Presumably your employers know about this?'

'I suppose so. It's just that no one's *said* anything. It's as if . . . I don't know . . . as if she'd ceased to *exist*. I've been feeling so frightened, thinking about what might have happened.'

'Try and stay calm, Megs. I'm sure it'll turn out all right.'

'It's just that I'm so *tired*,' said his daughter, sounding more overwrought than he'd ever heard her. 'I haven't slept much these past two nights.'

'Listen,' he said. 'Why don't you ask for some leave? You could come home for a few days – catch up on your sleep. By then, there may be news of your friend—'

'Three minutes, caller,' said the operator.

'I've got to go,' said Margaret, without replying to her father's last suggestion. 'I haven't any more money . . .'

'Wait,' said Rowlands. But there was nothing but the monotonous purring of the dialling tone.

'What did you make of that, Fred?' said Edith. 'Do you think something's happened to that girl?'

'I don't know. Presumably, if she's really gone missing, the police will have to be informed. Margaret didn't seem to know whether the powers-that-be at her place of work had taken any steps to trace her.'

'I'm sure they will,' said Edith. 'Her family will have to be informed, for a start.'

'But her family's in Kenya, remember?

'Well, even so, it's not really our business. I'm sure the girl will turn up, eventually. What about her fiancé? That young fellow we met at Christmas. I don't doubt *he'll* know where she is.'

'Perhaps.' But he wasn't convinced. On an impulse, he dialled a number – one he knew by heart. It rang several times, but there was no reply. 'Damn,' he muttered. 'He must be out on a case.' He stood for a moment, irresolute.

'Fred,' said his wife. 'I do wish you'd come and sit down. Your dinner's been ready this past hour.'

'Sorry,' he said. 'It occurred to me that Alasdair Douglas might be able to help, but he's not answering the telephone.' Another thought struck him. 'That chap who's been giving you driving lessons,' he said. 'Harris. Do you suppose *he'd* drive me up there?'

'What, *now*?' said Edith. 'It's a bit late to ask someone to turn out.'

'It's only half past seven. We could be there in under two hours.' But Rowlands knew that it was a hare-brained idea. Even if their genial neighbour were willing (and had the petrol) for such a journey, it might very well turn out to be futile. Because, after all, where was he intending to start on this quest for his daughter's missing friend? If indeed she *was* missing – she'd doubtless turn up in a day or two, as Edith had said. Then again, she might not.

'Is anything the matter?' came a voice from the top of the stairs. 'I heard voices and I wondered . . .'

'It's all right, Mother,' said Edith, at the same moment as Rowlands said, 'It's Margaret's friend Pamela. She's disappeared.'

'We don't know that for certain, Fred. You shouldn't worry Mother unnecessarily.'

'It's better to face things, I always think,' said Helen Edwards, coming downstairs. 'I learnt that during the last war – and the one before that. Now tell me what's going on.'

Briefly, Rowlands explained. 'I'm just trying to decide

what's best to do,' he said. 'If Margaret's right, and this girl's really gone missing, then . . .'

'I should think the most sensible thing would be for you to take your coat off and come and have your dinner,' said his mother-in-law gently. 'I can't see that much is to be achieved by haring off across the country at this time of night.'

Rowlands reluctantly agreed, if only because he didn't at that moment know what he was going to do once he got to Bletchley. Pamela Wingate's disappearance was really a matter for the police. It was possible that they were already on the case. What concerned him as much as if not more than the whereabouts of a young woman he'd met only once was his daughter's state of mind. He'd never heard her sound so miserable. Before he sat down to his belated dinner, he'd made up his mind.

'All right,' he said. 'But I'm going up there, first thing tomorrow. I mean to get to the bottom of this.'

Chapter Four

The 7.05 train from Euston was crowded with the by-now familiar mixture of military personnel returning from leave, women shepherding groups of small children ('Johnny, I'll not tell you again – use your handkerchief, not your sleeve.') and local businessmen – London-bound traffic being in the opposite direction, Rowlands supposed. He'd found a seat, but gave it up to a large woman carrying a shopping basket, who plumped herself down with a groan of relief. Muttering apologies, Rowlands edged his way past the knees of his fellow passengers and out into the corridor, where he lit a cigarette and contemplated what lay ahead. It wasn't a pleasant prospect – not least because he'd no clear idea where to start. Margaret had given out so little information about the organisation she worked for that he didn't even have the name of anyone to whom he could address his enquiries. Perhaps he should start with the landlady? There, at least, he had a name and an address. But even that was precious little.

It was a nuisance about Douglas's being away, he thought, pulling down the window by which he was standing in order to pitch out the stub of his cigarette. He could have used some of the Scotsman's sage advice in these curious circumstances. As it was, he'd have to manage as best he could on his own. After trying again, without success, to get in touch with the chief inspector, he'd made another call the night before. This – to Major Fraser – had been answered straight away, as had the granting of Rowlands's request for the day off from work. He was lucky in his employer (if that was an adequate description for his friend of many years), as in so much else, he thought.

The train, for a wonder, was on time, and it was just under an hour after leaving the metropolis that they pulled into the station, with the usual grinding of wheels and violent exhalations of steam on the part of the engine. Even if Rowlands hadn't known it was the stop – it being a direct service – the guard's booming announcement would have alerted him to the fact. 'ALL change! ALL change! BLETCH-ley STA-tion . . .' He was in this respect no worse off than any of the other passengers, since the signs bearing the name of this and other stations had been removed in the early months of the war, making announcements all the more essential, especially during the blackout. Whereas he, with his own personal 'blackout', was no more hampered by the lack of signs than he'd ever been.

He returned to the compartment where he'd been sitting, in order to collect his stick from the overhead rack where he'd placed it – to find himself, by this action, suddenly conspicuous.

'Do let me help you,' said a voice – rather a pleasant voice, with an intonation that denoted north of England origins.

'Thank you.' Rowlands felt his arm firmly grasped; he gently disengaged himself. 'I can manage quite well, as regards getting myself off the train – but perhaps you'd be good enough to walk with me as far as the ticket barrier?'

'Right-ho. Are you heading for BP, too?'

He recognised the acronym Margaret had used to refer to her place of work. At once he made up his mind. He'd been intending to go to Margaret's lodgings first – but that could wait. 'Yes, rather,' he said. 'Would you mind leading the way? It's my first visit, you see.'

'I don't mind a bit,' said his new friend. 'It's not far – just a seven-minute walk. Although I've done it in five.' She laughed. 'Anything rather than get a black mark for being late.'

'Then I'll walk as fast as you like,' said Rowlands. Having given up their tickets, they set off along the lane that led, so Rowlands's companion informed him, right up to the gates of what she also referred to as 'the Park'.

'Makes it sound rather grand, doesn't it?' she said. 'But it's really a bit of a monstrosity, with those red brick gables, and lots of domes and turrets stuck in odd places. The Victorians loved that sort of thing, I suppose.'

Rowlands agreed that they did.

'I remember the first time I came here, at the end of last year,' his companion said. 'Pitch black it was, with not even a sliver of a moon to light the way. I was terrified I'd lose my way, stumbling along in the dark—' She appeared to realise what she'd said, for she broke off suddenly. 'I'm sorry, I didn't mean . . .'

'That's all right,' he said. 'One does get used to getting by in the dark – as I expect you've found?'

'Oh yes. I'm quite accustomed to it now.' She'd been spending a couple of days' leave with an aunt in Bounds Green. 'The rest of my family are in Durham, so I don't get to see them very often.'

'That must be hard for you.'

'It's not so bad. We all have to put up with things we don't much like these days.'

'Yes.'

They must have come in sight of the house, for she said suddenly, 'Here we are! The jolly old barracks itself.'

'Thanks,' said Rowlands. 'I'm grateful to you for accompanying me, Miss . . . er . . .'

'Milward,' said the young woman. 'Marjorie, to my friends.'

'It was nice to meet you, Miss Milward.' He held out his hand. 'I'm Frederick Rowlands.'

'Oh! You're never Maggie Rowlands's father?' Suddenly she sounded wary.

'That's right,' he said. 'Do you know her?'

'I . . . Yes . . . That is . . . I have to go now,' she mumbled. 'Can't stop. Sorry.' Without another word, she darted past him and through the gate.

'Wait . . .' Rowlands went to follow her, and found his way blocked by the large, solid form of a sentry.

'Pass, if you please, sir.'

'Let me in, please. I've come to see my daughter, Margaret Rowlands.'

'You can't come in here without a pass,' said the guard.

'Then how do I get one?' demanded Rowlands. Around him, people were going in, unchallenged, through the open gate; he could hear their voices. They sounded young, high-spirited and absorbed in their own concerns.

'Going for a pint at the clubhouse later, old man?'

'Can't, worst luck. Bit of a flap on . . .'

Rowlands thought about accosting one of these young men, and asking whom to approach about getting a pass. Surely there must be a system whereby members of the public could visit such a place, given permission? If one could enter Whitehall or the Palace of Westminster, then why not 'BP'? This was England, after all, not Nazi Germany. You couldn't turn what was evidently just a country house given over to government offices into a fortress. Dispiritedly, he retraced his steps as far as the railway station, then, having asked the way of the station master, arrived, ten minutes after that, at Mrs Brown's boarding house in Shenley Road.

'You can't miss it,' said the man. 'It's two doors down from the Old Swan Inn. They'll do you a nice pint there, if you're stopping.'

The house itself proved to be much like such houses everywhere – at least if the smell (boiled cabbage and drains) was anything to go by. The woman who answered the door – the famous Mrs B, guessed Rowlands – seemed a pleasant enough soul, however. When she heard why he'd come, she said he'd better come in.

'You're the first person who's asked me anything about it,' she said, ushering Rowlands into a little parlour that smelt of coal dust and furniture polish. 'I was starting to think they'd both done a bunk, if you'll pardon the expression.'

'"Both"?' His blood ran cold. 'What do you mean by "both"?'

'Mean what I say, don't I? First one goes off – three days ago, it was – then the other . . .'

'Are you talking about my daughter Margaret?'

'That's what I said, didn't I? Not like her at all, to go off without warning. Thoughtless, I call it.'

'Let me get this straight,' he said. 'You're telling me that Margaret didn't come back to her lodgings last night?'

'That's right.'

Rowlands's thoughts were in a whirl. What on earth could have happened? It occurred to him that Margaret might have taken up his suggestion that she should come home for a few days. In which case, she should have turned up in Grove Crescent late last night. *So where was she?*

'May I use your telephone?' he asked.

'Don't have one. There's a telephone box on the corner. Or there's the one at the pub.'

This, being the nearer option, was where he went. Fortunately, the landlord was just opening up. 'Telephone's through there,' he said. It was an old-fashioned, wall-mounted affair. As he heard it begin to ring at the other end, Rowlands prayed that someone would be at home to take the call. After a longer interval than he had expected, it was Helen who answered. Edith was at the shops, she said.

'Has Margaret turned up?' he asked, after the briefest of preliminaries. The answer was in the negative. Having done his best to reassure his mother-in-law that there was nothing to worry about, he hung up and, with a heavy heart, retraced his steps to the lodging house.

'Any joy?' said Mrs B, then, when he shook his head,

'I've made us a nice pot of tea. You look as if you could do with it.

'Like I said,' she went on, when the two of them were once more seated in the little parlour, 'it just isn't like her – Miss Margaret, I mean – not to say that she was going away. She's a responsible young lady, she is – a credit to you, if I might say so. Not like the other one,' she added. 'Flighty piece, *I* call her. Not but what she couldn't charm the birds off the trees, when she wants something out of you . . . But not reliable. Not she. And with them both going off like that, I'm sure I don't know *what* I'll do.'

In her agitation, she stirred the spoon round and round in her cup. 'I mean, I'll keep the room ready for them for as long as I can, but there's a lot of demand for rooms to rent just now, you understand . . . And with only what Joe – that's my husband – brings back from the factory, well, you see how it is I'm placed.'

It was difficult to stem the flow of words, once she'd got started. 'You're telling me that Miss Wingate moved out three days ago?' Rowlands managed to interrupt at last.

The landlady took a noisy slurp of her tea. False teeth, thought Rowlands automatically. 'Well,' she said. 'It's not so much as she's moved out, as that she hasn't turned up. Same as with your young lady. Not a word of warning as to what they was planning to do.'

If they were planning to do anything, thought Rowlands. 'I take it, from what you've said, that my daughter left her things here?'

'She did,' was the reply. 'Would you be wanting to take them away with you, then?'

Rowlands said that if it was all the same to her, he'd rather leave them for now. 'But I wonder if I might take a look at the room?' he added. 'Just to see if Margaret's left a message of any kind.'

'You won't find anything,' said Mrs Brown. 'Don't you think I've looked? A note on the dressing-table would've been *something* . . . I said to my Joe, I said, "Wonder if that girl's had some kind of accident? Vanishing like that without a by-your-leave." Then when your Margaret went, I said, "Maybe they're in it together?" Not that I'd think anything bad of your girl, Mr Rowlands, but you never do know with girls these days.' Still talking, she led the way upstairs to a back bedroom, which seemed to Rowlands to be scarcely large enough for one, let alone two, young women. 'Well, here you are,' said the landlady. 'Nicest room in the house, though I do say so myself.'

Rowlands took a cautious step into the room. There was a smell of face-powder and some expensive scent – not one he recognised as Margaret's.

'Course, the untidy side of the room's Miss Pamela's,' said Mrs Brown. 'Never had to pick up after herself, I reckon. A lot of these girls is the same. Your Margaret's the tidy one – her bed's on *this* side.' She gave a snort of laughter. 'Not that it'd make much difference to *you*, I s'pose, whether a room was untidy or not.'

Rowlands smiled, although in fact the reverse was the case. His daughters had been taught to pick up after themselves from an early age, because not to do so could have turned their home into a hazardous obstacle course for their blind father. Small wonder that 'Miss Margaret' had developed the habit of neatness. He hoped that the garrulous Mrs Brown wasn't going to stand there all day. He wanted to make a thorough search of the room, in case there was a message the landlady had overlooked.

'I'll just be a few minutes,' he said. 'If I find anything, I'll let you know.'

She took the hint at last, and he heard her slippered feet descending the stairs. At once, Rowlands turned his attention to the half of the room that was – or had been – Margaret's. There wasn't much to it: a narrow bed, covered with an eiderdown. Her pyjamas were under the pillow (this gave him a pang). Her woollen dressing-gown was on a hook behind the door. Another wrap, made of artificial silk, hung there, too. This would belong to the absent Miss Wingate, he guessed. In the wardrobe, evidently shared by the two women, hung Margaret's sensible skirts and blouses, next to more extravagant frocks, in silk and wool jersey, that he supposed must belong to her friend. Shoes. The low-heeled brogues favoured by his daughter for daytime wear were missing; a pair of lighter design, for evening, was set to one side, next to a heap of wedge-heeled sandals and lizard-skin pumps – no doubt the property of Margaret's roommate.

On the 'dressing-table' (really just a deal chest of drawers, with a mirror propped against the wall) a similar disparity was to be found between the modest pot of cold cream and tin of talcum powder that belonged, Rowlands assumed, to his daughter, and the scent bottles and other expensive unguents preferred by the room's other occupant. Or former occupant. He opened the top drawer of the chest, which he deduced, from the orderliness of the contents (clean cotton underwear, and a pile of neatly ironed handkerchiefs) belonged to Margaret. The second drawer, with its tangle of silk underthings, confirmed this impression. He shut it hastily. Of personal possessions belonging to either woman, there were few – hardly surprising, in a room this size, he thought. On a shelf beside Margaret's bed were a few books; he shook these carefully, but no note fell out. And, on Margaret's side of the chest of drawers that separated the two beds, he found a framed photograph. He picked it up.

'Handsome lad,' said a voice from behind him. In his absorption, he'd missed the creak of the landlady's footsteps on the stair. 'Mind, they all look handsome in uniform . . . Boyfriend, is he?'

'I couldn't say,' said Rowlands stiffly. Perhaps, despite Margaret's denial that they were anything but friends, the photograph was of Jonathan Simkins, now flying missions for the RAF? Perhaps not. It wasn't his business, any more than it was that of the landlady. He was about to replace the picture, when he noticed that there was another photograph – a snapshot, this one – tucked into the frame. He guessed what it must be, before Mrs Brown spoke.

'That's you, isn't it? And the others must be your wife, and Miss Margaret's sisters. Very like you, isn't she – the middle one?'

'So I've been told,' he said. 'And you were right, there wasn't a message,' he added. Although he was now more certain than ever that something was wrong. For while he could believe that the insouciant Miss Wingate might decamp from her lodgings on a whim, leaving her expensive clothes behind, he couldn't for one moment accept that Margaret would be as careless with her own possessions. It was the photographs that had convinced him. Whoever the young man in uniform was, Rowlands was sure he meant something to Margaret; she wasn't the sort of girl to display such a photograph for effect. As for the snapshot, taken by Margaret herself last summer in the back garden of 44 Grove Crescent, he knew she wouldn't deliberately have left that behind, either.

At the police station, he met with no more success than he had at the gates of Bletchley Park. The sergeant behind the desk, to whom he addressed his concerns about Margaret, and about Margaret's friend, seemed to think this a matter for levity, rather than anything else. 'So you're telling me you've lost a young lady, sir – *two* young ladies, in fact?'

'That's right.'

'Well, now, I wouldn't worry yourself too much about it. Girls *do* run off, from time to time. Prob'ly gone to meet their boys, and forgot to let anybody know! Happens all the time – 'specially with all these young folks in the services. Chaps gets a forty-eight-hour leave, and want to take their girls out – stands to reason . . .' Something about Rowlands's appearance seemed to have struck him, for he added, 'Old soldier yourself, aren't you? I noticed the stick . . . Got an uncle who fought in France. All sorts of medals, he's got.'

'My daughter's friend has been missing for three days,' said Rowlands, trying not to let his exasperation show. 'And now I discover from her landlady that my daughter didn't return to her digs last night. It's quite unlike her. She isn't the type to go off without a word to anyone.'

'They never are – until they do,' said the policeman with a chuckle. Rowlands could have shaken him. 'She's twenty-one, you said? Old enough to make up her own mind about where she's going and who with.'

'You don't understand. She . . . they're both . . . doing government work – up at Bletchley Park,' said Rowlands.

This information, although it brought about a change in the officer's manner, achieved nothing more in the way of results. 'If they're with the Park, then it's best you approach the place directly,' said the sergeant. 'Up there they like to keep themselves to themselves, if you know what I mean.'

Rowlands did know, but this was no help to him. Having left his name, address and telephone number with the sergeant, in case any news of the young women's whereabouts came to the attention of the local police, he took his leave, feeling more frustrated – and a good deal more anxious – than he had before.

All the way back in the train, Rowlands racked his brains over what could have happened to his daughter, and how – as seemed all too likely – this might be connected to the disappearance of her friend. According to the landlady, she'd last set eyes on 'Miss Pamela' on the Tuesday morning, she said. '"Must dash, Mrs B," she says to me. "Early shift, you know . . ." And *that*,' said Mrs Brown, 'was the last I saw of her. Didn't come home that night, or the next one, neither.' It couldn't be mere coincidence, he thought, that two days after this, Margaret had disappeared, in much the same way. 'Went off as usual on her bicycle,' said Mrs Brown. 'Gave me a cheery wave, like she always did . . .' That had been at twenty minutes to four, she rather thought. '"Set your watch by her," I says to my Joe.'

It was a ten-minute cycle ride from Shenley Road to the Park. So she'd have been on her way to work, thought Rowlands. Because hadn't she mentioned, when she called on Thursday night, that Pamela hadn't turned up for work that afternoon?

But what had happened to Margaret *after* that, he hadn't been able to establish. All he knew was that she hadn't returned to Shenley Road that night, or since. So something must have happened to prevent her doing that, he thought. If so, then where was she now? Had she perhaps decided to go in search of Pamela herself? It didn't seem likely that his daughter would do anything so impulsive. Even so, he enquired at the railway station to see if the station master or either of the two guards who'd been on duty could remember seeing a young woman, dressed in a fawn coat and red tam-o'-shanter, get on a train sometime after seven-thirty, the time Margaret had phoned, on Thursday night. He even checked the rack outside the station to see if there was an unclaimed bicycle – with no more success. The whereabouts of the bicycle puzzled Rowlands almost as much as the whereabouts of his daughter. He was sure it must be at Bletchley Park, since that was where Margaret had been heading on Thursday afternoon, according to the landlady. If only he'd been able to gain entrance to the place in order to confirm this for himself! But if he'd been able to do that, he might already have found some clue as to Margaret's movements on that day. Round and round went his thoughts, in an agony of uncertainty.

When he told her of his wasted journey, Edith seemed at first surprisingly unperturbed.

'Don't you see?' she said excitedly. 'The two girls must have planned this together – one going off and then the other following. Perhaps they've gone to stay with friends of Pamela's . . .' She was grasping at straws, and she knew it.

Rowlands thought it best to say nothing. Useless to point out that, even if that were the case, Margaret would certainly have let them know if she intended to be away from her lodgings for a night or two. No one who'd been living, as they were, through the months of the Blitz, when the likelihood of returning from leave to find one's home obliterated and one's loved ones missing was all too common, would have failed to take such elementary precautions. Besides which, Rowlands thought but did not say, there was the small matter of taking unauthorised leave in a time of war. People had been shot for less.

As if these harsh truths had suddenly come home to her, Edith burst into tears.

'Oh, Fred,' she wept. 'What if something terrible's happened to her?'

The same thought had occurred to Rowlands, but he comforted her as best he could.

'It may be that you're right, and the two girls are together,' he said. 'There's safety in numbers.' Although even as he said it, he didn't really believe it.

It was still within office hours, and so he dialled the familiar number, and waited while it rang, once, twice . . .

'Whitehall 1212.'

Rowlands gave his name, and made his request. A few moments later, his friend came on the line.

'Mr Rowlands. Haven't heard from you in a long time. Must be a year . . .'

'At least,' he said.

The use of his surname rather than the less formal mode of address alerted Rowlands to the fact that the chief inspector wasn't alone – a suspicion confirmed when Douglas said, 'Can you hold on a minute? There's something I've got to deal with . . .' The indistinct sounds that followed were doubtless those of a conversation muffled by a hand put over the mouthpiece. At length he heard the other say, 'All right, carry on.' Then, after a pause, 'Fred? This is an unexpected pleasure! Edith's well, I trust?'

'Yes. But . . .'

'I take it this isn't a social call.'

'No.'

'Then what can I do for you?'

As succinctly as he could, Rowlands gave the reason for his call. Douglas listened without interruption. Only when Rowlands had finished speaking did he say, 'I think you'd better come into the office. There've been some developments. And no, I can't discuss them over the phone.'

A little over an hour later, the two men sat opposite one another in the chief inspector's office at Scotland Yard. It was warmer than Rowlands had expected, since the windows that overlooked the river were tightly closed, and the radiator next to which he was sitting was throwing out a powerful heat. The smell was of wax floor polish, dusty files and the chief inspector's pipe, which he smoked incessantly. To Rowlands's relief, they were alone, and so Douglas felt able to revert to the first-name terms he wouldn't have used in front of a subordinate. 'Listen, Fred. Before I say more, I need your assurance that none of what I'm about to tell you will go any further.'

'Agreed. But . . . what can I tell Edith?'

'You can't tell her anything. Or rather,' he added, seeing that his friend was about to protest, 'no more than the bare minimum. This is "most secret" information I'm about to share with you.'

'I don't care about that,' said Rowlands impatiently. 'All I want is to find Margaret.'

'We'll get to that,' said Douglas. 'But you've got to understand that nothing I tell you now can be repeated outside this room.'

Rowlands was on his feet. 'Are you saying you know where she is?'

'Sit down, Fred. Yes, I do know – and don't worry, she's safe and well. Which is more than can be said for the other lassie.'

'What?'

'Why do you think the police have been brought into this?' said Douglas. 'Pamela Wingate was found dead in a Mayfair flat on Thursday night. She'd been strangled. So you see this is now a murder inquiry.'

For a moment, Rowlands found himself unable to react. He felt as if the breath had been knocked out of him. 'My God,' he said at last. 'That poor child. Do you have any idea who . . . ?'

'We're questioning the boyfriend. It's his flat. So far he hasn't admitted anything,' said Douglas. 'And there are circumstances that suggest that . . .' He broke off. 'Let's just say it's not a straightforward case.'

'And Margaret?' said Rowlands. 'Where does she come into this? Pamela was her friend, it's true, but I can't believe she knows anything that can have a bearing on such a dreadful crime.'

'You may be surprised,' said Douglas. 'And you'd better prepare yourself. I'm going to take you to see Margaret now, but before I do, I'll need your word that you won't reveal a syllable of what passes between you.'

'You have it.' Once more, Rowlands was on his feet. 'Now tell me where she is.'

'Holloway prison,' was the reply. 'I warned you it'd be a shock.'

Chapter Five

It had been nearly fifteen years since Rowlands had last set foot inside the gates of the women's prison, to visit his sister – then incarcerated for assaulting a police officer during the course of a political protest. It wasn't an experience he was likely to forget – nor one he'd thought he'd have to repeat, in order to visit his daughter. Yet here he was once more, entering the wicket to one side of that ponderous gate, loomed over, he knew, by grim turrets that made no bones about the building's being a fortress. And yet (he reflected wryly) it had been easier to penetrate these massive walls than to pass through the relatively insubstantial wire fence that formed the boundary of Bletchley Park.

In the car on the way here, nothing had been said as to why Rowlands's daughter now found herself in such a place – nor how it was that he had been granted permission to see her.

'You'll find out soon enough,' Douglas had grunted; he, it seemed, was more concerned with the question of whether last night's bombing had rendered the route from Westminster to Holloway impassable or not, than with any discussion of what took them there. Perhaps for Rowlands's benefit, he kept up a running commentary on the progress, or otherwise, that had been made in clearing debris from the streets through which they were passing. 'We'll take Farringdon Road,' he said to the driver as they sped along the Embankment. 'It's pretty clear along there. Although Cripplegate's not what it was. You're lucky you can't see it,' he added to his friend. 'Smashed to pieces in a night – all but St Giles's church, and even that's half-ruined.'

Rowlands, who had seen the devastation of Ypres during the last 'show', made a non-committal sound. Memories of that scorched and flattened Flanders city, its once-magnificent Cloth Hall reduced to rubble, came back to him at Douglas's words. He didn't need to see the ruins of Clerkenwell now, to know what it must look like. There was that familiar, acrid smell of burning, too, which hung over London. In the past few months, it had become, in a very real sense, an infernal city.

'Saw a double-decker bus that'd fallen into a crater in High Holborn, middle of last week,' Douglas was saying. 'Devil's own job to haul it out again . . . St Paul's is still standing, though. Which, if you'd seen the firestorms around it two months back, might strike even an irreligious man as miraculous.'

As the inner gates of the prison clanged shut behind them, Rowlands gave an involuntary shudder.

'Unpleasant sensation, isn't it?' muttered the chief inspector. 'No matter how many times I set foot in a gaol,

I'm always glad to get out again.' Rowlands could only concur with this view, although what made the sounds and smells of the place infinitely worse was the thought that his beloved daughter was even now having to endure them.

'I want to know what she's supposed to have done,' he said, as the two of them, accompanied by the female prison officer, traversed the labyrinth of corridors that led to the gaol's interior.

'You'll find out in good time,' was the maddening reply; before Rowlands could demand a better one, the wardress who'd led the way came to an abrupt halt. There was a jangle of keys as she unlocked a door.

'In you go,' said Douglas to his friend.

Rowlands needed no second bidding.

'Daddy!' There was the sound of hurried footsteps on the tiled floor. A moment later, his daughter was in his arms.

'It's all right, Briggs,' said the chief inspector to the WPC who'd followed Margaret to the door. 'You can wait outside.'

'Sir.'

'Are you all right, Meg?' Mingled with the joy Rowlands felt at finding his daughter at last was anger at the circumstances in which he found her. 'What on earth are you doing here? Will someone tell me what's going on?'

'I haven't done anything wrong, Daddy . . .'

'I know that. What I *don't* know is why you've been put here.'

'Perhaps I can answer that,' said another voice from across the room. It was a voice Rowlands recognised.

'Miss Barnes,' he said. 'Well, well.'

'You don't sound surprised to find me here.'

'I suppose I'm not, very. And I've certainly got questions for you. But I want to hear what Margaret has to say first.'

'I . . .' said Margaret, then stopped.

'Go on,' said Iris Barnes, sounding faintly amused. 'You'd better tell your father all you know.'

'All right.'

'Perhaps we should all sit down,' said Alasdair Douglas. 'There's a chair just to your left,' he added to Rowlands. 'I'll take this one, opposite you ladies, if I may.'

The room – or cell, rather – appeared to be considerably larger than Rowlands had expected; even with the four of them occupying the space, it didn't seem unduly cramped. Most cells, he knew, were barely large enough for one inmate – two at the most. This seemed palatial, by contrast. The reason for this didn't, fortunately, strike him until later, when he and Douglas were in the car on the way back to Scotland Yard. Of course.

'That was the condemned cell,' he said. It wasn't the first time that he'd set foot in such a place, either.

'Och, it was the best place to put her, I'd imagine,' said the chief inspector, although he couldn't quite conceal his embarrassment. 'I mean, given that she had to be kept away from the other prisoners . . . It's not as if they've had much occasion to use it – unlike in the men's gaols, where it's occupied a good deal.' Yes, Rowlands was glad he hadn't known what the true nature of the room was until afterwards.

When they were all seated around a large deal table on the far side of the room, Margaret began speaking –

hesitantly at first, then gaining confidence. 'It all started on Thursday, after I'd finished work . . . Or rather, a bit before that, when Pam didn't come back. Only I thought . . . we all thought . . . well, that she'd taken an extra day's leave. It was only later that . . .' She broke off.

'Why don't you stick to telling your part of the story, and leave Miss Wingate out of it for the time being?' said Douglas, in a gentler tone than Rowlands had heard him use before.

'All right. But I do wish I knew what had happened to Pam. She hasn't come back, has she?' said Margaret eagerly.

'No, she hasn't come back,' replied the chief inspector.

'Oh dear. I had hoped . . .'

'Go on,' said Iris Barnes. It struck Rowlands that she probably knew a good deal more about the affair than she had so far let on.

'Yes. Yes, of course.' Margaret sounded flustered. Perhaps it was the thought of her friend that had thrown her. Rowlands's heart ached for her. She was too young to have to cope with this, he thought. 'Well, it was towards the end of the shift – just before midnight, I suppose. We were short-staffed because a couple of the girls had gone down with flu, and so Pam and I had been moved from the early shift to cover for them . . . Only Pam didn't come in that day either,' she added bleakly. 'I'd had my break at half past seven – that was when I phoned you,' she said to her father. 'I . . . I'd made up my mind that I had to make more of a fuss about the fact that Pam was missing. I mean, *somebody* had to know where she was, surely? I thought I'd start with my section head, and work upwards . . .'

She paused for a moment, as if nerving herself for what she had to say next. 'Before I could get to talk to him – we're not supposed to stop what we're doing until we're told we may – my section head came in, and told us all to stop work immediately. Then we were called out of the room, one by one, and told to stand by our lockers, while a search was carried out. When it got to my turn, I was told to hand over my keys, while one of the duty staff opened the locker in front of me. I . . . I knew there wasn't anything in there except a pair of shoes I was going to take to be mended. The heel had come off,' she added inconsequentially. 'Then I saw that . . . that there was something else in the locker. Some papers.'

'Documents of a technical nature, weren't they?' interjected Miss Barnes.

'Yes,' said Margaret. 'Although it was only later that I found that out. My section head told me I had to come with him at once . . . I couldn't even go back into the room to fetch my bag. He took me to . . . an office, I suppose . . . somewhere in the main building. I wasn't allowed to speak to anyone. He . . . he told me to wait there, and said that somebody would come for me.' She broke off, as if the telling of all this had exhausted her, then resumed. 'After I'd waited for . . . a while . . . I don't know how long exactly . . . somebody brought me a cup of tea.' She attempted a laugh. 'I was glad to have it, actually, because I hadn't had anything since the soup I'd had for supper, in the canteen . . . Anyway, I waited a bit longer, and then somebody else came with my things – my coat and bag – and said we'd be leaving directly. I thought he meant that I'd be sent home – back to my lodgings, I mean – but it turned out that there was a car waiting outside. I . . . I was told to get in, and then we drove quite a long way . . . it was dark of course, and so I couldn't see where I was being taken, but I guessed it must be London, because after a while we arrived at the outskirts of a city. Eventually things started to look familiar, even though I couldn't see much in the dark. We stopped outside a big building. I think it was Whitehall . . .'

'It was,' said Miss Barnes.

'We drove around to the back of the building and I was told I had to get out. Then I was taken to another office, where there were some people waiting . . .'

'One of them being myself,' said Iris Barnes. 'Which was perhaps fortunate for you.'

'Yes,' agreed Margaret. 'It was.' She was silent a moment. 'When I'd taken off my coat, and sat down, they . . . you . . . asked me if I wanted anything to eat or drink. I said I didn't. I was told that I'd have to answer some questions, before they'd decide what to do with me. Do you want me to say what it was I was questioned about?'

'I think we can leave it there for the moment,' said Miss Barnes. 'Let's just say that certain documents of a classified nature were found in your possession – or so it appeared,' she added, as Rowlands seemed about to protest. 'We needn't worry ourselves as to what exactly the documents were, or how important, or otherwise, they might have been to the conduct of the war. What was necessary to establish, over what must have been a gruelling few hours for you, Margaret, was whether you were the one responsible for taking them.'

'Of course she wasn't!' Having sat in silence throughout all this, Rowlands was no longer able to restrain his indignation at the treatment his daughter had received at the hands of the security service. 'Anyone with half an ounce of intelligence could have seen that.'

'Daddy, please . . .'

'You're absolutely right,' said Iris Barnes. 'And I'm glad to say that "intelligence" eventually prevailed. But you must see, Mr Rowlands, that it looked rather black for Margaret just then. Especially once we became aware of the other girl's disappearance a few days before.'

'I know all about that,' said Rowlands. 'I spoke to the landlady.'

'Did you, indeed?' Again, Rowlands thought he detected a note of amusement in the secret agent's voice. 'I might have known you wouldn't lose any time in getting to the bottom of things.'

'Daddy, I hope you haven't stirred things up any more than they already are,' said Margaret reprovingly.

'I couldn't say,' said her father. 'What I want to know from *you*, Miss Barnes, is why it was thought necessary to incarcerate my daughter in Holloway prison? You surely can't think she's guilty of stealing those documents you refer to? That's completely ridiculous, and you know it.'

'Yes,' said Miss Barnes. She was silent for a moment, perhaps weighing up what she was going to say next. 'Has it occurred to you, Mr Rowlands, that – given the circumstances – this might be the safest place for Margaret, just now?'

It was Rowlands's turn to be silent. 'You think Margaret's life might be in danger?' he said at last.

'It's a possibility,' was the reply. 'Seeing what's happened to the other girl.'

'You're talking about Pamela, aren't you?' said Margaret. 'I knew something was up! What's going on? What's happened to Pam?'

'I'm afraid your friend's dead. Murdered.' Iris Barnes's voice was crisp and brutally matter-of-fact.

Margaret gave a low cry of horror. 'I don't believe it! Who'd want to hurt Pam? She was so lovely.'

'Unfortunately, it's all too true, Miss Rowlands,' said the chief inspector. 'I was going to tell you, in good time, but . . .' He let the rest of the sentence hang in the air.

'I don't see any point in beating about the bush, when something like this is at stake,' said Miss Barnes. 'Bad news doesn't improve with keeping. It seems likely there's a connection between your friend's murder and the theft of the documents,' she went on, addressing Margaret. She paused to light a cigarette; then added, 'Care for one yourself?'

'Yes, please.' Margaret took the offered cigarette and lit it. 'Do you mean to say that Pam took those papers?' she said.

'We must assume so,' was the reply. 'Either she took them, or someone else did, and she found them. What seems probable – given that you and she knew one another – was that she was the one who put them in your locker.'

'But *why*?' Margaret sounded stunned by what she had heard. 'Pam would never have played such a dirty trick on me.'

'Wouldn't she?' The question hung in the air. 'How well did you know your friend, Margaret?'

'I . . . that is . . . Not very well, I suppose,' said Margaret. 'But . . . but . . . whatever you say, I'm sure she wasn't a traitor.' She was silent a moment. 'I want to know when it happened,' she said at last. 'I mean . . . when did she die?'

'She was found on Thursday night,' replied Douglas. 'By her boyfriend. The Honourable Hugh Montfitchet, to his friends.'

'But . . . they were engaged,' said Margaret. 'You don't think he . . . ?'

'Too soon to say,' replied the chief inspector gruffly. 'Although it was at his flat in Mount Street that she was found. He denies all knowledge of how she got there, o' course. He'd just gone on leave, he says, after a month at sea. Travelled up from Portsmouth that day on the 5.15 – ticket was handed in, so *that* part fits. Says he'd arranged to meet the girl at the Café de Paris at eight, but she didn't show up. He got tired of waiting after an hour, he says, and went to his club for dinner. Plenty of witnesses saw him up to ten thirty, when he says he went on to another watering-hole – The Blue Oyster – for a nightcap. Manager *thinks* he remembers a young chap in naval uniform answering to Montfitchet's description, but can't be sure. Time of death seems to have been between eight and midnight, which is when our young friend returned to his flat in Piccadilly – so he *could* have done it, between arriving back at his flat and going out again, although he *says* he only returned to Mount Street to change, and went straight out . . . So there's a period unaccounted for between 7.30 p.m. and 8.00 p.m., between when he left his flat and when he got to the Café de Paris, and again between ten thirty and midnight. Let's just say we're keeping Mr Montfitchet under observation for the time being,' he said, then, in a tone of concern, 'You're looking a bit peaky, Miss Rowlands. Shall I send WPC Briggs to fetch you a nice cup of tea?'

'I'm fine, really,' said Margaret, then, to Rowlands, who had been about to protest that his daughter had had enough, 'It's all right, Daddy. I need to hear this.' She sounded calmer, now. 'There's something I don't understand,' she went on. 'Pamela went missing on Tuesday afternoon. If she wasn't found until Thursday night, then there are two days unaccounted for. Where was she during that time – and who with, if she wasn't with Hugh?'

'That's what we're trying to find out,' said Alasdair Douglas. 'Maybe you can help us, at that.'

'I don't see how.'

'You were Miss Wingate's friend,' said Douglas. 'You shared a room with her. Worked in the same outfit, too, from what I can gather. Perhaps you can give us an idea who else she went about with?'

Margaret was silent a moment. 'I can try,' she said. 'But it won't help you much. Pam and I . . . well, we weren't really in the same "set" – especially after she got engaged to Hugh Montfitchet. She spent most of her free time after that with him . . . or . . . or his friends, when he was at sea. But I didn't really know them, either. I mean, she'd talk about the parties she'd been to, in London – but it was all rather vague . . . that is . . . I . . .' She broke off confusedly; then said, 'I'm afraid there's not much I can add.'

'Did she mention anyone particular that she was seeing?' the chief inspector persisted. 'Any name that you can recall?'

'I don't remember a name . . . That is . . . She didn't mention anyone else apart from Hugh.'

'Not to worry,' said Douglas heartily. 'If anything *does* occur to you, perhaps you'll let me know?'

'All right.' Margaret sounded utterly defeated. 'It's just so awful,' she went on, 'that anyone should want to hurt Pam.'

'These are ruthless people we're dealing with,' said Iris Barnes.

'And just who are they – these people?' said Rowlands.

'Why, our enemies,' was the reply. 'Although at present I'm not entirely sure *which* of them we're dealing with.'

'I still don't understand where Margaret comes into this,' said Rowlands. 'You've already said that you don't think she had anything to do with taking those documents, and she'd obviously nothing to do with Pamela Wingate's disappearance.'

'Yes, but whoever killed the Wingate girl doesn't know that,' said Miss Barnes, to whom he had addressed these remarks. 'Even though it was done with the utmost discretion, you can be sure that the news of Margaret's arrest will have got out. These things always do, in a closed circle like the one at Bletchley.'

Rowlands recalled Marjorie Milward's reaction when she learnt he was Margaret's father. 'The fact that those papers were found in Margaret's locker means she's now as much a target for our killer as Pamela Wingate was,' said the chief inspector. 'After all, he's no way of knowing how much the Wingate girl might have said to you about whatever it was she was up to,' he added, addressing Margaret directly.

Again, she fell silent, as if trying to make sense of all this. 'I don't understand it,' she said at last. 'Pam could be . . . well, a bit thoughtless at times – but I just don't see her as a traitor.'

'Perhaps she didn't realise what she was getting into until it was too late,' said Miss Barnes. 'When she *did* realise, she panicked. Which might account for the fact that she hid those papers where she thought no one would look for them – a friend's locker.'

'Do you think that's why she was killed?' said Margaret in a small voice. 'Because she changed her mind about handing over those documents?'

'Again, it's possible,' was the reply. 'This isn't the first such leak we've traced, so it may be that whoever the girl was feeding information to decided she was no longer a reliable source.' There was a moment's silence, as all of them considered this.

Margaret shivered. 'Poor Pam. Whatever she's done, she didn't deserve to die.' No one corrected her; although, thought Rowlands, treason was still a capital crime. But Pamela had been her friend.

'So you see,' said the chief inspector, 'this is the safest place for you at present. More than that, the fact that you're known to have been arrested might serve to put our killer off his guard.'

Rowlands could see the sense of this. Because, hard as this seeming loss of liberty must be for his daughter to endure, if it meant she was safe from harm, then there was no alternative. She, too, appeared to have accepted Douglas's line of reasoning, but then she burst out, 'It's just that . . . I can't bear the thought that people might believe that I could have stolen those documents or . . . or sold out to our enemies.' She sounded close to tears.

Rowlands reached for her hand, and squeezed it. 'No one who knows you could believe that,' he said. 'If I've understood what the chief inspector said, your being here is going to help him catch the man who did this awful thing.'

'That's about the size of it,' agreed Douglas. 'You've just got to sit tight for a wee while longer, Miss Rowlands, until it's safe for you to return to your work once more.'

'But will I be *allowed* to return to Bletchley Park?' said Margaret. 'Won't my . . . my *reputation* be tarnished, having fallen under suspicion of being a traitor?'

'I think I can safely say that there won't be any question of that,' said Miss Barnes. 'And now, unless either you or your father have any further questions for me, I'll be off. I've a war to run.'

She got up, and was making her way towards the door, when Rowlands said, 'I do have one other question. Do you think whoever's responsible for these crimes – the theft of the papers and the murder of Miss Wingate – is connected to Bletchley Park?'

Iris Barnes paused a moment before replying. 'Let's just say we're not ruling it out,' she said.

'In which case, don't you think it would make sense

to carry out further investigations at Bletchley?' said Rowlands. 'Given that it seems more than likely that . . .' He broke off, reluctant to put into words what it was he meant.

Miss Barnes had no such compunction, however. 'That there's a traitor at the Park?' she finished for him. 'The idea is certainly one we've considered. As for investigating further, that's something that should be left to the proper authorities. And I *don't* mean the police, saving your presence, Chief Inspector. A security leak such as this isn't really your concern.'

'Murder makes it my concern,' said Alasdair Douglas.

The car came for him at a quarter past six on Saturday morning.

'Might as well make an early start,' said the chief inspector. 'These intelligence johnnies work pretty odd hours, I gather, and so as like as not we'll find a few of 'em about first thing.'

Whether the hour was early or late made no difference to Rowlands, whose own sleeping patterns bore little relation to the hours of daylight or darkness; since he'd been blind, it had seemed to him more and more that going to bed and getting up at a certain hour was a matter of convention, and suiting others' convenience.

More problematic for him than the early rising was the question of what he should say to Edith about the nature of the investigation into which he had, it seemed, been conscripted. It had been bad enough telling her about Margaret's whereabouts; once her delight and relief that her daughter was safe and well had subsided, she'd demanded to know where the latter was at that moment – and why she couldn't come home.

'You won't like it when I tell you,' he'd said, and did so.

'*What!* I thought you said she was safe – not in prison!'

'Keep your voice down,' he said. 'You'll wake the others.' Their conversation had taken place late that night, after Rowlands had been dropped off in the police car – another thing to which Edith had objected.

'What the neighbours will think I can't imagine.'

'What does it matter what they think?' Now, he tried to reassure her. 'Margaret *is* safe – that's the whole point. She's in a place where nobody can harm her. And she's got her books.' This fact he'd discovered only as he was taking his leave of his daughter. 'Are you sure you're going to be all right, Meg?' he'd asked. 'It can't be much fun for you, being locked up like this – even if it *is* for your own good.'

'I'll be fine, Daddy. It's not so bad in here. I'm getting on with some research, as a matter of fact. The warden's been very kind about letting me have some books and a supply of writing materials.' She gave a tremulous little laugh. 'You'll have to take my word for it, of course, but the room itself isn't so bad. A bit austere, perhaps – but no worse than my rooms in college.'

'Well, if you're sure . . .'

'I'm sure.' She'd hugged him, then. 'You will find him, won't you, Daddy? The man who's done this dreadful thing?' He assured her that he'd do his utmost – although really, he thought, what *could* he do, practically speaking, that would be of any use? A blind man, with little knowledge of the world of secret codes and subterfuge.

'You may be wondering,' said Alasdair Douglas, as the Wolseley nosed its way out of Grove Crescent, and turned onto London Road, 'why I've asked you to come along wi' me?'

'The question did cross my mind.'

'My reason's twofold. First of all, you knew the deceased – albeit for a short time – and you met that chap of hers, too . . . the Montfitchet lad. Second, you've a knack for this kind o' thing. Somehow . . . I don't know how you do it . . . but you get people to talk to you.'

'It's because I'm blind,' said Rowlands. 'People think, because I can't see them, that I'm not judging them in the same way that a sighted person would.'

'Mebbe. All I know is, it gets results. Folk trust you. Which,' said the chief inspector,' can come in very handy when you're trying to find out whether they know anything, and if so, how *much* they know.'

'Hmph.' Rowlands wasn't sure that he liked this portrayal of himself as a kind of spy. Although it wasn't the first time it had been said of him.

'There's another reason why I wanted you to come along,' said Douglas. 'And that's the fact that your Margaret's caught up in all this. As a policeman, I can't allow myself to bring personal relationships into an investigation. But that needn't apply to you. You want to find out the truth, don't you, about who killed Pamela Wingate? For Margaret's sake.'

'Oh yes,' said Rowlands quietly.

His friend laughed. 'Then that makes you a dangerous adversary,' he said.

Chapter Six

This time there was no difficulty getting past the sentry at the gate. After the briefest of halts, during which the chief inspector confirmed that he was who he said he was, the car was waved through.

'Go on up to the house, sir,' said the soldier on guard. 'They're expecting you.' Rowlands, included in this general invitation, wasn't asked to identify himself, which was a relief – although of course, he told himself, it wasn't very likely that this was the same man who'd turned him away so ignominiously on the previous day.

As the police Wolseley began to make its way along the drive that led to the mansion, the driver, who been proceeding at a speed of no more than 15mph, slammed on the brakes.

'Bloody fool! Beg pardon, sir, but if I hadn't spotted him in time, he'd have gone across the bonnet . . . Hi, you! Look where you're going!' he shouted at the offender – evidently a cyclist – who'd shot out of a nearby turning without looking. The only reply was the defiant ringing of a bicycle bell, as the miscreant pedalled off.

'Silly ass,' agreed Douglas. 'You did quite right, Sergeant. Can't go killing members of the local populace, even if they *are* at fault. I must say,' he went on, as the car resumed its progress, 'they seem like an odd bunch around here, if that specimen was anything to go by. Fellow was wearing his pyjamas underneath his greatcoat. And a gas mask.'

'He obviously believes in being prepared.'

The chief inspector emitted a snuffle of amusement. 'Mind you, he's not the only oddball, judging by the general standard of dress,' he went on. 'Rum lot of coves altogether.' He spoke as the Wolseley nosed its way past what Rowlands would later discover was the first of a collection of huts. From these, a crowd of young men was just then emerging – Rowlands could hear their jovial shouts. Like boys let out of school, he thought. 'You'd think to look at them that they were a lot of undergrads,' said Douglas, confirming this impression. 'Oxford bags and shabby tweeds. Not a decent haircut in sight. As for the women . . .' Of course, thought Rowlands, there would be women; if not for present circumstances, his Margaret would have been one of them. 'You'd be forgiven for thinking you'd stumbled on a ladies' sewing circle, not a branch of British Intelligence.'

The Wolseley came to a halt on the gravel sweep in front of the house. Getting out of the car, Rowlands and his companion found themselves in the midst of a bevy of young women. Voices came at them from all sides: 'Gosh, I'm absolutely frozen. I swear there's something the matter with the radiators in our office. Can't wait to get into a nice hot bath . . .'

'Hot? You'll be lucky! "Have you seen the price of coals, duck?"' (This last delivered in a screeching voice, doubtless intended as a satire on the speaker's landlady.)

'Hurry up, Madge, do! I'm dying for a cup of tea . . .'

'Bacon and eggs for me, duck . . .' (The screechy voice again.)

'Excuse me, ladies . . .' Douglas's booming tones sounded all the louder over this feminine hilarity. As he piloted Rowlands through the door of the mansion, a ripple of women's laughter followed them.

'Hoots,' said the one who'd demanded bacon and eggs. 'Whut's the *for-rce* doing here, I wonder?'

'Shh, Madge, he'll hear you . . .'

'What if he does? He's hardly going to arrest me!'

Another burst of laughter.

'Silly young females,' muttered Douglas, as, having passed through a vestibule, he and Rowlands found themselves in a spacious entrance hall. 'How did they know I was a policeman? It's not that obvious, is it?'

Rowlands suspected that it was, but he said diplomatically: 'They'll have seen the car – and the uniformed officer at the wheel, I expect.'

'You're right,' said Douglas, evidently satisfied that his calling might otherwise have remained a mystery. 'Ah, now *that's* more like it!' he said in an undertone to his companion, as heels clicked smartly across the tiled floor towards them. 'Neat and trim as the very vessel of His Majesty's fleet on which she serves . . .'

This somewhat baffling remark became intelligible for

Rowlands when the 'trim little vessel' herself piped up. 'Chief Inspector Douglas? Commander Murchison says will you join him in his office?'

'Thank you, er . . .'

'Petty Officer Smedley, sir. If you'll come with me, sir.' The heels clicked away once more, leaving the two men to follow, up a flight of stairs and along a corridor to a door at the far end. This the petty officer opened without knocking, announcing as she did so, 'The chief inspector to see you, sir.' Rowlands she did not announce, which was fine with him. In spite of what Douglas had said to him in the car on the way here, he still wasn't sure what he was doing there.

The door closed behind them. From across the room, at a distance of perhaps fifteen feet, came a voice – addressing not the two men who'd just entered, but someone on the other end of the telephone: 'Yes, sir . . . Right you are, sir . . . I'll ensure you receive it in the next bag, sir . . .' Valedictions were exchanged and the receiver replaced in its cradle. 'My apologies for keeping you waiting, gentlemen,' said the speaker, now turning his attention to the new arrivals. 'That was the PM. He does like to be kept informed of what we're doing here. It's good to see you again, Chief Inspector – although I could wish the circumstances were otherwise . . . Perhaps,' he added, 'you'd be so good as to introduce me to your colleague?'

Douglas did so. 'Ah,' said Commander Murchison. 'You're Miss Rowlands's father, I take it? Then I don't quite see . . .'

'I've asked Mr Rowlands to join me in an advisory capacity,' said Douglas. 'As you've pointed out,

Commander, he has an interest in the case already, because of his daughter's involvement. And he knew the Wingate girl.'

'I see,' said the naval officer dubiously. 'I suppose it's all right, if you say so, Chief Inspector. But I should point out that these are highly confidential matters.'

'I'm sure Mr Rowlands understands that – don't you, Fred?' said the chief inspector. 'It isn't the first time he's had dealings with the secret service.'

'Very well,' said Murchison. 'Then let's get on with it, shall we? Do take a seat, gentlemen. May I offer you a cigarette?' He pushed a box across the desk towards Rowlands, who took one; it turned out to be a very good Virginian.

'I'd prefer my pipe, if it's all the same to you,' said Douglas.

'I'm a pipe man, myself,' said the other. 'Well,' he said, when all three had lit up. 'This is a bad business.'

'Aye,' said the chief inspector. 'It is that.'

'Perhaps you could bring me up to date with the investigation so far . . . starting with the girl's death . . . Miss Wingate, I should say. I understand you've arrested the man concerned?'

'Lieutenant Montfitchet. Yes, we've got him in custody.'

'A naval man,' said the commander, with faint disgust. 'Do you think he's mixed up in all this other business? Or was the girl's death merely a . . . how shall I put it . . . ?'

'Lovers' tiff that went too far?' supplied the chief inspector. 'We don't know, as yet. Doctor's report says she died between eight and midnight – they never *will* commit themselves to a more specific time. Montfitchet admits he returned to the flat at 7 p.m. to get changed, and then went out again. *If* he's telling the truth, and he didn't return to the flat again before midnight, he's in the clear . . . but we've only his word for it. The porter at the flats went off duty at 11.30 p.m., and the night porter didn't arrive at his post until a quarter past midnight – his bicycle had a puncture, he says. So our man *could* have got back earlier than he says he did. No one remembers seeing him at his club after 10.30 p.m., and the manager of the nightclub he claims he went on to afterwards can't swear that it was the same naval officer he saw.'

'Whatever the truth of the matter, it looks very bad for the service,' said Murchison, who seemed to take this as a personal affront.

'Then there's the question of how she – Miss Wingate – got into the Mount Street flat,' went on Douglas. 'If Montfitchet didn't let her in, then who did? She didn't have her own latch-key. There were signs that someone had been in the flat with her for some time before she was killed – two glasses had been used. There were traces of whisky in both. Two cigarette stubs – different brands – were in the ashtray. Glasses and ashtray wiped clean, o' course,' he added.

'Which suggests premeditation,' said Murchison.

'It does,' said the policeman. 'Although why Montfitchet would wipe off his own fingerprints, when it was his flat, doesn't make sense. Not unless the fingerprints belonged to someone else . . .'

A silence followed. 'One thing that seems pretty clear,' said Commander Murchison at last, 'is that

Pamela Wingate was passing secrets to somebody. Those documents that were found in Miss Rowlands's locker . . . the Wingate girl put them there, you think?'

'That's what we're assuming must have happened,' said Douglas.

'So it would seem,' went on Commander Murchison, 'that the girl – Wingate – must have had a contact, either here, at the Park, or outside, to whom she was passing these documents. A traitor, in fact.' His voice was bleak.

'Aye, that's about the size of it,' said the chief inspector.

A silence followed, which was broken at last by the naval officer. 'What are we going to do about it?'

'That rather depends,' said Douglas, after a moment's consideration, 'on how far it's gone. I mean, is this the first such instance you've had of documents going missing?'

'No,' was the curt reply. 'And I'm afraid I can't go into any more detail than that, other than to say that we've been aware that information was being passed to the enemy for a number of weeks. Perhaps months,' he added. 'Tracing it back, you understand, is a complex business, involving . . . well, let's just say that there are a number of different agencies concerned.'

'One of them MI6, I take it?'

'Amongst others. So you see, Chief Inspector, that discretion is of the utmost importance, in these investigations of yours.'

'Understood,' said Douglas, no less brusque in his response to these stipulations than the commander had been in making them. 'I'll need to question the people the Wingate girl was working with, o' course.'

'I've no objection to that. Just as long as you're careful

not to alert our traitor to the fact that we're onto him.'

'Or her,' said Douglas. 'But I take your point, Commander. We'll do our best to keep matters under our hats, so to speak . . . Which is where Mr Rowlands comes in . . .'

Rowlands, who had been listening attentively to what had been said by the others, was startled enough to exclaim, 'I? But what on earth can I possibly contribute? I know next to nothing about what goes on at Bletchley Park. Added to which,' he said, with a faint smile, 'as the commander might have observed, I'm blind. Hardly the ideal candidate for a life of espionage.'

'Tosh,' was the chief inspector's succinct reply to this piece of false modesty. 'Ye ken fine well that ye've helped me out more times than I care to recall. Mr Rowlands's blindness doesn't affect his brainpower,' he added to Murchison. 'I'll want him there while I'm conducting the interrogations,' he went on. 'Just lending an ear, ye ken, to see if anything untoward strikes him.'

'All right,' said Murchison, although he didn't sound wholly convinced. 'We'll have to think of a reason why you're here,' he said, addressing Rowlands. 'Blind or not, we can't have you wandering around the place without good reason.'

'Man from the Ministry, I thought,' said Douglas. 'You must have plenty of 'em poking their noses in, from time to time. Seeing how the money's being spent,' he added drily.

'Too true,' was the reply. 'Very well, Mr Rowlands. You can be here on "official business". I'll draft a memo to all departments. You'll report to me, Chief Inspector, as soon as you find anything out about this deplorable affair,' he added. 'I think it's best if we keep the matter between ourselves, as far as possible. The fewer people who know what's happened – or the steps we are taking to rectify the problem – the better, in my opinion.'

'Agreed,' said Douglas. 'I think, Commander, that we'd better start with a general look around the place. Put our heads into some o' these huts – the one where the Wingate girl was based, to start with.'

'That'd be Hut 6,' was the reply. 'But you won't be able to march right in, I'm afraid. That'd *really* put the cat among the pigeons! Bear with me a moment, will you?' He pressed a bell upon his desk, and a moment later, the door opened, to admit the efficient Petty Officer Smedley.

'Sir?'

'You're to escort these gentlemen to Hut 6 – and anywhere else they want to go,' said Murchison. He scribbled something on a piece of paper. 'If anyone objects, you can show them this.'

'Yes, sir.' She advanced towards where he was sitting, took the note from him, stepped back a pace and saluted.

'All right, Petty Officer. Carry on.' With which the two men understood that they, too, were dismissed. Whatever the lack of military discipline to be seen amongst some of the denizens of Bletchley Park, Commander Murchison evidently believed in maintaining a certain level of nautical smartness in his own realm.

Douglas's sergeant was waiting for them outside; he fell into step with the little party as it made its way from the house towards the nearest row of huts – a distance of a couple of hundred yards. There had been a good fire in Murchison's office; coming out from the warmth of this made the contrast with the raw February air all the more extreme. Rowlands was glad of his heavy tweed overcoat. The bustle of people going to and fro between the huts had died down during the time he and Douglas had been closeted with the head of the station, and a silence lay over the frosty lawns – although from time to time this was shattered by the roar of a motorcycle, signalling the arrival of a despatch rider.

'Been here long?' asked Douglas of the little Wren who was leading the way.

'Eight months, sir. Came straight from training.'

'You've done well to get promoted in such a short time.'

'Thank you, sir. At first I was disappointed not to get a ship but P5 . . . I mean, HMS *Pembroke V* . . . is a good berth, taken all in all.'

'Glad to hear it. So these are the huts we've heard so much about?'

'Yes, sir.'

'Now let's see. If this is Hut 1, then those must be 2 and 3.'

'Actually that's Hut 8, sir. Hut 6 is the one next to it, with Hut 3 on the far side of that.'

'Hmm,' said Douglas. 'I suppose it makes sense, once you know your way around.'

'Yes, sir. Here we are, sir. Hut 6,' said Petty Officer Smedley. She opened a door and they went in. A long, narrow corridor lay ahead of them, and there was a powerful smell of coke from the iron stoves that were the building's only source of heat. Their footsteps sounded hollowly on the linoleum-covered floor as the little party walked a few yards along the hallway, to where a door stood ajar.

From inside came the sound of typewriter keys tapping, and the subdued murmur of voices: 'Got those transcripts for me, yet?'

'Nearly done, sir.'

'Well, hurry up, there's a good girl. I haven't got all day . . .'

Perhaps alerted by the sound of footsteps, a head poked itself out of the gap in the doorway. 'What do *you* want?' it said rudely. 'You can't come in here.'

'Commander Murchison's orders,' said the Wren. 'These gentlemen are to be given access to Hut 6, and anywhere else they want to go.'

'Blast Murchison!' said the other. 'What does he mean, sending a lot of civilians along to my section? Who are you anyway?' he demanded, evidently addressing Douglas.

'Police,' was the curt reply. 'And who might *you* be, sir?'

'Name's Allingham. Harry Allingham,' was the reply. 'I'm in charge here.'

'Then you're just the man I want to see,' said Douglas. 'Is there somewhere we can talk in private, Mr Allingham?'

'You'd better come to my office,' said the other ungraciously. 'Although I can't spare you very much time, I'm afraid. I've a lot to get on with . . . Get back to your desks!' he shouted – presumably addressing the

102

other occupants of the room. 'This isn't a tea-break . . . See what you've done?' he added gloomily to the police inspector, closing the door of the room from which he had come behind him. 'Got the women all stirred up. I'll be lucky if I can get a decent eight hours' work out of them after this.'

The room into which he conducted them – Rowlands, Douglas and his sergeant (Petty Officer Smedley sensibly remained outside in the corridor) – was barely large enough to contain four people, and was sparsely furnished, with a desk, behind which Douglas seated himself ('No leg room,' he muttered. 'Government issue, no doubt.') and a deal chair, to which he directed Rowlands. 'I'll need another chair for my sergeant,' Douglas said placidly. 'And one for the young ladies and gentlemen I'll be talking to.'

'I say, what's all this about?' demanded the man whose office had just been commandeered. 'Waltzing in here and making yourself at home, without a by-your-leave. I want to know what this is about.'

'It's a murder inquiry, Mr Allingham. As of now, I'm taking over your office as an interview room. I realise it's something of an inconvenience for you, but . . .'

'A *murder* inquiry?' The young man seemed genuinely flabbergasted. 'Wh-who's been murdered?'

'Young woman by the name of Pamela Wingate. I gather she worked in Hut 6.'

'Pamela? B-but she's off sick, surely? Taken a week's leave . . .'

'Who told you that?' said Douglas sharply.

'I . . . I don't remember exactly. Somebody must

have said something. Happens a lot. People drop out. Nervous exhaustion, mainly. And they complain of sore eyes . . . the huts *are* poorly lit . . . And chilblains . . . that's the cold, of course. I've had several go down with bronchitis . . .' In his excitement, he was babbling. 'I think I just assumed . . .'

'Well, your assumption was wrong,' said the chief inspector. 'The girl was found dead two days ago.'

'I . . . I don't believe it.'

'I'm afraid it's true.'

'B-but . . .' After this, Allingham seemed unable to bring out another word.

It was Rowlands who took charge. 'Why don't you sit down,' he said, indicating the chair from which he had just risen.

The young man did so. 'Sorry,' he said, after a moment. 'It's a bit of a shock, that's all.'

'All right, sir,' said the chief inspector, when the other had regained his composure. 'Perhaps you can tell me when you last saw Miss Wingate?'

Allingham took a moment to think about it. 'I . . . I'll need to consult the log,' he said at last. 'But I think it was probably 4 p.m. on Tuesday, when she went off duty, after the early shift. Yes, that must have been it, because she didn't come in on Wednesday, when she was slated to do the afternoon shift – that's from 4 p.m. to midnight,' he added helpfully. 'Left me short-staffed, because I was already missing a couple who'd gone down with the flu . . . I say, are you taking all this down?' he added nervously, having become aware of Douglas's sergeant busily scratching away in his notebook.

'A necessary precaution, Mr Allingham,' said Douglas. 'It'll save having to ask you these questions again. What did you think of Miss Wingate?'

This sudden change of tack seemed to disconcert the witness, as it was no doubt intended to. 'I . . . I didn't think much about her. I mean . . . I didn't know her that well . . .'

'Come now, Mr Allingham! She was one of your team. You must have formed *some* impression of the young lady.'

'Well, of course, I . . .' Once more he seemed to falter. 'She worked for me,' he brought out at last. 'I didn't really know her *socially*.'

'Tell me what you did know,' said Douglas, his manner easy and pleasant – always a danger sign, thought Rowlands.

'Can't say I had much to do with her – or with any of the women, come to that,' said Allingham. 'M-my job's to keep them working at . . . whatever it is they're supposed to be working at . . . How much do you know about what we're doing here, Inspector?'

'*Chief* Inspector. And *I'm* the one asking the questions, Mr Allingham. I know it's secret work you're engaged upon. That's not my affair. What I *do* want to know is what Miss Wingate's part in all this was. And what you thought of her as a person.' Douglas suddenly seemed to lose patience. 'Don't give me any flannel about your not knowing the girl. You saw her every day. What was she like?'

'Pretty,' was the subdued reply. 'Vivacious. A bit of a liar.'

'Indeed?' Douglas's tone did not betray the quickening

of interest he must have felt, thought Rowlands. 'Can you give me an example of what you mean?'

'Oh . . . nothing much, you know. Just little things. She . . . she was often late for work . . . overslept, no doubt . . . but she'd always come up with a reason, so that you couldn't penalise her for it. A flock of sheep had got onto the road when she was cycling in from her lodgings . . . that was one corker, I recall. Or she'd been delegated by one of the section heads to help carry some files from the main building and got lost in the corridors. That was another. Afterwards, you'd find it was a complete fabrication.'

'Harmless fibs, rather than lies, wouldn't you say?' Douglas's tone was bland.

'I suppose so,' was the reply. 'Except . . . I can't put my finger on it, exactly . . . it was more than that.'

'You didn't like her.'

'I . . . I wouldn't say that. She could be, well, charming – when it suited her.' This seemed to Rowlands, listening in his corner, to fit with his own assessment of the dead girl's character. 'I suppose I didn't really trust her. She could be . . . underhand. Once I caught her in Hut 8, with no good reason for being there. We're not supposed to go out of our sections here, you know. She gave me some story about having a message to deliver to John Havilland – he's the section head for Hut 8. I didn't believe her for a moment, but what could I do? I'm sorry she's dead, but I can't say I'll miss having her in my department,' said Allingham. He attempted a laugh. 'Rather too hot to handle, if you know what I mean?'

'I do. Thank you, Mr Allingham, that'll be all for the

present. If you could show my sergeant where he can find a couple more chairs, I'd be grateful. And I'll need a list of all the people who work in Hut 6.'

'Yes, yes, of course.' Allingham got up to go. 'Will there be anything else?' There was no sign of the truculence with which he had greeted the arrival of the police. Now he was all compliance.

'A cup of tea for myself and my colleagues would be nice,' said Douglas. 'And then you can send the first of the young ladies in.'

Chapter Seven

The young woman who came into the office a few minutes later was not unknown to Rowlands. He realised this as soon as she replied to Douglas's first question. 'You are Miss Marjorie Milward?'

'That's me. Oh!' Because she'd evidently caught sight of Rowlands. 'You're Maggie's father. I say, what's this all about?'

'One thing at a time, Miss Milward,' said the chief inspector. 'I want to ask you about another of your work colleagues. Pamela Wingate.'

'Pam? Oh, Lord! What's she gone and done now?'

'I'm sorry to say that she's been found dead, miss.'

'*What*?' Her horrified reaction seemed unfeigned. 'But that's awful. Was it a car smash? Pam was always dashing about the countryside, breaking the speed limit with some chap or other in a fancy car . . .' Her voice faltered. 'Sorry,' she said, making an effort to compose herself. 'It's just that it's come as rather a shock. We weren't friends, particularly, but . . .' She found a handkerchief and blew her nose.

'Take your time,' said Douglas. 'Sergeant, perhaps you could fetch Miss Milward a glass of water?'

'I'm all right. really. Poor Pam. When did it happen?'

'Thursday night. And it wasn't a car accident,' said the chief inspector. 'Miss Wingate was murdered. As someone who knew her, Miss Milward, if only as a work colleague, I have to ask you: do you know if she had any enemies – anyone who would want to harm her?'

There was a moment's silence, during which Marjorie Milward considered her reply. 'I . . . I really couldn't say,' she said at last. 'I mean, it sounds like such a preposterous question – who'd want to kill such a ravishing creature?'

'Was she? "Ravishing", I mean,' said Douglas. He refrained from saying that when he had seen the young woman in question she had looked anything but that.

'*I'll* say,' was the reply. 'Made the rest of us look like country mice. *Real* silk stockings, not lisle, if you know what I mean? A real fur coat. *And* she was hand-picked by Molly himself, as one of his 'Misses' – only the top-drawer types are good enough for dear old Moll. He and Pam's father were at school together, don't you know?'

'Molly?' The policeman's tone was one of polite enquiry. 'I don't think I . . .'

'Oh, sorry.' Although Miss Milward didn't sound in the least abashed by her faux pas. 'Mostyn Box. Professor Box, if you want his proper title. He's the one that runs things here – even though Commander M thinks *he's* the Grand Panjandrum.'

'I see,' said Douglas. 'So Miss Wingate was hand-picked as one of Professor Box's assistants, was she?'

'So Pamela said . . . but she might just have been boasting, as usual. Oh dear, what a spiteful little cat I am! She did have a tendency to lay it on a bit thick, though. Comes of being a child of the Legation, or whatever she was. Oh, do make me stop!' she cried. 'Here's poor Pam *dead* and I'm saying all these horrid things about her . . . I am sorry about it, truly I am, although it may not sound it.'

'Murder's an upsetting thing,' said Douglas. 'Takes people in all kinds of ways. But you haven't answered my question, Miss Milward. Do you know if Miss Wingate had any enemies?'

'I suppose she might've,' was the reply. 'She did put some people's noses out of joint. But as for who they might have been . . . I mean, she was always surrounded by people – men, that is. She'd talk about this one and that one, but it was just names, you know? One week it'd be Johnny who was taking her to the officer's mess; the week after that, Dickie would be giving her dinner at The Ritz . . .'

'She had lots of men friends, then?'

'Well . . . yes . . . I suppose so. Can I ask you something, Chief Inspector? Was it a man who killed her?'

'We don't yet know for certain. But it seems likely.' Which was as much as Douglas was prepared to divulge, Rowlands guessed, about the circumstances of the murder. Strangulation, more often than not, was a man's method of killing.

'Then I don't know why you're wasting your time here,' said the forthright Miss Milward. 'It isn't likely to be one of the chaps at Bletchley – they're much too shabby a crew to have interested the likes of Pam Wingate! She'd set her sights higher than some Bletchley boffin in a baggy tweed jacket and flannels.' Having delivered this withering assessment of her colleagues, Miss Milward returned to the subject of her earlier enquiry. 'You still haven't told me why *you're* here, Mr Rowlands. Is it because of Maggie? *She's* all right, isn't she?'

'Yes,' said Rowlands. 'She's all right. Just in need of a few days' rest, that's all.' This was the fiction upon which he and the chief inspector had agreed.

'Oh, I'm so glad!' said Marjorie. 'When she didn't come into work, we were all a bit worried. It's not like Maggie to . . . to *disappear*, without a word. I hope she'll be feeling better, soon. Do send her my love, won't you?'

Rowlands said that he would.

'Nice girl, that,' said Douglas, when Miss Milward had taken herself off. Rowlands agreed. And yet, he thought, they're all nice girls – and boys. Yet one of them might be a traitor – or indeed, a murderer. It was a chilling thought.

A Miss Phyllida Hanbury-Withers was next on Douglas's list. After Miss Milward's pleasant north country tones, Miss Hanbury-Withers's voice – and manner – were altogether more 'county'. When informed of Pamela Wingate's untimely death, her remarks were brisk and to-the-point: 'Jolly bad show. Can't say I'm surprised, though.' Asked to explain this remark, she was no less trenchant. 'The Wingate's sort get themselves into scrapes. Drink and drugs and so forth. So it's highly likely she'd have come to a sticky end.' Told that the other woman's death had not been an accident, Miss Hanbury-Withers remained unfazed. 'All I can say is, whoever did for Pamela Wingate did the world a favour.'

'And just why do you say that, miss?' asked the chief inspector.

'Believe in speaking my mind,' was the reply. 'Not to put too fine a point on it, the Wingate was a pain in the neck. Always trying to get out of doing any work, so she could buzz off with her smart chums.' The scorn with which she pronounced this last phrase said all that needed to be said about Miss Hanbury-Withers's view of metropolitan 'smartness'. Perhaps she realised she'd gone too far, for she added, in a less acerbic tone, 'Look, I'm sorry she's dead, and all that – but a lot of people are dying, all over the place, these days. Not least from Hitler's bombs. My job – and that of the rest of us at Bletchley – is to do what we can to stop that happening. So if you've nothing more to say to me, Inspector' – Douglas did not attempt to correct her – 'I'll go back to what I was doing.'

'Phew!' said the chastened police officer, when the young lady had gone. 'And they call 'em the weaker sex! She can't have been more than twenty-two, that lass, and yet she put me in mind of an old aunt of mine. Holy terror. Used to clip me around the ear if she caught me nodding off during the Sunday sermon.'

'No love lost between her and Miss Wingate, I fancy,' said Rowlands.

'I'd say you were right,' was the reply. 'The Wingate lass doesn't seem to have been very popular with any of the womenfolk here.'

Rowlands wasn't sure that this was entirely accurate. Whether she'd been universally popular or not, Pamela

Wingate had had at least one friend – his daughter Margaret. But then Margaret never had a bad word to say about anybody.

The door opened and the next member of Harry Allingham's team of female operatives was ushered in. This was a Miss Mavis Lacey, late of St Anne's College, Oxford. By contrast with that of the rather grand Miss Hanbury-Withers, her manner was brisk, dry and decidedly academic.

'Pam Wingate? Didn't have much to do with her. Different sets, you know. She was in with a rather *sociable* crowd. Went up to London a lot. For parties, one assumes.' Her tone indicated that she found it hard to believe that such people existed. 'Whereas like most of the rest of us, I'm here to do a job of work. Pam Wingate wasn't, as far as I could tell.' Then, just as Rowlands was wondering how old this formidable young woman might be – surely not out of her twenties? – she laughed. 'I must sound like an awful prig! But honestly, Inspector' – Douglas had given up correcting this error – 'it's hard for the rest of us, slogging away, hour after hour, and day after day, without a break, when there are people like Pam who seem to get away with murder . . . I say, what's this all about? Is Pam in some kind of trouble?' When put in the picture, Miss Lacey had the grace to fall silent. 'How perfectly beastly,' she said at last. 'She and I weren't friends, as I said – but I wouldn't have wanted anything bad to happen to her.'

Douglas acknowledged this comment with a faint grunt. 'Tell me,' he said, 'about Miss Wingate's visits to London. How often would you say they took place? Every week? Or more often than that?'

'I couldn't say for certain,' was the reply. 'As I said, we were in different sets. To be perfectly frank, I wasn't all that interested in Pam's social life. At a guess, I'd say she was away most weekends. She was often late into work on a Monday, and she'd ask people to cover for her. I mean, we all do it from time to time,' she admitted. 'Forty-eight hours isn't long, and if one misses the last train back, it's a matter of catching the milk train, and running like mad from the station to get in before one's missed. One relies on one's colleagues to stick up for one. Only with Pam, it got to be a regular occurrence.'

'She was engaged, wasn't she?' said Douglas. 'No doubt she wanted to spend as much time as possible with her young man . . .'

'No doubt,' said Miss Lacey drily. 'Quite a few of us here are engaged, as a matter of fact. Most of us accept that we can't always have time off when we want it.'

Rowlands was reminded of his wife's old friend Maud Rickards. Just so might she have sounded when faced with an especially feeble excuse from an undergraduate brought before her for some misdemeanour. A few more questions followed, but it was obvious that there was little more to be learnt from the conscientious Miss Lacey, who was evidently anxious to get back to her work.

'Hmm,' said Douglas, when the door had closed behind her. 'Didnae get much change out o' *that* one! Still, you might say we're building a picture.'

'Of a limited sort,' said Rowlands. 'No one seems to have known very much at all about Miss Wingate. Including me,' he added.

'I was going to ask you about that,' said Douglas. 'You

met the lass. Spent Christmas with her, too. What did *you* make of her?'

'Not a lot,' was the reply. 'I've been racking my brains, but my chief impression is of a pleasant enough girl. A bit too fond of the sound of her own voice, I suppose. Lots of stories about embassy parties and lion-shooting in Africa . . . I suppose you've notified her parents?' he added, brought up short by this recollection. 'Father's in the diplomatic service, I believe.'

'Well, that's the strange thing,' said the chief inspector. 'There's no one of the name of Wingate in the Kenya office. It was your Margaret who mentioned Kenya as the Wingate girl's family home, and so naturally we made enquiries in that direction. But not a trace of a Wingate could we find.'

'Perhaps,' said Rowlands, 'it's her *step*father who works for the Foreign Office? They might have different surnames.'

'We thought o' that,' was the reply. 'But none of the families we contacted had a daughter – or stepdaughter – of the right sort of age, who was stranded in England for the duration. We didn't stick at Kenya, either,' he added. 'Thinking that your girl might have made a mistake about the country – it's a big place, Africa – we tried all the embassies we could find. Nigeria, Uganda, German East Africa, Gold Coast, Bechuanaland . . . We cabled them all. Not a sniff of a Wingate.'

'How very strange,' said Rowlands. 'And it *was* Kenya, by the by. I heard Pamela herself mention it, several times.'

'Well, if the family was ever there, they're not there now.'

'So that means . . .' began Rowlands, but at that moment Petty Officer Smedley put her head in.

'Sylvia Pritchard to see you, sir. Go on in,' she admonished the young woman who had been hovering just outside the door. 'He won't bite.'

'No, indeed,' said the chief inspector, for whom this last remark had probably not been intended. 'Come in, Miss Pritchard. Take a seat. I've just a few questions for you about your colleague Miss Wingate.'

'I . . . I don't think I can tell you anything useful. I hardly knew Pamela Wingate. She wasn't my friend. I mean . . . she was all right, I suppose. But I don't think she thought very much about me at all.'

'But you saw her every day,' her interrogator reminded her. 'You must have formed *some* impression. Was she easy to work with? Passed the time o' day with you, at all?'

'I . . . I've told you, I hardly had anything to do with her.' The girl sounded close to breaking down. 'I don't know why you're asking me all these questions,' she muttered. 'I had nothing to do with Pamela. *Nothing!*'

'All right, miss, have it your own way,' said Douglas. 'I realise you ladies are all rather upset by what's happened. It can't be very nice to know that one of your number's been murdered . . .'

'Oh!' Her shocked gasp seemed unfeigned. 'Murdered! I . . . I . . .' She burst into tears. A moment later, she had rushed out of the room.

'Let her go,' said the chief inspector. 'I can talk to her again when she's calmed down. Poor little mouse. Seems frightened of her own shadow.'

'She's certainly frightened of something,' agreed Rowlands. 'Or some*one*. I'd like to know who.'

Douglas grunted an agreement. 'Aye,' he said, preoccupied with filling his pipe. 'But with that type, the more you harry them, the less you get out of 'em. No, we'll leave that lass to stew for a bit, while we get on with tackling the laddies.'

As it was now getting on for midday, and the three men (including Douglas's sergeant) had had nothing in the way of refreshment since that morning, apart from a cup of tea, the chief inspector proposed that they should stroll over to the main house, where, he was reliably informed, one could obtain a hot meal in the cafeteria. And so, shepherded once more by the efficient Petty Officer Smedley, they made their way back along the path, skirting the frozen lake – on which, to Douglas's amazement, some people were skating – and joining a growing throng streaming out of the huts on either side. Ahead of them ambled a group that, to judge from the snatches of conversation that drifted back towards them, included the head of Hut 6.

'I s-say, Allingham. W-what's all this I hear about P-Pamela? It isn't t-true, is it?'

'Don't ask *me*,' was the reply. 'I know as little as you do, Fitzie, old man. Girl's turned up dead. That's all *I* know.'

'D'you s'pose Montfitchet did her in?' said another voice, with a satirical intonation.

'Couldn't say. Might've done,' said Allingham. 'All I know is—'

But he never did say what it was he knew, because at that moment, Douglas – who, although a heavy man, could walk fast enough when he chose – caught up with him.

'Ah, Mr Allingham,' he said, falling into step with the Hut 6 section head. 'Introduce me to your friends, would you?'

'I . . . er . . . Very well, Inspector . . . that is, *Chief* Inspector,' said Allingham. 'This, er, is Cyril Fitzpatrick . . .' The man with the stammer, Rowlands surmised. 'The man to his left is David Solomons. And *this* bright lad is—'

'Jock Colquhoun, at your service,' said the man who'd asked whether Hugh Montfitchet had 'done in' Miss Wingate. 'Always glad to help the police with their enquiries – isn't that the phrase?'

'It is, sir. Although at present we're just having a pleasant chat, wouldn't you say?' Douglas's friendly tones did not mean that he gave way in the slightest, as those who'd attempted to trifle with him in the past had learnt to their cost. 'As your colleague Mr Allingham will have told you, I'm the police officer in charge of investigating this case. This is Sergeant Jones, who'll be assisting me.' He didn't offer Rowlands's name. 'I assume you're all heading in the same direction – that is, to the canteen? I'll join you, if I may.' It was not a request. 'We can have our little chat over lunch.'

Whatever the four young men might have felt about having their free time commandeered in this way, they made no objection. When, having collected their lunches from the self-service counter, the seven of them (the petty officer having absented herself for the time being) sat themselves in two opposing rows at one of the long tables with which the room was furnished, Douglas wasted no more time.

'Now then, gentlemen,' he said. 'I want to know as

much as you can tell me about the last time any of you saw, or spoke to, Pamela Wingate.'

There was silence for a moment. Then Solomons, who had contributed little to the conversation up to this point, said, 'I last saw her on Tuesday afternoon . . . that is, I talked to her. It was only for a few minutes,' he added.

'What was the conversation about, if you don't mind my asking, sir?' Again, the chief inspector's polite tones did not disguise the fact that he meant to have an answer to his question.

The Mancunian sounded taken aback. 'Nothing much. She . . . she was supposed to give me some intercepts that had come in that morning. She said she'd put them on my desk. I told her I hadn't seen them.'

'You gave her a well-deserved rocket, as I recall,' said Jock Colquhoun, with what seemed to Rowlands a certain malicious relish. 'Not that she didn't deserve it. Lazy little baggage . . .'

'I say, that's a bit uncalled-for,' protested Allingham.

'Why?' said the other. '*De mortuis nil nisi bonum* and all that rot? I speak as I find.'

'I . . . I . . . th-think you're being a b-bit unfair,' said the young man who'd been introduced as Cyril Fitzpatrick. 'P-Pamela wasn't lazy. She c-could be a bit d-distracted, s-sometimes. But she always d-did very good work for me.'

'Oh, the chit was clever enough,' said Colquhoun dismissively. '*When* she could be prevailed upon to give her mind to her work. She was one of Molly's Misses, after all. Blue blood, beauty *and* brains. Only the best for Molly . . .'

'I'll be talking to Professor Box later,' said Douglas.

'First I want to hear a bit more about Tuesday. You spoke to Miss Wingate at what time, Mr Solomons?'

'I suppose about two o'clock or half past,' said the other. 'We'd still a couple of hours to go before the end of the shift, and I wanted to get on with those intercepts. When they couldn't be found, I instituted a search.'

'And did you find them?'

'Eventually. After I'd wasted another half an hour getting people to turn out their desks, I found them under a pile of papers on my own desk – although I could have sworn they weren't there when I first looked.'

'Hmm,' said the chief inspector. 'And what were you doing while all this was going on, Mr Colquhoun?'

'I don't recall, exactly,' said the young man. 'I work in a different office, and so . . .'

'Yet you overheard Mr Solomons giving Miss Wingate a "rocket", as you put it, about the missing intercepts,' Douglas reminded him.

'Well, yes,' admitted the other. 'But then everyone in the office would have heard it. Dear old Solly – that is, Solomons here – rather lost his temper with the girl, and she gave as good as she got. Told him she had her own work to get on with, thank you very much, and that she hadn't the time to waste putting *his* mistakes right.'

'When you've been working long hours, with no respite, for weeks at a stretch, tempers tend to get frayed,' put in Allingham.

'You don't say so, sir?' Douglas's tones could not have been drier. 'So you didn't speak to the young lady yourself, Mr Colquhoun?'

'I might've done,' was the off-hand reply. 'I was in and

out of my office several times during the course of the day, so it's hard to say. The women,' he explained, 'tend to get on with their work in *their* room, and we get on with ours, in our own part of the hut. I might have spoken to her once, I suppose, but I can't remember what about.'

'B-but . . .' stammered Fitzpatrick. 'That w-wasn't the last time we saw her . . . P-Pamela, I mean. Don't you remember? She was at the s-station, w-waiting for the London train. Y-you pointed her out to me.'

'Was it *that* afternoon?' asked Colquhoun casually. 'I'd forgotten. Well, if you say so, old man, then it must have been . . . We were going up for a lecture at the Royal Society,' he added. 'Old Routledge on Recent Developments in Radio Waves. Interesting stuff – although not really my subject. I'm a chemist, not a physicist. Yes, now you mention it, I do remember seeing Pamela Wingate on the platform at Bletchley station. Couldn't miss her, really, in that coat she was wearing. Mink, I'd guess. S'pose she was meeting the boyfriend. Funny that he didn't offer to come and pick her up in that flashy motor of his. Maybe he couldn't get the petrol.'

'What time would this have been, sir?' said Douglas in an even tone. Anyone who didn't know him well would have thought it merely a routine enquiry.

'Time? It was about ten to five, wouldn't you say, Fitz? We were waiting for the seven minutes past train. Didn't get in till a quarter past.'

'I see,' was Douglas's only rejoinder. 'And what of the young lady? Did she say where *she* was going – or whom she might be meeting?'

'Don't think she said anything, did she, Fitzie? Might have passed a remark about the weather.'

'She was w-worried about being late,' said Cyril Fitzpatrick.

'Oh? What exactly did she say, sir?'

'Not very m-much. Just . . . "I hope the train isn't too delayed, because I'm late already", or some such. I expect she d-didn't want to keep him waiting. M-Montfitchet,' added the young man.

'She said it was Lieutenant Montfitchet she was meeting, did she?' said the chief inspector casually.

'Not that I recall. I j-just assumed.'

'Indeed, sir. You've been most helpful – as have the rest of you gentlemen. I'll need a statement from you all as to your movements on the day in question. My sergeant will take down a written account, which you'll sign when you've read it. Routine procedure in a murder case.'

'So she travelled to London by train,' said Rowlands, when – the half-hour allocated for lunch being over – the four young men had returned to their labours in Hut 6. 'I suppose that gives you a line of enquiry.'

'Not much of one,' said Douglas gloomily. 'If she'd gone by car, we'd have had a better chance of tracing it, given that there aren't too many private vehicles on the roads these days. But I'll get a man onto it. *Somebody* must have noticed her, either while she was on the train or when she got off at Euston station.'

'I wonder if anyone met her?'

'Oh, I think she was met all right,' said the chief inspector. 'Even if she wasn't met from the train, somebody had a car waiting outside it. I think she was taken away – *collected*, you might say – by this person or persons, and then brought to a place where she was kept, or persuaded to stay, for the next two days. That's the missing part of the puzzle. We know where she was until a quarter past five on Tuesday afternoon, because Fitzpatrick and Colquhoun saw her get on the train. Even though I wouldn't trust that conceited young chap as far as I could throw him' – Rowlands guessed it was Jock Colquhoun he meant – 'I've no reason to suppose he was lying – about *that*, at any rate. Whatever else he may or may not have lied about, I've yet to decide. No,' went on the policeman, 'I think we can safely say that was the last sighting of the lady, before she turned up dead in Montfitchet's flat.'

Having finished their lunch (a slice of Woolton pie for Douglas, which he pronounced 'quite tasty', and an omelette, made from powdered eggs, for Rowlands, which was not), the two friends, leaving Sergeant Jones to write up his report, made their way out of the house and across the stable yard that lay to one side of it. Here, in the building known from its earlier domestic function as the Cottage, they had arranged to meet Professor Box, whose domain it was. As they reached the building ('Rather quaint,' said Douglas. 'Not at all what you'd expect a nerve-centre of British Intelligence to look like.'), the door opened and someone came rushing out, almost colliding with the chief inspector, who was at the head of their party. Before he could react, the man burst out rudely, 'What are you doing here? Don't you know this is a restricted area?'

'Police business,' said Douglas curtly, to which the other, not at all nonplussed, replied, 'Police? If you've come about my stolen bicycle, you needn't have bothered. It's been found.' He chuckled. 'Matter of fact, it wasn't stolen at all – just mislaid. Found it chained to the fence outside Hut 3, where I must have left it.'

'Indeed, sir?' said Douglas, as if humouring a small child. 'That *is* good news! But we haven't come about your bicycle. We've an appointment to see Professor Box.'

'Why on earth didn't you say so?' said this exasperating individual. 'He's in his office. I'd go straight in, if I were you.'

'Thank you, sir. That was my intention,' said Douglas. 'Mad as a hatter,' he muttered to Rowlands, as the man who'd lost and found his bicycle hurried away. 'At least he's put on some more respectable clothing since the last time we saw him.' From which Rowlands surmised that this must be the eccentric in pyjamas they'd encountered on their arrival at Bletchley Park, who had narrowly escaped throwing himself, and his bicycle, under the wheels of the police vehicle.

Chapter Eight

Inside the Cottage, they found Professor Box talking to one of his staff. 'Run these cribs down to Hut 8, would you, Miss Leavis?' he was saying, as they came in. 'I meant to give them to Dr Twining just now, but he dashed off before I could do so. Tell him I'll have the rest of them by three o'clock this afternoon.'

'Yes, sir.'

'Thank you, Miss Leavis. I know I can rely on you . . . Ah, you must be Chief Inspector Douglas,' he said, having spotted the arrivals. 'And this is your colleague, I take it?' Douglas confirmed that this was so. 'Miss Leavis, perhaps you'd be good enough to ask one of the other girls to bring us some tea?'

'Of course, sir.'

The door had barely closed behind the obliging young woman when Box remarked, 'Marvellous girl, that. Extremely capable. If even *some* of the men we've got here were as good at their jobs as she is at hers, we'd be winning this war, hands-down. As a matter of fact,' he added, 'I recommended her for a pay rise only the other day. She should be earning the same as the men, really – considering she's doing the same job as they are – but things are the way they are, I suppose. Most unfair, in my opinion.' Rowlands decided that he liked Professor Box very much. 'Do sit down, gentlemen,' the latter went on. 'If you can find a seat. Bit of a squash in here, I'm afraid, but we do the best we can. Now.' Suddenly, his rather rambling manner give way to a sharper tone. 'What exactly can I do for you?'

'I'd like to ask you some questions, if I may, sir, about a young lady I believe you employed a few months ago,' was the reply. 'A Miss Pamela Wingate. I take it you are aware that she has been murdered?'

Professor Box sighed. 'Yes, yes, indeed,' he said. 'The poor child. Most distressing. And you are correct, Chief Inspector – she did work for me, for a time. Charming girl,' he added reflectively. 'Good head on her, too. That was why I recommended her for transfer to Hut 6. Thought she might find the work more interesting.'

This was so unlike everything else they had so far heard that Douglas seemed nonplussed. 'Are we talking about the same girl? I meant Miss *Pamela* Wingate . . .'

'So did I. As I said, she was a valuable member of my team. Rather wasted in this section, unfortunately – considering that so much of what we do is necessarily of a routine nature. Have you much idea of what we do here, Chief Inspector?'

'Not at all,' was the reply. 'Except that it's top secret.'

'Yes, there is that,' the other said carelessly. 'But I

believe I can trust you . . . and your, ah, associate . . . not to divulge what I am about to tell you. You've heard of Enigma, I suppose?'

'I . . .' began Douglas, but Professor Box swept on.

'It's a German code, which we've been trying – with some success – to break, for the past two or three years. This' – he must have indicated something on the desk in front of him – 'is an Enigma machine. Looks like a glorified typewriter, doesn't it? Lovely little machine. Of course, this is an old model. We've obtained others since, which are much more up to date . . .' He broke off as a soft knock on the door was followed by the entrance of a young woman with the tea tray. 'Thank you, Miss Butler. Just leave it there, would you? Do help yourselves, gentlemen. Sugar's on the tray in front of you. Now,' he went on, as the door closed behind the girl once more. 'Where was I? Ah, yes, Enigma. The way it works is like this: the machine is set up to encipher messages at one end, and then to *de*cipher them at the other end – that is, when the message is received. The operator at, say, the German end of the process types a letter on this keyboard, which sends an electric current through these rotating code-wheels. This, in turn, lights up *another* letter on the adjacent lampboard here. *That* letter is noted down, and then the subsequent letters that make up the entire message are noted down in turn, and then the whole encrypted message is radioed in Morse code to its intended recipient. Do you see?'

'Well . . .' said Douglas doubtfully, but Rowlands, who had had experience, not only of using a typewriter, but also of operating a telephone switchboard, thought that he *did* see.

'I suppose,' Rowlands said hesitantly, 'one would need another Enigma machine set up in the same way, in order to decipher the message?'

'Precisely,' said Box. 'The coded letters are then tapped into the machine, one by one, and – one by one – the real letters are illuminated on the lampboard. Beautifully simple, isn't it? Or it would be,' he added, 'if the machine's settings were not changed every twenty-four hours.'

'I can see that that would complicate matters,' said Rowlands.

'Oh, it does, it does!' laughed the other, evidently relishing the challenges thrown up by these relentless variations. 'But I don't think I caught your name, Mr . . .'

'Rowlands. Frederick Rowlands.'

'Perhaps you'd like to try the machine?' said the professor, with the eagerness of a small child showing off a favourite toy. 'I'm afraid it's not set up at present, but . . .'

'Mr Rowlands is blind,' said Douglas, perhaps intending to save his friend from embarrassment.

But Rowlands had already stepped forward and, guided by Box, ran his hands over the keyboard of the mysterious machine. It was, as the other had said, not unlike a conventional typewriter in some respects: the arrangement of letters on the keyboard, for example – or so Box informed him – 'Good old QWERTYUIOP. And the same arrangement above.' – guiding Rowlands's hands, as he spoke, to the lampboard above the rows of keys. Then there were the wheels, with their serrated flanges, which could be turned to any one of twenty-six positions. It was these, said Box, now evidently mounted upon his favourite hobby-horse, that made the process of decryption so fiendishly difficult. 'Although,' he added modestly, 'we have had our successes. I myself invented the "rodding" system, which one might explain as follows. Suppose there was a word of six or more letters, likely to appear in a given message. One selects places worth looking at in the text by checking for what I call "clicks" . . . In other words, you set the assumed plain letter against each section of the text and look for settings on the rods where the same letter appears twice . . . Do you follow me so far?'

'I think so,' said Rowlands.

'No,' said Douglas.

'It's really quite straightforward,' said Professor Box. 'With the charts we've set up to pick out all the "clicks" as quickly as possible, you can find the "double-clicks" very rapidly. Then you set the rods up to see if it will work. Very often it does,' he added cheerfully. 'Of course, we've other systems for identifying repeated letters – and indeed, whole words. I call these my "cillis".'

'Sillies?' Douglas sounded thoroughly confused.

'Procedural errors by Enigma operators,' explained the professor kindly. 'These are of two kinds: using a recognisable, instead of a random, setting – for example, the operator (call him Fritz) might use his girlfriend's name (call her Cilli) as a message setting – or failing to alter the position of the wheel before sending a new message. Human error, you know,' said Box. 'It's what we've been relying upon, until quite recently. Unfortunately, in the past few months, our adversaries' – he spoke as if they were opponents in a game of chess – 'have tightened up their security procedures. But we persevere . . .'

'I suppose one would need to produce a kind of crib, in order to be able to decipher the messages on a regular basis,' said Rowlands diffidently.

'Exactly so,' said Professor Box. 'Using the more banal material – such as weather reports and call-signs – one can build up a lexicon of sorts. Once we've broken a code in one particular message, the decrypt gets passed on to the Machine Room, where our young ladies type it up on our own Enigma machines, which are actually adapted Telex machines. It is then passed to the cryptographers in Hut 6, and from there to Hut 3, for translation and cross-referencing. It's an exhausting business, checking and cross-checking every message that comes in, to see if certain names and places recur.

'Was that Dr Twining we met coming out of your office just now?' asked Douglas. 'Excitable gentleman.'

'That's him,' was the reply. 'He's convinced that the decryption process can be carried out by this machine, instead of by human agency. Of course,' he added, 'even the most sophisticated machine will still need human beings to run it, and to provide it with the material on which it's to work.'

'It sounds like something out of a story by Mr Wells,' said Rowlands.

'Oh, it is!' The other laughed. 'Really quite astonishing, the things Twining's achieved with that marvellous machine of his . . . But I'm sure he'd prefer to tell you about it himself.' Rowlands wasn't so sure of this, guessing that the irascible Dr Twining might be considerably less communicative about his invention than Professor Box had been about his own manual system for decoding Enigma messages. As if he had suddenly become aware that, in his enthusiasm, he might have been indiscreet, the eminent cryptographer said, 'Now I really must get on. I hope you find whoever's done this dreadful thing. Good day, gentlemen.'

But Douglas wasn't to be dismissed so easily. 'I've just a couple of further questions, sir, before we take our leave. You said that Miss Wingate was transferred to Hut 6 – when would that have been, I wonder?'

'End of last year, I think. I'd have to ask my secretary to check. We have quite a high turnover of girls here.'

'So Miss Wingate would have been working in Hut 6 around the time that some documents went missing from the building next door – Hut 8, that is,' went on the chief inspector. 'The documents in question later turned up in another young lady's locker. But we're pretty sure it was the Wingate girl who took them, and hid them there.'

'Poor child! I wonder what drove her to do such a thing?' said the professor sorrowfully.

'That's what we're trying to find out, sir,' was the reply. 'We know Miss Wingate went to London on the day she disappeared. We don't know who she was intending to meet, but . . .'

'You say she took the documents, but didn't carry them away with her?' Box sounded puzzled. 'Then I fail to see . . .'

'My guess is she panicked,' said Douglas. 'Hid the documents and then, afraid she'd be found out, fled to London, to meet whoever it was she'd arranged to meet.'

'Do you suppose that's why she was killed?' said Box.

'Because she failed to come up with the goods, so to speak?'

'It's one theory,' said Douglas. 'Speaking of that particular day – that is, last Tuesday – I wonder if you can tell me what your own movements were, Professor, between, say, 8 a.m. and 5 p.m., when Miss Wingate was last seen at Bletchley Park?'

Box thought for a moment. 'I'd have been here,' he said. 'My secretary, Miss Meredith, will be able to tell you exactly. Why are you interested in those particular hours?'

'Because last Tuesday at just after five was the last time Pamela Wingate was seen alive,' said Douglas. He got to his feet. 'You've been most helpful, sir,' he said.

'I thought it was interesting, what he said about Pamela,' said Rowlands, as, having collected Sergeant Jones along the way, they walked across the frozen lawn towards the row of huts on the far side of it. 'He seemed to have a higher opinion of her intelligence than some of the others we've spoken to.'

'Mebbe so,' was the gruff reply. 'Then again, she was a pretty young female, by all accounts, and our learned professor likes to surround himself with such ladies, if the sample I saw just now was anything to go by . . . What was it young Colquhoun said about "Molly's Misses"? Blue blood, beauty . . .'

'And brains,' said Rowlands. 'That's the crucial thing, if you work at Bletchley.'

'Speaking of Colquhoun . . .' Douglas went on, in a speculative tone.

'Ah,' said Rowlands. 'I wondered about him, too.'

'I mean, it's a moot point whether he'd have admitted to being the last – or *one* of the last – to see Pamela Wingate, if his friend hasn't spilt the beans,' said the policeman. 'Even if he's not actually lying about what he knows, he certainly isn't telling us the *whole* truth.' They had by now reached Hut 8 – domain of the eccentric Dr Twining. 'We'll have to tick *him* off the list, I suppose,' said Douglas, referring to the eminent scientist. 'Seeing as the girl was working in the next building. Although I don't imagine he'll have much to tell us. Head in the clouds, these scientist types.'

Just then there came the crunch of gravel on the path behind them. 'I say, Chief Inspector . . .' It was Petty Officer Smedley, sounding a little out of breath. 'Commander Murchison sends his compliments, and might he have a word before you leave?'

'Certainly,' was the reply. 'I'll come and find him when I'm finished with Dr Twining. Shouldn't be too long.'

If this was intended as a polite dismissal of the Wren's services, it failed in its aim, for she said brightly, 'Jolly good. I'll take you to Dr Twining's office, shall I? It's just this way . . .' Breezing past the three men, she pushed open the door of the hut and went inside, leaving them with no choice but to follow. Hut 8, like its adjacent twin, Hut 6, had a smell of coal-fired stoves, cigarette smoke and pencil shavings, with a lingering residue of something that was probably stale milk – presumably for the cups of tea that seemed a regular part of the routine of Bletchley Park life. At the end of a corridor, Petty Officer Smedley knocked upon a door, then opened it.

'What do *you* want?' said an irritable voice from within.

'Gentlemen to see you, sir.'

'Tell 'em I'm busy.' At which point Douglas, who was just ahead of Rowlands, with the sergeant bringing up the rear, must have insinuated himself into Twining's office, for the latter said, 'Oh, it's you again, is it? I told you – my bicycle's been found.'

'This isn't about your bicycle,' said the chief inspector sternly. 'I'm investigating a murder.'

But if he'd thought to shock the cryptographer into a more seemly frame of mind, he was disappointed, for the other said merely, 'I rather supposed you *would* be – since that sort of thing's your department, wouldn't you say? Although what it's got to do with me, I can't imagine. Now, if you don't mind, I really am rather busy.'

'The young woman who was found murdered was one of your staff,' said Douglas, showing no inclination to bring the interview to an end before he was ready. He settled himself in the only vacant chair, in what was evidently a tiny office, leaving Rowlands hovering awkwardly in the doorway. Petty Officer Smedley and Douglas's sergeant remained, perforce, in the corridor. 'She worked in the hut next to this one, and so . . .'

'Hut 6, I suppose you mean?' said Twining carelessly.

'That's right, sir. And what I wanted to ask you was . . .'

'I doubt if I could tell you the names of any of the people who work in Hut 6 . . . Well, apart from Allingham, of course, and that other chap . . . what's his name . . . stammers a bit . . .'

'I think you must mean Mr Fitzpatrick,' said the policeman.

'That's the one. Not a bad codebreaker,' said Twining, with the first sign of warmth Rowlands had heard him express. 'As for the women . . . to be frank, I can hardly tell them apart. There's one good mathematician among them, but I haven't seen her around for a day or two.'

Rowlands wondered if it was Margaret to whom he referred. Whoever it was, it seemed as if this – her prowess in maths – was the only detail he'd retained about her. 'The name of the young lady we're interested in was Pamela Wingate,' said Douglas. 'She went missing a week ago. Found dead on Thursday night.'

'Where was this, exactly?'

'I beg your pardon, sir?'

'It's a simple question. Where was she found?'

'Mayfair,' said the chief inspector. 'In her fiancé's flat, as it happens, but—'

'Then what the *devil*,' said Anthony Twining, 'has any of this got to do with Bletchley Park?'

'I should have thought it was obvious,' said the policeman stiffly. 'She worked here.'

'So do several thousand other people,' said Twining. 'Statistically, a proportion of them will die from some cause or other. A motor accident or a bomb blast. We're trying to do something about *that*, of course – if given the chance,' he added pointedly. After a few further questions, eliciting the same vague answers, had established that Twining had no memory of ever having met Pamela Wingate, the two men went to take their leave. Only then did the cryptographer betray an interest – and it wasn't in the last hours of the dead woman. 'I say, you,' he said. 'I didn't catch your name . . .' Since he was the only other person in the room, Rowlands realised that it was he himself who was being addressed. He supplied his name. 'Ah. Rowlands, is it? I've been wondering about you ever since you came in.'

'Mr Rowlands is here in an advisory capacity,' said Douglas.

'I don't give a fig about that,' was the reply. 'You're blind, aren't you?' Twining went on, again addressing Rowlands. 'I wasn't sure at first, because you disguise it awfully well.'

'Yes,' said Rowlands. 'I'm blind. Shrapnel injury, during the last war.'

'Marvellous,' was the unexpected reply. 'I don't suppose I could borrow you for an hour or two?'

'Well . . .'

'Only I've being exploring the possibilities offered by the *aural* nature of the communications we've been receiving, with regard to this new machine of mine. I don't suppose you know Morse code?'

'As a matter of fact, I do.'

'Splendid. Then you're just the man I'm looking for. Shall we say four o'clock? I'll have finished this bit of work by then.'

Rowlands hesitated a moment, torn between a certain fascination with the project on which this extraordinary man was engaged, and a feeling that he ought not to be distracted from the matter in hand – which was tracking down the killer of Pamela Wingate. Before he could reply, Douglas intervened. 'If Mr Rowlands wants to join you for an hour or so this afternoon, I've no objection. Although I'd like to leave by six o'clock, if it's all the same to you. The roads were fairly clear on the way up, but there's a chance of snow tonight.' It was accordingly arranged that Rowlands would call by the cryptographer's office at the suggested time, which was in an hour. 'Maybe you can get a bit more out of him,' said the chief inspector, as, piloted by Petty Officer Smedley, they made their way back towards the house. 'Cold fish, isn't he? Seemed completely uninterested in the fact that a girl's been murdered on his watch.'

'I thought he was like all the scientists I've met,' said Rowlands. 'Only interested in the business in hand. Which is probably a good thing for all of us, in this instance.'

'No doubt you're right,' said Douglas. 'I just wish he'd given a bit more of his attention to *my* particular bit of business. Still, I've a few leads to follow up as a result of our interrogations today, so it hasn't been an entirely wasted journey. But what a strange crew they are,' he added in a wondering tone. 'You'd hardly know there was a war on, the way they carry on.'

Within a few minutes, they were back inside the rambling Victorian mansion that lay at the heart of the Bletchley Park operation – a curiously fitting location for this most secret and eccentric of enterprises, thought Rowlands, as they crossed the spacious entrance hall and began to ascend the stairs. As they did so, they encountered someone descending in a hurry. Immovable force met immovable object as the two parties, neither willing to retreat, danced around each other. At last the man – for it was a man, Rowlands gathered – managed to slip past, his exasperated 'Well *really!*' signifying his disapproval of this invasion by outsiders.

Nor did his appearance seem to gratify the chief inspector. 'I've seen some funny sights here,' he muttered darkly, 'but I never expected to meet one of *his* kind! Should've thought he'd be more at home in Hampstead or Soho, with his long hair, and "artistic" clothes . . . Blue shirt and orange bow tie,' he elucidated for Rowlands's benefit. 'More the kind of thing you'd find at one of these artists' hangouts.'

'Mr Wilcox is a writer,' said Petty Officer Smedley. 'He's published ever so many books.'

'Hmph,' said Douglas, as if that explained it all.

When they entered Murchison's office, it was to catch the end of conversation between the commander and another visitor – an American, by the sound of him, although this particular American accent – drawling and curiously mannered – wasn't one with which Rowlands was familiar.

'I'm telling you, Commander, when this gets out, heads are gonna roll.'

'It won't get out.' Murchison seemed more on edge than he had at their previous encounter, thought Rowlands, even though only a few hours had passed. 'I'll see to that.'

'Better make sure you do, that's all.' Then the man – whoever he was – was gone, brushing past Rowlands and the chief inspector, without another word.

A brief silence followed this exchange, before Murchison – still sounding vaguely rattled – addressed Douglas. 'So, Chief Inspector. Any progress with your enquiries?'

'I wouldn't go so far as to say "progress",' was the reply. 'I've talked to a few of your people – Professor Box being one, and that Dr Twining another – but it doesn't strike me that either of them had much to tell me.'

Murchison didn't seem surprised by this. 'They're busy men,' he said.

'So they told me, sir.' Douglas sounded disgruntled. 'As for the young people in Hut 6 – they were a little more forthcoming, seeing as they knew the young lady . . . Miss Wingate, I mean. I've now got a clearer idea of her movements on Tuesday last – up until a quarter past five, when she caught the London train.'

'I see,' said Murchison. He sounded troubled. 'Any idea to whom the girl intended to pass the stolen documents?'

'Not at present, sir, no. But we're working on it.'

'Good show,' said the commander. 'Keep me posted, won't you, Chief Inspector? I don't need to tell you that this is a very serious matter, as regards national security. It could compromise the whole of our Atlantic defence. If the Germans get to hear that we've broken their Enigma code . . . well, I won't answer for the consequences, that's all. I mean, if we can't trust our own people with this most secret material, then we really are in a bloody mess.'

Rowlands checked his watch. One of the older Braille models, issued to him when he'd joined St Dunstan's in 1917, it was still going strong, over twenty years later. Edith had said she'd buy him another one, for Christmas, but he was attached to this – or it was attached to him; he couldn't say which was the more accurate description. Certainly it had felt almost a part of him since the day he'd first strapped it to his wrist, his fingers feeling uncertainly for the raised dots around the face that signified the hours and minutes. A quarter to four. Leaving Douglas and his sergeant together to review the day's interviews in the room set aside for this purpose, he left the main building once more, and made his way along the now-familiar route towards Hut 8. It was still very cold; he guessed it would already be getting dark. The air had a crisp, icy snap to it; sounds carried far in the frozen stillness. The cawing of rooks, high above in the elm trees; the softer cry of a moorhen from the lake; the crunch of his own footsteps on the gravel path – all sounded sharp and distinct.

As he neared his destination, the gravel gave way to a concrete apron on which the huts were set, deadening the sound of his approach, or so he supposed. Because it was obvious that whoever was standing just outside Hut 8, between it and Hut 6, in point of fact, was unaware of his presence. Voices, a man's and a woman's, were raised in urgent conference. 'I've told you, no one's going to find out, if you keep your mouth shut . . .' Rowlands knew the voice, with its Aberdonian accent: it was young Colquhoun.

'But, Jock, you *promised*. You *said*, after what happened with Pam . . .' He knew that voice, too: it was the girl's – Sylvia Pritchard's. During the interview with the chief inspector, she'd sounded scared. She sounded no less scared now.

'Shut up! Don't keep on about that woman. Hasn't she done enough harm, with her meddling?' Something must have alerted Colquhoun to the fact that they were not alone. 'Shh . . . somebody's coming . . .' There seemed little point in trying to conceal his presence any longer, and so Rowlands, making a show of being unconcerned, walked boldly up to the door of Hut 8. 'It's him – the chap who was with that policeman,' he heard Colquhoun say. 'What's *he* doing here, I wonder?'

Chapter Nine

Still brooding on what he had heard, Rowlands made his way along the corridor to Twining's office, knocked, and, at an interrogative sound from within, went inside.

'Come in, come in,' said the cryptographer, when he saw who it was. He seemed at once more affable and more communicative than at their last encounter when, Rowlands reminded himself, the chief inspector had also been present. Perhaps Twining was one of those whom the presence of policemen made uneasy. 'Glad you could join me. I don't suppose,' Twining went on, 'that you know anything about electrical circuits?'

'Not a great deal,' admitted Rowlands. 'I've operated a switchboard, though.'

'Excellent. And you're familiar with a typewriter, I expect?'

'Well, yes . . .'

'Then you'll already know a good deal about the machine I'm planning to construct. It's a kind of super-typewriter, which can identify symbols. It can write, but it can also read, up to a point. It will be able to carry out a whole range of tasks – mathematical and otherwise – requiring little or no intervention from a human operative. My argument, do you see, is that any calculation a human being can perform, a machine can perform just as well, if not better – and much, much faster.'

Rowlands nodded, not sure where all this was going, but interested, nonetheless. He suddenly saw how the eccentric and irascible Twining might be a kind of genius.

'Of course,' the cryptographer went on, 'this machine of mine has yet to be built. My work here at Bletchley is rather a sideline . . . I say, won't you sit down? I can't offer you tea, because the trolley's just gone round, but I do have some cigarettes somewhere.'

Rowlands said that, if it was all the same to Dr Twining, he'd smoke his own brand. Having refused one of Rowlands's Churchman's, Twining went on talking, clearly in an expansive mood.

'You manage your blindness very well, I must say,' he observed, having watched as Rowlands lit his 'gasper' – which he did in his usual way, by striking the match away from him, so that its flame came level with the end of the cigarette he held between his lips: a trick from his army days. 'I notice that you carry a stick, but it seems to me you'd get by, at a pinch, without it.'

Rowlands agreed, adding that he relied a good deal on his hearing.

'Quite so,' said Twining. 'I imagine you can judge distances in much the same way as bats do – using sound frequencies.'

Privately amused at being compared to a bat, Rowlands said that he supposed this was so.

'It's a factor I hope to introduce into my machine,' said Twining. 'Using sounds, as much as visual clues, I mean. Although I haven't worked out how, yet. Once this war's over, I'll be able to get on a bit faster. But in the meantime I'm obliged to devote all my time to the Bombe.' He must have seen Rowlands's startled look, for he said, 'I don't mean the kind that causes explosions . . . *this* one aims to prevent them, rather.' He got to his feet. 'Come and meet Victory.'

Mystified, Rowlands followed the other out of his office and back along the corridor to the exit. After the stuffy atmosphere of Hut 8, the air outside was bitingly cold. As they crossed the concrete apron towards another of the huts, he wondered whether Colquhoun and his girlfriend, if that was what she was, were still hanging around. The substance of their conversation still troubled him.

'In here.' Twining, who was leading the way, pushed open the door of another hut, and they stepped inside. At once, a whirring sound, as of a large machine, perhaps of the type once used in the manufacture of cloth, drew Rowlands's attention to the far side of the otherwise empty building. Although it was not quite empty. Because at that moment, someone who was standing next to the machine spoke.

'It's still circling through the combinations,' said this voice – not one Rowlands had heard before. 'Nothing doing yet, though.'

'Well, there won't be, until they change the settings at midnight,' replied Twining. He didn't bother to introduce the man, leaving Rowlands standing awkwardly on the sidelines, until the other spoke.

'I don't believe we've met. I'm Graham Weston.'

Rowlands supplied his own name and the two men shook hands.

'Oh, he's not one of ours,' said Twining. 'He's just come for a look . . . or rather, a *listen*.' He sounded amused by his own mild joke. 'Come closer,' he said to Rowlands. 'And tell me what you think.'

Rowlands did so, struck anew by the sounds the thing gave off: a whirring, as of the giant spinning machine of his imagination, followed at length by a decisive click . . . or was it more like a *clunk*? From where he stood, a few feet away, he got the sense of a very large structure, taller than he was, and perhaps twice as wide as it was tall. 'Impressive,' he said, although it seemed to him an inadequate response. Twining seemed gratified enough by this, however.

'Wait until you've heard what it can do. This is just a trial run, to perfect some modifications my colleague here is making. You see, once we've provided it with the data from Enigma—'

'Anthony . . .' Weston's voice held a warning note.

'It's all right,' said the cryptanalyst. 'He's a friend.'

'Even so . . . after what's happened, I should have thought you'd be a bit more careful.'

'I can promise you,' said Rowlands, guessing that this wasn't the first time that Twining had broken Bletchley rules of confidentiality, in order to show off his invention, 'all this is very much over my head. I've got only the vaguest idea of what the Bombe machine looks like – and not the slightest understanding of how it works.'

'Then come and feel for yourself what it looks like,' said Twining, not at all perturbed by this. 'Mr Rowlands is blind,' he explained to Weston. 'So he's hardly going to be able to draw a plan of the Bombe to give to the enemy.' So saying, he drew Rowlands towards the now silent machine, and exhorted him to touch it. When Rowlands did so, he found that the surface of the thing consisted of row upon row of wheels, or cogs, each about six inches in diameter. It was these that, when set in motion, produced the whirring and clicking sounds. Conscious that the Bombe was only at rest, and that the wheels might again begin to spin, Rowlands withdrew his fingers – not wanting to lose any of them to the Spinning Jenny, as he privately christened it.

'Very impressive,' he said again. 'Although I feel rather like one of the blind men asked to describe an elephant . . . my impressions being of a similarly partial nature.'

'Make no mistake about it, our "elephant" is going to win us the war,' said Anthony Twining. 'Just as soon as we can get him to work properly.'

Leaving Twining and his colleague discussing something called a 'diagonal board', which would, in Weston's opinion, greatly improve the efficiency of the machine, Rowlands walked back to the house, where he found the chief inspector and his sergeant ready to depart.

'Seems to me I've got as much out of this crowd as I'm going to get, for the time being,' said Douglas. 'Trouble is, you can't get a straight answer to a question from most of 'em. Either they'll tell you it's classified information, or they'll go haring off on some completely different tack. How'd you get on with the professor?'

'I learnt a good deal about his wonderful new thinking machine.'

'But nothing to the purpose,' said the other with a groan. 'Like I said, they've got their heads in the clouds, these folk.'

'They look at things on a different scale, I think,' said Rowlands, as the big Wolseley moved cautiously along the drive towards the gate – Sergeant Jones evidently taking no chances, in the blackout, with regard to any more reckless cyclists he might encounter. 'I suppose you could call it seeing the bigger picture.'

'That's as may be,' was the disgruntled reply. 'Myself, I'm more concerned with the *smaller* picture. Like finding out who killed that girl.'

Several days passed, with no further developments – at least none of which Rowlands was aware. He went back to work – a large order for camouflage nets had come in from the War Office, and he had to deal with the usual bureaucratic hitches to do with this, as well as all the rest of his regular commitments. Work was exhausting for another reason, which was that none of them were getting much sleep. The nightly bombing raids that had plagued London since the autumn of last year were still going on – although these had now spread to the major ports. Plymouth, Portsmouth, Bristol, Swansea, Merseyside, Clydeside, Newcastle and Hull were all being pounded to smithereens, that spring of 1941. Not that the reports on the wireless said as much – but one could work it out for oneself, reading between the bland phrases referring to 'enemy action in our coastal regions' and the need to remain 'calm and resolute' in the face of this. Kingston-upon-Thames, where the Rowlandses lived, had become a target early in the war, due to the presence of the Hawker aircraft factory in Canbury Park Road. The bomb disposal squad was often to be found at work in the surrounding streets, defusing bombs that had failed to detonate. Difficult and dangerous work, Rowlands thought, with a pang of sympathy for the young 'sappers' entrusted with this task.

He was just glad that his own street hadn't yet suffered a direct hit, although there'd been a number of near misses. On Saturday night there'd been a particularly bad raid, with some damage to the town centre, and the sewage works in Lower Marsh Lane hit – so Rowlands learnt from a neighbour, who'd been doing fire-watching duty. He and Edith and Joan, and Edith's mother, had spent the best part of the night in the Anderson shelter. As the four of them huddled on the narrow benches beneath its corrugated iron shell, listening out for the all-clear, he wondered how his eldest daughter was coping in her prison fortress. Solid as Holloway gaol undoubtedly was, it was still much closer to central London than his own present location – and potentially a more dangerous spot. He prayed that, wherever Margaret was, and whether under bombardment or not, she wasn't too frightened.

Sunday passed in a grey blur, of church (prayers for Our Brave Fighting Men in North Africa, and a collection for those bombed out of their homes in the East End), Sunday lunch (a leg of mutton, for which Edith had saved up their meat coupons), an after-lunch snooze, followed by cups of tea and Edith's home-made scones, and a concert on the wireless (Elgar's *Enigma Variations*). Tired after a day of doing not very much, Rowlands decided to turn in early. It was then, at around a quarter to ten, that the telephone rang. He leapt up, his heart pounding.

'Sorry to disturb you so late,' said a voice he knew. 'Only I thought you'd like to know that the funeral's tomorrow. I take it you've got a black tie?'

At half past nine the next morning, there was a knock on the door. He went to answer it, a little surprised at this early summons, because the funeral wasn't until eleven. It wasn't the chief inspector who stood there, however.

'Hello, Daddy.'

'Meg!' He hugged her close. But his delight was succeeded at once by apprehension. 'What are you doing here?'

It was Douglas, now walking up the path to the front door, who answered. 'I thought, seeing as she was the lassie's friend, she ought to be there.' Further explanations were cut short as Edith, alerted by the sound of their voices, came hurrying out of the kitchen, followed closely by her mother.

'Margaret! We've been so worried . . .'

'It's all right, Mummy. Don't make a fuss.'

'*Fuss*! I've been out of my wits . . .'

'Why don't we talk about this inside?' said Helen Edwards. 'Much better than standing about in the cold.' Although they oughtn't to stay long, warned the chief inspector, as they still had to drive to Brockley Cemetery.

At which reminder of the reason why her daughter

and the policeman were there, Edith said, 'It's a dreadful business. I'm so sorry for that poor girl's parents. Do please pass on my condolences.'

'And mine,' said Mrs Edwards.

'I will,' said Margaret. An awkward silence followed.

'I really think—' began Edith, but before she could say what it was she thought, her daughter said quickly, 'I'll need some black gloves – could I could borrow yours, Granny? And perhaps a hat. My beret doesn't seem quite the thing.'

While the two of them were out of the room, in search of these items, Edith turned angrily to the chief inspector. 'I know I'm not supposed to ask questions, but why on earth is my daughter being kept in *prison*? She hasn't done anything wrong!'

'You're right,' was the reply. 'And there *were* reasons... I needn't go into those now. What I *can* tell you is that Miss Rowlands is going to be returning to her job very shortly. Just as soon as we can arrange a suitable companion for her.'

Rowlands guessed this meant a police guard. But Edith had focused only on the first part of what Douglas had said. 'She's going back to Bletchley? But that's marvellous – why didn't you say so before? Margaret, Chief Inspector Douglas has told us the news,' she added, as their daughter returned with her grandmother. 'You'll be glad to get back to your work at last.'

'Yes,' said Margaret evenly. 'I will.'

The funeral was being held at St Mary's Church, Lewisham. 'The aunt lives nearby,' said Douglas, as the Wolseley drew up in front of the church.

'An aunt? So you did find her family?'

'She . . . Miss Coulson . . . found us,' said the chief inspector. 'She saw the report of the murder in the newspaper.' Further discussion was forestalled until later, as the three of them entered the church – a draughty Victorian building, smelling of incense, candle-wax and decaying hymn books.

As Margaret took her father's arm, he sensed that this was as much to give herself courage to face the ordeal ahead, as it was to guide him in the right direction. He squeezed her hand. 'It'll be all right,' he whispered, wondering if it ever really would.

The church was sparsely filled – a fact that the hollow echo of their footsteps along the aisle only served to emphasise. 'Hugh's here,' said Margaret, in a low voice. 'It must be so awful for him.' She and her father, with the chief inspector on Rowlands's right, took their seats in one of the pews a few rows behind Montfitchet and the friend he'd come with – Gilbert Burton, it transpired. The two young men were seated next to a woman Margaret guessed must be Pamela's aunt. There were no other family members present. 'I suppose they must all be in Kenya,' she whispered.

Some of the Bletchley crowd were also there, it emerged. 'Marjorie's come . . . I hoped she would. She's with Sylvia . . . and Jock.'

So Colquhoun and his girlfriend had decided to put in an appearance, had they? thought Rowlands. He wondered if Douglas had noticed them. When he'd reported the substance of the conversation he'd overheard that day at Bletchley to the chief inspector, the other had seemed surprisingly unconcerned. 'So you think that Colquhoun's mixed up in all this?'

'It certainly sounded like it.'

'The question is, how? We know he caught the train to London that she was on, but he had an alibi – he was with Fitzpatrick at that lecture.'

'So he says. And there's more to it than that,' said Rowlands. 'What do you think he meant when he said Pamela had been "meddling"?'

'I haven't the least idea. But I'll find out, never fear,' was Douglas's confident assertion. 'If Colquhoun's our culprit, he'll give himself away before too long.'

'I should think you'd have more success with Miss Pritchard,' said Rowlands. 'She certainly knows more than she's let on.'

'Och, I'll talk to the lassie again, if you insist,' said Douglas. 'Although I can't see that timid little mouse getting mixed up in a murder, can you?' Rowlands wasn't so sure. The girl was hiding something. What it was remained to be seen. Rowlands was still puzzling over all this, when the doleful notes of the 'Dead March' sounded, and the bearers carried the coffin in. Then for the next few minutes his thoughts were preoccupied only with the dead woman, for whose sake they were all assembled, and with the living one, her friend, who sat weeping quietly at his side.

The service was mercifully short, there being no hymns, and only the briefest address by the officiating clergyman, deploring the waste of a young life cut off before its time. Stripped of pomp and circumstance as it was, it reminded Rowlands of some of those hastily arranged burials he had attended as a soldier during the last war, when a dead comrade – or what remained of him – was hurried into the ground, with only the most perfunctory ceremony. Still, the words, now as then, were a comfort. The coffin was borne out at last, leaving those who wished to attend it to the graveside in Brockley Cemetery to follow.

Rowlands and his daughter accordingly got up, and were walking slowly along the aisle towards the west door, when there came an outburst from behind them: 'Couldn't you leave me alone, today of all days?' It was Hugh Montfitchet.

'Now then, sir, no need to take on,' said the chief inspector, to whom this reproach had presumably been addressed – but the other wouldn't be silenced.

'*Hounding* a fellow, when he's at his lowest ebb . . .' The words, spat out in a fury, echoed hollowly in that vast space.

'Come on, old man,' said another voice – it was Gil Burton's – in conciliatory tones. 'You're upset. A stiff drink is what you need.'

'That's your answer to everything, isn't it?' snapped Montfitchet. 'As for *you*,' he added fiercely to Douglas, 'you needn't think I'm going to answer any more of your damn fool questions. I've already *told* you everything I know.'

'Come on, old man . . .'

'Oh, leave me *alone*, can't you?' With that, Montfitchet strode off, his footsteps ringing on the tiled floor, leaving the others standing, nonplussed, in the aisle.

'As you can probably *deduce*, Inspector – assuming

that's what you are – he's rather cut up about all this,' said Burton. He himself didn't seem particularly upset; if anything, he sounded amused by his friend's behaviour, thought Rowlands.

'And you are, sir?' said Douglas.

'Name's Burton. Before you ask, I don't know anything about the affair. Wasn't even in town when the body was found. Staying with friends in Sussex, as it happens. So no sense in giving me the third degree.'

'Friend of Lieutenant Montfitchet's, are you?' said Douglas, paying no attention to what had just been said.

'As this gentleman will confirm,' said Burton, acknowledging Rowlands for the first time. 'We met at Christmas, didn't we – albeit briefly?'

'That's right,' said Rowlands.

'As for my friendship with dear old Hugh,' the young man went on, 'I'd say we've known one another forever. We were at school together. Same jolly old college at Cambridge, too. There! Now you know the whole story. I'm just here to give moral support to an old pal.'

'Very commendable, sir. You're not a naval officer, I take it?' said the chief inspector, falling into step with the young man, as the four of them, with Rowlands and Margaret bringing up the rear, made their way towards the exit.

'I should have thought that was pretty obvious – unless one supposes that I've left my uniform at home,' was the reply. Again, Burton seemed to think better of his facetiousness, for he added, 'I've what's generally known as a "nice little desk job" in the War Office. Bad eyes, you know . . . Or was it flat feet?' He seemed unable to resist this provocative note. Once outside the church, he immediately lit up a cigarette. 'Thank Christ that's over,' he remarked; then, evidently spotting his friend in the group of mourners about to make its way across the road to the cemetery, he went to join him. 'Look, old man, I'm going to cut the rest of the show, if you don't mind. Graveyard scenes give me the horrors. I'll drop you off and wait for you in the car.'

Montfitchet muttered something Rowlands didn't catch, to which his friend replied, 'That's the ticket. Keep your pecker up, as the actress said to the bishop. I'll just bring the car round, old man.' Then he sauntered off.

Douglas, seizing this opportunity, took his place. 'Lieutenant Montfitchet . . .' he began; but before he could go on, the other said, 'Look, I'm sorry about just now. I . . . I spoke out of turn. It's just that it's all so bloody upsetting.'

'Quite understandable, sir,' said Douglas. 'And I won't trouble you any longer than I have to. But I wondered if you'd heard anything from Miss Wingate's family?'

'No. Should I have?'

'We've been trying to get in touch with them, sir, and I thought—'

'Pam never introduced me to her family,' said the young man. 'They're all in Africa, as far as I know.'

'So you weren't aware that Miss Wingate's aunt had telephoned the police?'

'Never knew she had an aunt. Was that the quaint old body who was sitting next to me? Thought she might have been an old servant. Look, I've got to go. I was only

155

waiting for my friend, but – as is his wont – he's let me down.' And with that, Montfitchet strode off.

'We should join the rest of 'em, too,' said Douglas to his companions. 'Don't want to lose our party, do we? What I find strange,' he went on, as the three of them got into the car and set off on the short drive to the cemetery, 'is that, apart from this one aunt, the family haven't tried to make contact. And Montfitchet says he'd never met or heard from any of them. Odd, considering he was engaged to the girl.'

'It's wartime,' said Rowlands. 'People tend to skip the formalities.'

The service of committal was already in progress as Rowlands and his companions joined the others at the graveside. The familiar words floated, crisp and stark, through the cold spring air:

'Man that is born of woman hath but a short time to live, and is full of misery. He cometh up, and is cut down, like a flower; he fleeth as it were a shadow, and never continueth in one stay . . .'

Well, that part – about being cut down like a flower – was true enough, in the present case, reflected Rowlands bleakly. The death of a young person was always worse than any other kind, especially when it had been brought about by violence. At last the coffin was lowered into the grave. Someone – he supposed it was Hugh Montfitchet – stepped forward, to throw a handful of earth after it. There was a stifled sob from someone else – one of the girls, he thought. Margaret, standing beside him, shivered a little in the biting wind, and slipped her hand into his. Poor little lass, this was very hard on her, he thought. When it was over, an awkward moment of indecision followed, as no one wanted to be the first to leave. At last, people started to drift away, and Rowlands and his daughter began walking back towards where the cars were parked. From behind them, came the sound of hurried footsteps on the gravel path.

'Maggie?' said a voice. It was Marjorie Milward. 'I saw you in church. Oh, Maggie, isn't it awful?'

'Yes. Poor Pam.' The two girls fell back a few paces, talking in low voices.

Rowlands moved away a little to give them privacy. As he waited for his two companions to join him once more, he was not wholly surprised to hear another voice he recognised.

'Come to see if you can spot the guilty man?' said Jock Colquhoun sarcastically. 'Isn't that what you policemen do at funerals?'

'I'm not a policeman,' said Rowlands pleasantly. 'I'm here with my daughter. As for "spotting" anyone, I'm not in a position to do that, even if I wanted to. Of which,' he added, with a smile, 'I think you're also well aware. What's on your mind, Mr Colquhoun? Having second thoughts about the accuracy of the statement you've given to the police?'

'No. I . . . I just wondered what you were doing here, that's all.' Colquhoun sounded abashed, as if he had been caught out in a piece of mean-spirited behaviour – which in a way, he had, thought Rowlands.

'And I've just told you,' he replied. 'But if you've any further questions, I suggest you address them to the chief inspector,' he went on, his sharp ears picking up the sound of his friend's voice from a few feet away.

'No thanks,' muttered the young man. 'I've had enough of being grilled. Come on, Sylvia,' he added to his companion. 'We'd better get a move on, if we want to catch that train.' With that, he was gone. A rather irascible type, thought Rowlands, wondering what it was that had so unsettled Colquhoun. He was prevented from further speculation by the arrival of Margaret and her friend.

'Daddy, this is Marjorie,' his daughter began.

'We've already met.' Rowlands smiled. 'It's good to see you again, Miss Milward.'

'I'm so glad that Maggie'll be coming back to BP soon,' said Marjorie. 'We've missed her cheery presence. Well, must be going. Train to catch, you know.' The two young women kissed, and then Rowlands was alone with Margaret once more.

'Look, about your going back to Bletchley,' he said. 'I'm not sure it's such a good idea . . .' But before he could say what was on his mind, they were joined by Douglas and his companion – Pamela Wingate's aunt, it emerged.

'So you're telling me you'd no idea where your niece was living, or what she was doing?' Douglas was saying to that lady, whose voice Rowlands now heard for the first time. A quiet, rather timid voice, with a genteel accent – not at all what he had been led to expect, from having met Miss Wingate.

'Yes, that's right. It must be two years or more since I last saw her.' Miss Coulson gave a tremulous laugh. 'She wasn't much of a one for keeping in touch, our Pammie.'

'It must have come as a shock when you saw the report in the newspaper.'

'Oh, a *dreadful* shock! I couldn't believe it at first. But then when I read a bit more, and saw that it . . . it *happened* in Mayfair . . . well, that's our Pammie, I thought. She always did set her sights high.' The elderly lady seemed momentarily overcome with emotion.

'Miss Coulson's been telling me a bit about her niece,' said the chief inspector to Rowlands and Margaret. 'It seems Miss Wingate lived with her in her flat in Ladywell until just before the war broke out. Went to school in the area, too. In fact, Miss Coulson was the one who brought the girl up.'

'I did my best,' was the reply. 'Although we never had much . . . I think that's what made dear Pammie so . . . so keen to get *on* in life . . .' Again, her voice faltered.

'There, there. Don't upset yourself,' murmured Douglas. 'I've suggested that we might all go and get a cup of tea somewhere,' he added to the others. 'Miss Coulson knows a place not too far from here.'

'Oh *yes*,' said the latter. 'They do *quite* nice cakes there. And they *know* me, of course,' she added shyly.

'Miss Rowlands here was a friend of your niece's,' said the chief inspector to Pamela's aunt, when the four of them were seated at a table in the said teashop, in Lewisham High Street.

'Oh!' cried Miss Coulson. 'I'm *so* glad. I know Pammie had *lots* of very nice friends – at least, so I gathered – but you're the first I've met.' She hesitated, then went on, 'How was she when you last saw her? I mean . . . did she seem happy?'

'I think so,' replied Margaret. 'At least . . .' She broke off whatever it was she'd been going to say. 'Yes, very happy,' she said. 'She'd just got engaged, and—'

'Oh *yes*, the inspector mentioned that. He even pointed out the young gentleman at the funeral. An Honourable – fancy that! Pammie would have *loved* being married to an Honourable.'

There was a brief silence, while the other three digested the implications of this. But it was Margaret who asked the question that was, Rowlands guessed, in all their minds: 'Then Pamela didn't grow up in Kenya?'

Miss Coulson gave a startled laugh. 'Kenya? Bless you, no.'

'But I thought she said that her parents . . .'

'Her parents are dead,' said the elderly lady firmly. 'Both died of the influenza, when Pammie was a baby. I think, dear, you must be confusing her with somebody else.'

'I think I must be,' said Margaret sadly.

'It bears out what Allingham said – that the girl was an accomplished liar,' remarked Douglas on the way back into town. They'd dropped Margaret at home, where she was to spend the rest of the day with the family, before heading back to Bletchley the following morning. 'Oh, I wouldn't say that,' replied Rowlands. 'A bit of a storyteller, perhaps. She wouldn't be the first to make herself out to be grander than she was, poor young thing.'

'Wonder if that chap of hers – Montfitchet – knew about her humble background?' said Douglas. 'Might have been a reason to break off the engagement, if he'd found out she'd been telling lies.'

'Surely not? He seems like a decent enough young fellow. Not the sort to mind about all that kind of thing. And even if he *did* find out, it'd hardly be a motive for murder.'

'You'd be surprised,' was the reply. 'Chap discovers that the girl he's been walking out with is a fraud. Loses his temper. You'll admit he's got a bit of a temper . . . Think I'll get him in for further questioning.'

'That's up to you, of course,' said Rowlands. 'But – even if they did quarrel about Miss Wingate's tall stories – it doesn't really make sense of the Bletchley Park element . . . the disappearance of the documents, I mean.'

'Och, I've got that side o' things covered, never fear,' said the policeman with a satisfied air. 'Matter o' fact, your Margaret's going to keep an eye out for anything untoward in that department.'

'I don't want Margaret getting involved. It's too dangerous. You said so yourself.'

'She'll have one of our best women officers looking after her,' said Douglas. 'Anything she thinks isn't quite right, WPC Briggs'll be on the phone to me PDQ.'

'I still don't like it.'

'It was Margaret's idea, as a matter o' fact,' said the other. 'She's a plucky little lass, that girl o' yours. "I want to do it for Pam," she says to me. "If it helps to catch the man who killed her, then count me in."'

Chapter Ten

Life resumed its familiar routine for Frederick Rowlands, as it did for thousands of his fellow Londoners, that spring of 1941. He'd wake with nerves jangled from a night of broken sleep, already tired out before the day had begun. No matter how early he woke, there never seemed time for more than a hasty breakfast, with Edith short-tempered because of having to make their rations stretch to last the week, when anyone could see they'd run out by Thursday. He'd hurry to catch the train – which would be packed with the bodies of his fellow passengers – their various smells of bad breath, stale sweat, cheap scent and cigarettes made more intense by the tightly closed windows. He'd make his way – sometimes by Underground, but more often these days on foot – through the wrecked streets, to the relative quiet and security of the office. Here, he'd occupy his thoughts with the minutiae of filling orders and despatching them, or whatever else landed on his desk that day. Then he'd repeat the journey he'd made to work in reverse, travelling back across London as the blackout came down, and the metropolis braced itself for another night of bombing. All the talk was of this: which part of the city would 'cop it' tonight. One lived in a permanent state of dread, which was almost more exhausting than the terror of the raids themselves.

March moved into April, and suddenly, after what had seemed an endless winter, spring had arrived. You could smell it in the air – in the freshness of new growth on the trees in Regent's Park, and smell of spring flowers drifting from the borders in those areas of the park that hadn't been given over to growing vegetables. One evening, a few days into the month, Rowlands left the office at six, and began the walk that would take him to Waterloo station. It was a route he'd followed many times before – he could do it in under an hour – and tonight, there was no particular rush, since Edith would be at her WVS meeting. So he took his stick and set off, glad of the chance to blow the cobwebs away. Leaving the park by York Gate, he turned along Marylebone Road, and from thence into Park Crescent and Portland Place.

Passing in front of the portals of Broadcasting House, at the top of Langham Place, he wondered whether this part of the city would be spared tonight, or if the sandbags heaped against the front of the famous building would once more be necessary for its protection, as they had been on so many previous nights. He sent up a prayer to the gods who presided over such things that the BBC would be able to continue its essential task of bringing hope and comfort, to say nothing of accurate news bulletins, to the many millions in the United Kingdom and around the globe who relied on its services.

At that moment he felt somebody take his arm – a woman, to judge by the smallness of her gloved hand, and the faint waft of some exotic scent (*could it be* Je Reviens?), as she drew him closer to her. 'It's kind of you,' he said. 'But I can really manage all right.'

'I know you can, Fred,' said a voice he knew. 'But if it's all the same to you, I'd like to walk with you a little way.'

'Of course,' he said, wondering what it was she wanted from him. That this wasn't an accidental meeting, he was certain. With Iris Barnes, things were seldom accidental.

'Well,' she said, as they began walking in the direction of Oxford Circus. 'This reminds me of that time in Barcelona, when we walked along Las Ramblas, dodging the bullets – remember?'

'Yes,' he said, although it hadn't happened exactly like that. They'd spent a week together in that war-ravaged city. 1937. How long ago it seemed!

'I miss those times,' she said, with what sounded like genuine regret. 'One really felt one was making a difference, whereas now . . .' She let the sentence tail away.

'Now we're caught up in a war, just as we were then,' said Rowlands. The sounds of traffic grew louder as they reached the intersection with the busy shopping street. Even though many of its larger stores had suffered extensive damage during the recent spate of bombings, it was still thronged with crowds of shoppers heading home after spending their saved-up clothing coupons.

'This feels different,' said Iris Barnes. '*Then* things were clear-cut. One knew what one was up against. *Now* it's as if we're fighting in a thick fog. It's hard to see who one's opponents are.'

It didn't seem all that different to Rowlands, whose memories of the Spanish Civil War were of the murderous in-fighting that had taken place between the various factions on the Republican side, as much as of the war against Franco's fascists. But he said nothing. If anyone knew about such things, he thought, it was this long-time member of the secret services.

'Ah, there's a taxi!' she said, stepping off the pavement in order to hail it. Then, as the vehicle drew alongside, 'Come with me, won't you? There's someone I want you to meet.' He started to say that he really ought to get back, but she cut across him. 'Please,' she said. 'It won't take long.'

He remembered this about Iris Barnes: she had always been good at getting her own way. With a feeling that he was probably letting himself in for more than he had bargained for, he climbed into the cab beside her. She gave an address in St James's, which turned out to be that of a private members' club.

'It's women only,' said Miss Barnes. 'But I can sign you in as my guest.' A few minutes later, they were seated in front of a good coal fire, in what Rowlands guessed, from the smell of leather-bound books, furniture polish and fresh flowers, to be a library. A servant came to take their order. 'It's a bit late for tea, don't you think?' said Miss Barnes to Rowlands. 'Two whiskies, please,' she told the waiter, then, 'Has my other guest arrived?'

'Not yet, madam.'

'Show her in here as soon as she does, will you?'

'Yes, madam.'

'Olga arrived back in England by a rather circuitous route a few days ago,' she said to Rowlands. 'She's been in Spain for the past few months, doing some work for us. I wonder what you'll make of her?' As she spoke, there came the tapping of heels on the parquet floor. An aura of expensive perfume wafted towards them. 'Ah, here she is!' cried Miss Barnes. She summoned the waiter. 'Bring another whisky for my guest, will you? Hello, Olga.' This was to the new arrival. 'Sit down, won't you?'

But the woman did not at once take up this invitation. 'Who is this?' she said, evidently referring to Rowlands. Her tone was suspicious.

'A friend,' said Iris Barnes. 'Now do sit down. How were things in Madrid when you left?'

'Quiet,' was the reply. 'You would not know there was a war. Not like London, with the bombs dropping every night!' The accent was hard to place. It wasn't Spanish, thought Rowlands. Polish, perhaps?

'Olga here has been very useful to us,' said Miss Barnes to Rowlands. 'Because of her, we have had an invaluable insight into the workings of the Abwehr – the German secret service,' she added, for his benefit. 'Here come our drinks.' She waited until the waiter had placed the tray, with the three glasses of whisky and a jug of water for those who wanted it, on the low table in front of the fire. Only when he had gone did she go on. 'A toast, I think, don't you?' she said, when the glasses had been handed round. 'What shall it be? "Confusion to our enemies"?'

'To freedom,' said the woman called Olga. So they all drank to freedom.

'Now then,' said Miss Barnes, once this ceremony had been performed. 'To business. What have you got for me?' The other woman rummaged for a moment in her handbag. She must have handed Iris something, for the latter said, 'All right. I'll look at these later. Did you have any trouble getting hold of the material?'

'No. I waited until he was asleep before I went to his office. He was careless, as always. He had left the papers on the desk. It was easy to photograph them. I was back in his bed within ten minutes.' She laughed – a throaty, self-satisfied laugh. 'He was snoring like the pig he is.'

'Good. But take care. If he were to suspect . . .'

'He will not suspect. I am careful.'

'Even so. You have the capsule, if necessary?'

'Yes. But it will not be necessary.'

'All right. When do you return to Madrid?'

'Next week.'

'Excellent,' said Miss Barnes. 'You have all you need?'

'I need money for expenses.'

'Let me have a note of how much.'

'I will do so. Now,' said Olga, setting down her glass with a decisive click. 'I am going to play baccarat. I find it steadies the nerves.'

Then she was gone, leaving a whiff of *Tabu* behind her.

Iris Barnes laughed. 'Nerves?' she said. 'That woman doesn't know the meaning of the word. Just as well, given the kind of risks she has to take. It's not an easy life, being a double agent.'

'I can imagine.'

'Of course, she's only one of a number we've got working for us – but she's one of the best. A Polish patriot.' So Rowlands had been right. 'She trained as a dancer in Paris, which is where we recruited her. She caught the eye of a senior German intelligence officer. When he was posted to Spain, to take over the Abwehr networks there, she went with him. Oh yes, Olga's been very useful to us.'

'She's Polish, you say?'

'On her father's side. Mother was French. Jewish, you know. So she didn't need much persuasion to come over to our side,' said Miss Barnes. 'She has expensive habits, as you may have gathered. Expensive tastes, too. A pity you couldn't have seen her, really. That Chanel two-piece she was wearing must have set her back a pretty penny . . . or us, rather.'

'Why did you ask me to come here?' said Rowlands.

'I thought it might interest you,' was the reply. 'And it could have a bearing on that little matter at the Park. Thanks to Olga and her kind, we've been able to keep quite a sharp eye on the information that's been passing through German intelligence during the past few months. We'd be the first to spot any if leaks were coming from our own side.'

'And?'

'That's the odd thing,' said Iris Barnes. 'There *aren't* any – or not as far as we can tell from the coded traffic passing between Abwehr sources and our agents. If intelligence *is* being leaked, then it isn't getting through to the enemy . . . or, rather . . .' She hesitated a moment. 'Not the *Nazi* enemy, at least.'

'Then who?'

'That remains to be seen,' was the enigmatic reply. A brief silence elapsed, during which Rowlands considered what she had said, and wondered what exactly this extraordinary woman had in mind, in telling him of this. At last Iris Barnes let out a sigh. 'I could sit here all evening, talking over things with you,' she said. 'But Whitehall calls, I'm afraid.' She got to her feet. 'I'll get the taxi to drop you at Waterloo.'

'There's no need.'

'I insist. I've kept you from your wife and family long enough. How's Margaret, by the way?'

'Keeping busy, from what I can gather,' he said, as the two of them made their way to the foyer of the club.

'Cab, please, George. Soon as possible,' said Miss Barnes to the porter. 'That's good,' she went on, replying to what Rowlands had said. 'She's a bright girl. She should go far.'

'Yes, I—'

'I wonder,' said Iris, as if another thought had suddenly occurred to her, 'if you'd care to come to a party on Saturday?'

The car arrived while Rowlands was still tying his bow-tie – or trying to; it had been a while since he had last had to go through the rigmarole, and his fingers seemed to have forgotten how to do it.

'Let me,' said Edith, seeing that he was struggling. As she deftly flicked the ends of the tie into place, the object of her ministrations wondered aloud whether his evening clothes were still up to scratch, even after they'd been thoroughly brushed and aired.

'You're sure the moth hasn't got at them?'

'Quite sure.' Her handiwork completed, Edith stood back and surveyed him. 'In fact, considering how old that suit is, it's really stood up very well.'

'Which is more than you can say about the wearer.'

'Stop fishing for compliments. You look fine. Now you'd better go, or that young woman of yours will be wondering where you've got to.'

'She isn't my "young woman", as you well know. I'm only going to this wretched party because it might be of use to the investigation.'

'I know, I know.' She helped him on with his overcoat and was handing him his hat (a soft hat, thank goodness; this was only a black-tie occasion) when Joan came downstairs.

'Gosh,' she cried. 'Don't you look swish? I wish *I* could go to a party.'

'It's for your father's work,' retorted Edith. 'Not the sort of party you'd enjoy.'

'But I *would* enjoy it! All that lovely food and . . . and champagne.'

'When the war's over,' said Rowlands, 'I'll take you to The Ritz for a champagne supper, I promise.' With which he made his exit, to the strains of Flanagan and Allen's 'Nice People', as sung by his youngest daughter.

The party – or reception, rather – was being held in one of the grand buildings in Grosvenor Square, the identity of which only became obvious to Rowlands as he was admitted into the foyer. For here, American voices predominated, and the smell of American cigarettes rose all around.

'They're all in there, sir – through the double doors,' said the butler, perhaps seeing him hesitate.

'Thank you.' With the feeling that he was here under false pretences, he made his way across the expanse of marble floor, to where the sounds of talk and laughter were loudest. Just as he was wondering whether he'd have to give his name to the man on the door, and what he would say if his presence were questioned, he was relieved to hear a familiar voice.

'You got here, then?' said Iris Barnes, slipping her arm through his. 'Come and meet some people.'

'Gladly,' he said. 'Although before I do, you might explain what I'm supposed to be doing here.'

'Let's just say you're here as an interested observer.'

'Iris . . .'

But she had already drawn him towards the group just inside the doors of the reception room. Introductions were performed – a cultural attaché here, a naval officer there – of which Rowlands retained not one word. Courteous American voices pressed refreshments on him: 'This man needs a drink. What'll you have? Scotch and soda? Or on the rocks?' At least it wasn't champagne, he thought – the stuff didn't really agree with him. Beer would have been his preference, but the whisky (pre-war quality, too) slipped down easily enough.

'General McCormack was just saying that it's the first time he's attended a party where the balloons were bigger than the building,' said Miss Barnes. 'I told him we don't do things by halves, in this country.' Rowlands smiled politely, but his incomprehension must have been obvious, for she added quickly, 'Of course. You won't

171

have seen the barrage balloon in Grosvenor Square. There's a group of WAAFs manning it – if "manning's" the right word for a lot of women . . . They've christened it Romeo, apparently. Heaven knows why.'

'Fine bunch o' gals,' said the general. 'Guess they hafta get their fun somehow.'

'Do ya think they might give the navy a chance?' said the young officer whose name had eluded Rowlands. 'Or is it only the Brylcreem boys they go for?'

'I think you'll find that Americans are quite popular with English girls – whatever service they belong to,' said Miss Barnes. 'Of course, if America comes into the war, that'll become very much more the case.' Laughter followed this sally, which was delivered in characteristically deadpan style.

'You're an army man, I guess?' said McCormack to Rowlands, who had, as instructed, worn his medals.

'I was in the last "show", sir,' he replied. 'Now I'm just a private citizen.'

'Nuthin' the matter with that,' said the general, clapping Rowlands heartily on the back. 'Evenin', Commander. I was jus' sayin' to this gennelman here that we need good people on the ground, as well as in the military,' went on McCormack, who'd said nothing of the kind, as far as Rowlands recalled. 'Wouldn't you agree?'

'Well, yes, I suppose so,' said the man he'd addressed, diffidently. It was Angus Murchison. On reflection, Rowlands wasn't surprised to find him in that gathering. 'Good evening, Rowlands. Miss Barnes. I wondered if I'd see you here.'

'Oh, you know me. I never miss a party,' said Iris

airily. 'Especially when there are so many distinguished guests. Isn't that the Secretary of State for War I see over there, talking to the ambassador?'

'It is,' replied General McCormack.

'They seem to be getting on awfully well,' observed Iris. 'But then, it's hard not to warm to a man who's just announced to the British press how glad he is to be here.' Which indeed the newly appointed American ambassador had done, on his arrival at Bristol airport the previous month, Rowlands knew. It had been all over the newspapers.

'I'll say,' said Murchison. 'Jolly good show.'

'I think we'll leave them to it,' murmured Iris in Rowlands's ear. 'Let's go and get something to eat, shall we? I'm famished.' She took his arm once more, and they began making their way through the crowd, towards where supper had been set out. As they did so, snatches of conversation floated towards Rowlands, from the various groups clustered near the buffet tables.

One of these, consisting, presumably, of military men, was discussing the progress of the war: 'If the USA comes in, there are gonna hafta be some changes in the chain of command, that's for sure . . .'

Another group – this one evidently made up of women – was canvassing the vexed question of the servant problem: 'You simply *can't* get the help, these days. They can get better wages working in a factory, that's the problem . . .'

Across the room, a dance band started up, playing a medley of popular tunes – 'In the Mood' blending smoothly into 'A Nightingale Sang in Berkeley Square'.

The smell of hothouse flowers mingled with that of expensive cigars – both overlaid by the enticing smell of rich food. It was as if the war had receded beyond the walls of the elegantly appointed building in which they stood, for this crowd of well-dressed and well-fed people (to pass through the crowd was to become aware of both facts).

'It looks as if the embassy caterers have done us proud,' said Iris, as she and Rowlands took their places in the queue for the buffet. 'I could live for a week on what some people are piling onto their plates. I'll help you, shall I? There's cold chicken, ham, a whole salmon . . .'

But Rowlands was distracted from making his choice by a familiar voice, coming from the far end of the buffet, where drinks were being served.

'I say, give us another Scotch, there's a good fellow . . .' It was Gil Burton. He sounded half-cut, thought Rowlands.

With him was young Montfitchet. 'Steady on, old man. You've had enough.'

'Damned if I have. I *said*, give me another Scotch.'

'What's *he* doing here, I wonder?' said Rowlands to his companion, as, their plates now full, they moved away from the crush around the buffet tables.

'Hugh Montfitchet, you mean?'

'It was his friend I was referring to,' said Rowlands. 'He was at Pamela Wingate's funeral, too.'

'Well, he would be. They're pretty inseparable, he and Montfitchet. School chums, and all that,' said Iris vaguely. 'Young Burton works in the War Office . . .

private secretary to the minister, I gather. He's quite a charmer, by all accounts. Of course, he gets himself into a lot of scrapes, as that type tends to, but he must be good enough at his job, or he'd be out on his ear. Margesson doesn't suffer fools gladly, I'm told.'

'I see,' said Rowlands, thinking that he would never understand the ways of the ruling class. Still, it wasn't his affair whether or not a rather louche young man got on in the world or not.

'There are a couple of chairs over there in the window,' said Iris, interrupting these thoughts. 'Let's get them before anybody else does.' Thus ensconced, they could eat their supper in peace, and converse in relative privacy. 'This reminds me of the time we first met, at Celia West's party, all those years ago,' said Rowlands's companion nostalgically, as the strains of 'Bewitched, Bothered and Bewildered' floated over the heads of the crowd towards them. 'I was just a struggling journalist, hoping to get a column in *Woman's Own* or *Peg's Paper* – "How the Smart Set Live", or something along those lines. *You* were hunting a murderer – or so someone told me later. I can't remember who it was, now.'

Rowlands had a pretty good idea. The only other person who'd known what he was up to on the night in question had been Alasdair Douglas, with whom he'd been working on the case. The murderer had been right under their noses at that party, but they hadn't realised it until afterwards – Rowlands himself having been distracted, to say the least, by the presence of the woman to whom Iris had referred. Celia West – or Celia Swift as she was now. It had been two years since they'd last met, in Ireland. The passage of years hadn't changed the way he felt about her then, or now.

He made no comment upon what she'd said, beyond a grunt. 'Good ham, this,' he said.

'The best Virginia ham, I've no doubt,' said Iris. 'Probably flown in specially. No rationing for *this* crowd!'

Suddenly, Rowlands was tired of all this beating about the bush. 'So what *am* I doing here?' he said. 'If I'm meant to be an observer, then what am I supposed to be observing?'

'It's quite simple, my dear Fred. You're here to help us – the service I work for, that is – find out who's been leaking secrets. Our American cousins are just as concerned as we are with what's been happening. I'm sure there are quite a number of their operatives amongst this crowd. Why do you think old Murchison's here, in his best bib and tucker? The fact that Bletchley's security has been compromised is a matter of grave national importance, which might affect the whole conduct of the war. No wonder the Yanks are in a blue funk.'

'What exactly do you want me to do?'

'Just keep your ear to the ground, as you always do,' said Iris. 'Tell me if anything strikes you as strange, or untoward.'

'I'll do my best,' he said. And for the next hour or so that was what he did, following in Iris Barnes's footsteps as she circulated, dropping in on this conversation or that, as the fancy took her. She seemed as much at home in this milieu as she had been on a similarly grand occasion, mingling with the cream of the German film industry and members of the Nazi high command at the Hotel

Adlon in Berlin in 1933, or, more recently, in Barcelona, fraternising with Republican revolutionaries during the Civil War. But she seemed no less at ease in the company of wing commanders and four-star generals. 'Ah Miss Barnes! Just the woman I want to see! What's your view of the Balkan situation?'

It was during this particular conversation that Rowlands, who had been listening to what was being said with interest, if only the most general understanding of the issues being debated by these eminent chiefs of staff, heard something that made his ears prick up. It wasn't what was said – a question about whether the partisans in Greece would throw in their lot with the Allies, or capitulate to the Axis, as Yugoslavia had done – but who had said it. It was the man whose name he'd never learnt – the American who'd been in Murchison's office that first day, and who had made that remark about 'heads having to roll'. It had seemed to Rowlands at the time a rather menacing remark, albeit delivered in an off-hand manner. He'd been struck, then as now, by the man's distinctive intonation: it was certainly an American accent, but not one with which Rowlands was familiar, being both more exaggerated, with its drawling consonants, and more patrician, than any he'd previously come across.

'Of course, now Yugoslavia's fallen, Hitler just has to secure Greece to cut off access to the Romanian oilfields,' said the American, adding, with what seemed to Rowlands an undisguised satisfaction, 'I'd say it doesn't look good for the British.'

'Oh, I don't know,' said Iris, her clear tones penetrating that fug of male self-satisfaction and cigar smoke. 'Once the Greek partisans come over to our side, I think Hitler will have a fight on his hands.'

'Which you'll make sure to bring about, I guess?' said the man, with an unpleasant edge in his voice.

But Iris Barnes was equal to this. 'I?' she replied with a laugh. 'What makes you think *I* have anything to do with it? I'm only a journalist. I merely report what I find.'

'Sure you do.' This time there was no mistaking the hostility in the other's tone. 'I must've been mixing you up with somebody else.'

'I think you must have been,' replied Iris Barnes sweetly; then to Rowlands, 'I could do with another drink, couldn't you?' With that, she walked off, with Rowlands in her wake.

'I know that man,' said Rowlands to his companion, once he judged they were out of earshot.

'Joe Anderson, you mean?' She paused to light a cigarette. 'Oh, sorry. Would you like one?'

'I'll smoke my own, thanks. Is that his name – Anderson? What does he do?'

'Do? That's easy. He's a spook. One of theirs,' she added. 'American secret service, that is. I met him in Washington in '39. Bit of an odd fish, but he's on our side.'

'Are you sure about that?' Briefly, Rowlands told her of his encounter with the man in Murchison's office that time. 'I'm sure it was him,' he said. 'There can't be two people with that accent.'

'You'll find plenty of them in Boston,' said Iris, but she didn't seem unimpressed by Rowlands's revelation. 'Do you think he recognised you?' she said.

'How on earth could I tell? We didn't exchange a word just now – and the Bletchley meeting was *very* brief. If I hadn't heard him speak, I'd never have made the connection.'

'Well, it's not particularly surprising to find someone like Anderson poking his nose into our affairs. The Americans are obsessed with finding out what's going on at Bletchley. They think we should be sharing all our intelligence with them. He was probably just picking Angus Murchison's brains.'

'You don't suppose . . .' Rowlands began to say, then broke off.

'Suppose what? That our friend Anderson was the one who bumped off Pamela Wingate – having first coerced her into stealing the documents for him? I think that's a bit far-fetched, Fred. It's true that the Americans want a share in our intelligence, but not to the extent of committing murder to get it.'

'When you put it like that, it does sound absurd,' he said.

It wasn't long after this that the party began to break up, with some going on to engagements elsewhere, and others anxious – as Rowlands was himself – to get home before the air raid sirens announced the onset of another night's bombing. He had already taken his leave of Iris, and collected his hat and coat, when an altercation broke out in the room behind.

'Take your hands off me! I'm *perf-ickly* cap'ble of walking . . .' A moment later, Gil Burton, flanked by a couple of other men (aides of some sort, Rowlands guessed) came stumbling into the foyer. He had obviously become considerably drunker in the hour or so since Rowlands had first become aware of his presence at the party. 'I *said* take your hands off me!'

'Pipe down, Gil. You're making a scene . . .' It was Hugh Montfitchet. 'It's all right,' he said to the men who'd manhandled Burton. 'I'll see him into a taxi.' Then, addressing his friend again, 'You are a bloody fool, Gil. Insulting our hosts like that. Did you mean to get us thrown out?'

'Course not. Bloody Yanks can't take a joke. All I said was—'

'We all heard what you said. Now put your coat on, and we'll get out of here before you cause an international incident.'

As the drunken man, still muttering under his breath, did as he was told, he must have caught sight of Rowlands. 'You again!' he cried. 'Why do I keep seeing you everywhere?'

'Hello, Mr Burton. Time you went home, I think.'

'Ev'rywhere I go, *there* you are.'

'Come on, Gil.'

'Sneaking about and . . . sh . . . shp . . . *spying*.'

'I'm sorry about this,' said Montfitchet to Rowlands. 'He doesn't know what he's saying.'

'That's quite all right.' It was a relief when, at that moment, a footman announced the arrival of a car for 'Mr Rowlands' and he could take his leave. It had been an interesting evening, he thought.

Chapter Eleven

It was the Monday morning after the party, when Rowlands let himself into his office. Miss Symonds wasn't in yet. He wondered if she was all right. *Where was it she lived again? Pinner ... or was it Ruislip?* He hadn't heard anything on the wireless this morning about its having been hit last night – but then you didn't always.

He'd just sat down at his desk and was considering how best to tackle the first task of the day without his sighted assistant – the post would have to wait, but there were some telephone calls he could make – when that instrument, as if it had anticipated his thought, burst into strident voice. Thinking it was probably Jean Symonds, ringing to say she'd been delayed, he seized the receiver with alacrity.

'Hello?'

'Rowlands? That you?' It wasn't Jean.

'Hello, Douglas. What can I do for you?'

'There've been developments. The Wingate case.'

'Oh?' He felt a surge of anxiety. 'It's got nothing to do with Margaret this time, I hope?'

'Well, as a matter of fact, it was she who alerted me.'

'To what?'

'I think it's best if I tell you in person. I'll pick you up in twenty minutes.'

'I can't leave the office unattended,' he protested – but Douglas had already hung up.

Fortunately, Miss Symonds came in at that moment. 'Sorry I'm late, Mr Rowlands.' She sounded out of breath. 'The house two doors down took a direct hit last night. A family of five.'

'Did they get out in time?'

'I'm afraid not. The only one they managed to save was the old lady, Mrs Roberts. Mrs Scott's mother,' she added. 'The others . . . Mr and Mrs Scott and the three children . . . were all killed.'

'I'm sorry,' said Rowlands gently. 'Do you feel all right to carry on?'

'Yes, Mr Rowlands. There's nothing to be done, after all, is there?' said the young woman, a little too brightly. 'Shall I make us a cup of tea, before we get started?'

'I have to go out, I'm afraid. Can you cope for a while, do you think?'

'Oh yes. I've plenty to be getting on with,' said Miss Symonds, still in the same artificially cheerful tone. 'It's just a pity about the old lady. Quite confused, she seemed. Kept asking where her daughter was, and the kiddies. Poor old duck.'

* * *

'So what's this all about?' said Rowlands, when he was once more seated beside the chief inspector in the police Wolseley. 'You said you'd heard from Margaret.'

'That's right. It's about that girl – Sylvia Pritchard. The little mouse . . .'

'I know who you mean,' said Rowlands. 'What about her?'

'She's got something to tell us, apparently. Your Margaret didn't say what, but I don't imagine she'd waste our time with trivialities.'

'No,' said Rowlands, with the creeping sense of unease he'd felt when he first heard that his daughter would be – however indirectly – assisting the police. Her place was in a university, not working as a go-between for Douglas and his minions. But he kept this thought to himself. In wartime, everything one had believed fixed and certain was turned on its head.

They reached the gates of Bletchley Park in just over an hour, and were waved through, as they had been before. After the barest of preliminaries, they found themselves seated in Murchison's office. Margaret and Sylvia Pritchard were already present; the latter had obviously been crying.

'Now then, Miss,' said Douglas, not unkindly. 'No need to take on. I gather you've something to tell us?'

At which the young woman's sobs grew louder. 'I . . . I never meant to get anybody into trouble,' she said indistinctly. 'It's just that . . . I've been so *worried* about Jock . . .'

'Buck up, Sylvia,' said Margaret. 'You'll have to tell them, you know – so it's best if you do it now.'

'All right.' With which the story began to emerge –

haltingly, and with many sniffs and sobs. How she'd told him and *told* him that it was wrong, and that he'd only have himself to blame if they caught him. How he'd *promised* her, after what happened to Pam, that he'd stop what he'd been doing . . .

'And what *had* Mr Colquhoun been doing?' The chief inspector's tone was studiedly neutral.

Sylvia Pritchard must have picked up something else in his expression, however, for she burst out, 'They won't arrest him, will they? He told me he was only doing it to help bring the war to an end.'

'You still haven't said what it was he was up to,' said the policeman.

'Tell him, Sylvia.' Margaret's voice was gentle.

There was an agonised pause before Sylvia Pritchard spoke again. 'He . . . he said they weren't really our enemies, the . . . the Russians. We were on the same side, he said, if we could only see it. We . . . *our* side . . . ought to share intelligence with *their* side, so that we could beat the Germans together . . . He . . . he got hold of some papers . . . circuit diagrams, I think he said they were . . . I didn't really understand what he meant.'

'Good God,' said Commander Murchison softly. 'So it was Colquhoun who was passing secrets to the enemy all along.'

'He said they *weren't* the enemy . . . not really,' wept the girl.

'He stole those papers,' said Douglas, ignoring this.

'It wasn't stealing,' said Sylvia. 'He was going to put them back, afterwards. He said he needed some concrete proof, to show them.'

'Show *who*, exactly?' Murchison again.

'He said he knew somebody, up in London . . . It was Pamela who gave him the name.'

'Did she indeed?' said the chief inspector. 'And what *was* the name of this person?'

'I . . . I don't know,' was the reply. 'Jock never said. Only that it was somebody he knew . . . from when he was at Cambridge, I think.'

'So you're saying that Mr Colquhoun intended to pass these documents on to this unnamed person in London?' Douglas persisted.

'I think so,' said Sylvia. 'She . . . Pamela . . . was going to make contact with . . . with the man first. She said this . . . this person . . . was very well connected. He'd know exactly whom Jock needed to approach, on the Russian side.'

'It sounds as if Miss Wingate had the upper hand in the affair,' remarked Douglas drily.

'Oh, I wish he'd never got involved with her!' cried the girl. 'Jock's a good person. He'd never do anything for personal gain. But she . . . Pamela . . . saw Jock taking those papers, from Hut 8. She said if he didn't do as she said, she'd expose him. It would have been the end of his career.'

And the end of him, thought Rowlands. 'So what you're saying is that Miss Wingate and Mr Colquhoun were in it together?' he prompted her, when she fell silent. 'Was it he – Jock – who hid those papers in Margaret's locker, then?'

'He . . . he never meant to drag Maggie into it,' was the tremulous reply. 'He just needed somewhere to hide them – the documents, I mean. It was after we'd heard that Pamela had disappeared. He knew there'd be an investigation . . . especially when the documents were found to be missing. He panicked, I suppose. Maggie's locker was the first that came to hand. When we heard that she . . . Maggie . . . had been arrested, Jock was horrified. We both were. He said he'd never intended to go through with it.'

'Be that as it may, he was committing treason,' said Douglas sternly. 'I'll need to talk to him at once. Where is he?'

'I don't know.' Sylvia spoke so quietly that it was an effort to hear her. 'I haven't seen him since the day before yesterday.' She and Jock Colquhoun had both been on the late shift, she said. There'd been a 'flap' on, and so they'd all been working flat out, trying to decipher the latest batch of intercepts, before the codes changed at midnight. No, they hadn't talked; there was seldom time for more than a quick hello, before one got down to it. 'And Jock was in a different room from the one in which I was working. All of us – the women, that is – are in the main room, while the men have their own area, so you see . . .'

'We get the picture, miss,' said Douglas. 'What I want to know is what happened at the *end* of the shift. This would have been early on Wednesday morning, would it not?'

'About eight o'clock, that's right. I . . . I saw Jock was leaving, and I went to catch up with him. We . . . we sometimes went to the canteen for breakfast, or . . . or he'd walk me back to my lodgings. But that morning . . .'

'Wednesday morning,'

'Yes. He . . . Jock . . . seemed in an awful hurry. When I caught up with him, outside the huts, he . . . he didn't seem to want to stop. Said he had a train to catch.'

There was a brief silence, broken only by the scratching of Sergeant Jones's pencil as he noted all this down. 'Did Mr Colquhoun say where he was going?' said Douglas.

The young woman hesitated. 'I . . . I assumed he must be going to London, perhaps to try and find this man . . . the one Pamela had mentioned. He said he knew the name, so . . .' She let the sentence tail off. 'Or it might have been for one of his meetings. Jock's a communist,' she added, with a shade of defiance. 'It's what convinced him that the Russians were our friends.'

Murchison, who had remained silent throughout the interrogation, now emitted an exasperated hiss. 'Friends!' he said. 'Now I've heard it all! It's no thanks to that young man that Comrade Stalin isn't now in possession of our most secret intelligence. I want you to find him, Chief Inspector – and as quickly as possible, before he does any more damage.'

'Right you are, Commander.' The chief inspector pushed back his chair, and began to get to his feet. 'You'd better get Miss Pritchard's statement typed up, Sergeant,' he said to that officer, who had been diligently taking notes throughout. 'Then get her to sign it.'

'Sir.'

'W-what's going to happen to me?' said Sylvia Pritchard.

The senior policeman was silent a moment. 'I think,'

he said at last, 'that's for Commander Murchison to decide. 'He'll have his own views on the matter.'

'I do indeed,' said Murchison, and his tone was not a reassuring one, as far as Miss Pritchard was concerned. 'Now that the police have finished with you for the time being, we'll have some questions of our own to ask you. You must be aware,' he went on, as the girl gave a frightened sob, 'of how extremely serious this is?'

'Margaret, you'll stay with Sylvia, won't you?' said Rowlands to his daughter, as he got up to follow the chief inspector. 'That is, if Commander Murchison will permit it?'

'I was just going to suggest it,' said the naval officer, with a slight softening of his tone. 'Perhaps,' he added to Margaret, 'you'd take Miss Pritchard to wash her face, before we get started on further questions?'

In Hut 6, they were halfway through the morning shift. The usual atmosphere of frenetic activity prevailed. 'Jock? No, he hasn't been in for a couple of days,' said Harry Allingham. 'Pretty inconsiderate, if you ask me. He knows we're under pressure.'

'Did he give any notice that he was going to be away?' asked the chief inspector.

'Not that I recall. Although I must confess, I don't always listen when people tell me things. There's too much going on, as a rule. Things needing urgent attention. So I might very well have missed something . . . Hi, you're not telling me *Jock's* disappeared as well?'

'I'm not telling you anything, sir,' said Douglas.

'That just about puts the tin lid on it!' grumbled the

cryptanalyst. 'He's one of my best men. Now you're saying he's taken French leave, just when we're at our most frantic . . .' Then, to one of his female colleagues, 'I say, Miss Hanbury-Withers! Hurry up with those decrypts, can't you? I haven't got all day.'

The rest of Colquhoun's colleagues were no more forthcoming as to where he had gone than Allingham had been. 'H-he goes up to London s-sometimes,' said Cyril Fitzpatrick. 'F-for meetings.'

'What sort of meetings?'

'I c-couldn't tell you.'

'You were with him that day – the day Pamela Wingate disappeared,' said Douglas. 'Attending a lecture – or so you said.'

'We d-did attend the lecture,' said Fitzpatrick. 'At least . . . I did. Jock arrived late. He'd had some things to do beforehand, he said, and so he didn't get to B-Burlington House until the lecture w-was almost over.'

'Why didn't you mention this before, sir?' said Douglas coldly.

'I d-didn't think it was important,' replied the young man.

'Which is what we've been grappling with from the start of this case,' remarked the chief inspector gloomily, as he and Rowlands walked back towards the house. 'None of these people . . . scientists, I should say . . . seem to have the least idea of what is, and what isn't, important. A man's disappeared, leaving not a trace, and we've a pretty good idea he's been betraying secrets. Yet none of 'em seem in the least bit concerned.'

'Have you discovered whether he actually went to London on Wednesday morning?' asked Rowlands.

'My sergeant's at the railway station now. But we've no reason to doubt it. The girl says he was agitated that morning. Something on his mind. Said he was going to catch a train. Where else would he be going?' Rowlands admitted that he didn't know. 'It's the only lead we've got,' said Douglas, as they reached the entrance to the house, through which the usual stream of young people was flowing – it being lunchtime. 'Stands to reason that—'

They were interrupted at that moment by the arrival of Sergeant Jones, sounding a little out of breath. He'd bicycled to and from the station, on a borrowed machine, this being the preferred method of transport at Bletchley.

'He caught the 8.15 all right, sir. Station master knows him well. Often travels up from Bletchley on that line.'

'So the ticket was to London, then?'

'That's right, sir. Euston station. A return ticket.'

'Was the return part of the ticket handed in?'

'No, sir.'

'Then what the blazes happened to it – and to him?' said the chief inspector.

'So if Miss Pritchard's to be believed,' said Commander Murchison, when the three men met for the last time that day, 'Colquhoun was a communist, who'd been passing secrets to the Russians for some time.'

'Looks like it, sir.' An uncomfortable silence followed.

'I suppose he killed the Wingate girl, too?' said Murchison. 'I mean, given that she was his accomplice –

or so it would appear,' the commander went on. 'I couldn't get much more out of the Pritchard girl than she told us before. But it seems clear that Pamela Wingate put him up to it. No doubt they had a falling-out. He killed her – then hid the documents he'd stolen in his panic.'

'It's a possibility, sir,' replied Douglas. 'Although we won't know for certain what happened until we question him. He – Colquhoun – was certainly on the train Miss Wingate caught to London on the nineteenth of February, because his friend, Fitzpatrick, confirmed it at the time. He seems to have given Fitzpatrick the slip – apparently, he didn't turn up at the lecture they were both supposed to be attending until later. One can assume he followed the girl to wherever it was she was going, killed her, and then placed the body in Montfitchet's flat.'

It occurred to Rowlands that this version of events didn't take into account the missing two days. Pamela Wingate had made that journey on the Tuesday afternoon. Her body hadn't been discovered until the Thursday. But he said nothing, knowing his friend would be all too aware of this, and the difficulty of making it fit with the rest of the facts.

'It hardly bears thinking about,' said Murchison. 'If Colquhoun had succeeded in passing those documents to the Russians, things would be in a pretty pickle. As it is, the situation's bad enough. If, as we suspect, he'd been passing information to his communist "friends" for some time, then doubtless *they* passed it on to their German allies – fatally compromising our security, with regard to the war at sea. No wonder our ships have been suffering such heavy losses from the wolf-packs.' Murchison was silent a moment. 'This is a disaster, Chief Inspector,' he said at last. 'Nothing short of a disaster.'

'Yes, sir.'

A longer silence followed, which none of those present seemed inclined to break. 'I want you to find this man, Chief Inspector.' Murchison's voice was not quite steady. 'Find him and bring him to trial. I for one won't rest until he pays the penalty for what he's done.'

But the ensuing manhunt yielded no results, even though it stretched as far as Aberdeen, where Colquhoun's mother lived, and where it was supposed he might have taken refuge. Jock Colquhoun had simply vanished into thin air.

'O' course, he'll likely be travelling under a false name,' said Douglas, two days into the investigation. 'But we've a fair description. Even disguised, he won't be able to avoid detection. Our men are trained to spot things you can't easily conceal. Height. Build. Posture. Why, the way a man walks is often what gives him away.'

'What about the old stone in the shoe trick?' asked Rowlands, who had once been taken in by just this device.

Douglas ignored him. 'Mark my words,' he said. 'He won't escape us for long.' He was right, as it turned out, although not in the way he had meant.

The following day, which was a Saturday, Rowlands was planning to spend his free afternoon in the garden. The recent spell of beautiful weather had brought everything out at once, it seemed. His vegetable garden needed attention. The grass needed mowing. With Edith and her mother out shopping, and Joan at Guides, he was looking forward to an uninterrupted few hours' work. And so when the telephone rang as he was about to change out of the suit he'd worn to the office that morning and into his gardening clothes, he was tempted to let it ring. Who'd be ringing at a weekend? He'd already half-guessed the answer to *that* one.

'You're in,' said the voice at the other end of the line, when Rowlands reluctantly picked up the receiver and announced himself. 'I was beginning to think I'd missed you.' Then, before the other could say anything more, the chief inspector went on, in a grimmer tone, 'There's been a development. We've found Colquhoun. Dead, as it happens.'

'Ah.' Rowlands hesitated before asking the obvious question. 'Was it suicide?'

'Looks that way,' was the laconic reply. 'I'm just heading up there now. Thought you might like to come along.' The body had been found earlier that day by some men working on the railway track, a few miles beyond Bletchley, Douglas explained, after Rowlands had been collected in the Wolseley. The corpse, he went on, had been partly hidden by some bushes on the embankment, which was why it hadn't been discovered sooner.

'Do you think it was concealed deliberately?' asked Rowlands.

'Too soon to say,' was the answer. 'Until the pathologist's taken a look at him and determined the cause of death, we can only speculate as to how he ended up where he did.'

'Are we assuming that he fell – or was pushed – from a moving train?' asked Rowlands.

'We're assuming nothing just yet,' said the chief inspector. 'But something o' the sort does seem likely.'

'Did he leave a note?'

'Confessing to his crimes, you mean?' said Douglas, with grim humour. 'Now that *would* have been a tidy outcome. Unfortunately, he didn't. Nor were there any incriminating documents about his person – nothing on him, in fact, except a wallet with three pounds ten shillings in notes, some loose change, a box of matches and a packet of Senior Service, half of 'em smoked.'

'No latch-key?'

'He was staying in digs, like all these Bletchley Park people.'

'Even so, he'd have needed a key, working the kind of hours he did. Unless his landlady was an insomniac.'

'I'll be talking to the landlady later,' said Douglas. 'Perhaps he'd mislaid his key.'

The scene of the crime – or accident, or whatever it was – proved to be a bleak stretch of terrain, covered with scrubby undergrowth and clinker, just outside Leighton Buzzard. 'The train would have been slowing down as it approached the station,' said Douglas. 'So it would've been moving at a steadier speed. If he was going to do it, that would have been the time.'

'While he had more control over his movements, you mean?'

'Aye. That was my thinking.'

'Or while whoever pushed him had control,' said Rowlands.

'I've already told you, we're keeping an open mind about that,' the chief inspector replied. 'Find anything?'

he said to one of the police constables who was engaged in searching the area around where the body had been found.

'There's this, sir,' replied the young policeman, scrambling down the steep slope that ran from the track to halt smartly in front of his superior officer. He produced an object wrapped up in a piece of sacking. 'It was in the bushes a few feet from where the deceased was lying.' This turned out to be a heavy-duty spanner. 'Course, it might have been dropped by one of the railwaymen,' added the constable.

'And again it might not,' said Douglas. 'All right, Baker, get it to the lab, fast as you can.'

'Do you think that was the weapon he was killed with?' asked Rowlands.

'We won't know for certain until the lab boys have taken a look at it,' said Douglas. 'And we'll have to see what the PM turns up, as the cause of death.' The post-mortem, he added, would be carried out at the local hospital. The pathologist wouldn't have anything for them until three o'clock. 'We can get a pint first. I hear they do a decent drop of beer at the Old Swan.'

'Fractured skull,' said the pathologist, before the chief inspector had even opened his mouth to ask the cause of death. 'As for *when* it happened, I can't be any more precise than to say it was within the past four days.'

'Which we already knew,' said Douglas grimly. 'Any idea how he got the injury? Given that he appears to have fallen from a moving train.'

'You don't say?' said the doctor. 'Well, the superficial

cuts and bruises he's sustained . . . *here* and *here* . . . would be consistent with that. The fatal wound *might* have been acquired if he struck his head against something when he fell. A sharp rock or a piece of metal could have done it.'

'A piece of metal?' echoed Douglas. 'Such as a heavy spanner?'

'Something with a sharp edge, yes. If you look at the way the posterior cranial fossa has been depressed, you'll see that—'

'Yes, yes,' said Douglas hastily. He took a step back from where he had been standing beside the mortuary table, almost landing on Rowlands's foot. 'Sorry,' he muttered, then, addressing the doctor once more, 'So you're saying that a blow to the head might have killed him?'

'A blunt force trauma, yes. Either that or he struck his head when he fell, as I said.'

'Thank you, Doctor. Anything else I should know?'

'He'd had a fair bit to drink, before he fell,' was the reply. 'Stomach contents showed he'd imbibed the best part of a bottle of whisky. Drinker, was he?'

'I couldn't say,' said the chief inspector. 'That's another thing I'll need to find out.'

It was a relief to leave the mortuary, with its oppressive chemical stink covering up worse smells. Even though Rowlands couldn't see the pathetic remains that had been lying on the mortuary table, he had enough experience of such horrors to have conjured up, from these unpleasant odours, and from the pathologist's words, an all-too vivid impression of how poor Colquhoun must have looked. He took a deep breath of the fresh spring air, conscious that he had been trying not to breathe too deeply while they'd been in the presence of death. 'I know what you're going to say,' said Douglas irritably. 'That it's looking less and less like suicide.'

'I didn't say a word.'

'I know that superior look of yours,' replied the policeman. 'You think he was murdered, don't you?'

'Let's just say I think it's a strong possibility,' said Rowlands. 'If he was passing secrets to the Russians, and started to think better of it, then somebody might have decided he'd become dangerous, and had to be silenced.'

'It's one theory,' admitted Douglas grudgingly. 'We'll see what comes back from the laboratory about that spanner. If there are traces on it that support the notion that he was hit on the head, then we'll have to think again. But for the present, my money's on the fact that he was running away. He knew the game was up and so he jumped.'

Colquhoun's lodgings were in Fenny Stratford, a village on the outskirts of Bletchley. The landlady, a Mrs Driver, showed them into a room on the ground floor, which Rowlands guessed had once been the sitting room, before the necessities of the present emergency had required its requisition. 'I've never touched a thing,' said the woman, in a truculent tone. 'It's just as he left it. Never lets me in, even to dust,' she added.

'Which is obvious, from the state of the place,' muttered Douglas to his sergeant and Rowlands, once the landlady had taken herself off. Certainly the room was in a very untidy state, with drawers pulled out, and their contents scattered on the floor, and piles of books toppling from every surface – facts Rowlands only discovered when he followed the two policemen into the room, and found himself trampling on a sea of paper.

'Do you think somebody's been in here before us?' he said to Douglas, who merely grunted.

'Hard to say. If they have, then it's not obvious what they were looking for.'

A brief search of the room turned up nothing that pointed to the fate that had overtaken Jock Colquhoun, apart from some scribbled jottings – the beginnings of a letter, evidently – pushed under a pile of books. Alerted to these by Sergeant Jones, Douglas glanced through them.

'Hmm. Looks like he was writing to the Pritchard lass. "*Dear Sylvia,*"' he read aloud. '"*Just to say that I won't be able to make it this evening after all . . .*" It breaks off there. Then he has another go, from the look of it: "*Sylvia, I know you were upset when I . . .*" Same again. Seems like he was having trouble saying what it was he wanted to say. Here's his final attempt: "*Dear old girl, I don't expect you to understand, but I've got to go through with this . . .*" Now *that*,' said the chief inspector with a note of triumph, 'sounds as if he was telling her he meant to end it all.'

'Or it could mean something else entirely,' said Rowlands.

His friend gave a sniff. 'You're hard to please,' he said. 'Not every man sets down his last words in perfectly formed sentences. He was upset. Agitated. Stands to reason he'd stumble over his words.'

'I don't agree,' said Rowlands. 'Surely if a man's

contemplating suicide, he'd take the trouble to make it as plain as possible? And Colquhoun was an intelligent man. Then there's the matter of that key.'

But the landlady could tell them nothing about the key – or rather, the fact that it was missing from the dead man's effects. 'All I know is, he was *given* a key, when he first came here – like all my young gentlemen. Whether he's gone and lost it since, I couldn't say. They're supposed to pay five shillings to get a new one cut if that happens,' she added resentfully. 'Who'll pay it *now*, I'd like to know? It shouldn't have to be me.'

After which interlude, they drove back to London, there being little more to be done for the present, said the chief inspector.

'What'll happen to the girl?' said Rowlands.

'The Pritchard lass, you mean? It depends,' replied the other, 'on what view the powers-that-be at Bletchley take of her part in all this.'

'You surely don't believe she knew what Colquhoun was involved in?'

'Hard to say,' said Douglas. 'She knew he was up to no good, that's for sure. And – if he hadn't decided to take the quick way out – he'd have been looking at a long prison term, at the very least.' Rowlands was silent for a few minutes, as the powerful car sped on its way towards the metropolis.

'She could have kept quiet about what she knew,' he said. 'There's that in her favour.'

'Aye, true enough. Fortunately it's not for me to decide whether the girl's innocent or guilty,' said the chief inspector.

Chapter Twelve

If Rowlands had hoped for more definite evidence that Jock Colquhoun's death had been neither accident nor suicide, he was disappointed. The results of the tests on the spanner, when they came back from the police laboratory, turned out to be inconclusive.

'Nothing to prove it was ever the weapon,' said Douglas, relaying this information on the telephone. 'No blood or human hair. Some cotton fibres were found – which suggest it might have been wiped, before it was thrown away . . . *if* it was thrown away, and not merely dropped by one o' the railwaymen. The fact that it was lying out in the open for four days didn't help, either. What with all that rain we had last week.'

'I get the picture,' said Rowlands gloomily.

'Besides which . . .' Alasdair Douglas's voice had a guarded note. 'The chief constable wants the whole affair shut down as quickly as possible. No sense in prolonging speculation, in a case like this, he says. Not where national security is at stake.'

'But—'

'I know, and you know, Fred, that there's more to this case than meets the eye. Somebody killed that girl. Whether that "somebody" was Colquhoun or another may never be clearly established – not without spending a lot more time digging around for further evidence. Time my superiors are of the opinion I should be spending on something else.'

'Alasdair . . .'

'Hear me out, will you?' said the other fiercely. 'What we're left with is this: Pamela Wingate was colluding with Colquhoun to pass secrets to the enemy. She got scared, and threatened to turn him in. He killed her, then took his own life. It's a nice, straightforward story.'

'Except that it's the wrong story,' said Rowlands.

Then, for a while, that seemed to be that, as far as the Wingate case was concerned. Rowlands was back at work, more than a little relieved that his detecting days were over for the time being. The nagging doubts he'd voiced to Douglas were pushed to the back of his mind, preoccupied as it was with the exigencies of getting through the next day, and the day after that. Bombing raids continued on a nightly basis, rendering sleep impossible; one learnt, as one had during the war in the trenches, to sleep with one eye open, and with an ear cocked for the demonic whine of the high-explosive bombs that were being dropped by the ton on London – or rather, for the moment the sound stopped. As long as one could still hear it, one knew oneself safe – or at least, still alive. The grim tally of those who were not so fortunate continued to rise. Some days, he found himself wondering whether they could stand it another day, and yet he knew they would, because they had to.

Letters came, at intervals, with news from the world outside the capital. Margaret's were full of the usual inconsequential stuff – a concert the entertainments committee was getting up; a cycling expedition into the countryside around Bletchley Park – but there was one item, slipped in casually amongst the rest, that interested her father. Sylvia Pritchard had been granted indefinite leave to recover from 'nervous strain', wrote Margaret. So the powers-that-be must have decided there wasn't enough evidence to prosecute her after all, thought Rowlands. For which he was glad.

His sister, Dorothy, wrote from Cornwall with news of the family. She and Jack and the boys were in good spirits, she said: Billy sounded as if he was enjoying his training (he had joined the RAF six weeks before) and Walter's medical studies in Edinburgh were going well, from what she could gather. In the eight years since he had fled Germany as a child and taken refuge with Dorothy and Jack, the news from Walter's family in Berlin had become increasingly sparse. Now it had dried up altogether. Danny, the Ashenhursts' fifteen-year-old adopted son, had been a great help to Jack, running the hotel (which now housed several families who'd been bombed out of their homes in Portsmouth and Southampton). Victor, the youngest, was doing all right at school, as far as his mother could tell – 'although like all boys of his age, he spends most of his time making model aeroplanes'. He was impatient to join up, like his older brother, Dorothy added. 'Luckily, he won't turn eighteen for another five years, by which time I hope this dreadful war will be over.'

'Let's hope so,' said Edith, as she finished reading the letter aloud at the breakfast table. 'I think we've all had about as much as we can stand.' Which was uncharacteristically defeatist talk for Edith, but last night's had been a particularly bad raid. The ack-ack guns had been going all night, making any chance of sleep a remote possibility. Even though they were twelve miles from the city centre, the sounds of war were inescapable. Rowlands made his way to work through a city made strange by yet more disruption. Burst water and gas mains added to the confusion, with traffic having to be diverted to avoid the resulting mess, while the stink of ruptured sewers mingled with the choking pall of smoke and dust rising from shattered buildings, creating a foul miasma that reminded Rowlands uncomfortably of his days in the trenches.

He arrived at the office feeling as if he'd already done a day's work before the day had begun. Miss Symonds arrived a few minutes later, and – after a perfunctory exchange of civilities – the two of them worked in a silence broken only by the tapping of typewriter keys, and the intermittent ringing of the telephone. At half past five, his secretary put the cover on her typewriter. 'If you'll just sign that last batch of letters, Mr Rowlands, I'll take them to the post on my way home.'

'Yes, of course, Miss Symonds.' When she had gone, closing the door behind her, Rowlands sat for a moment thinking about the day, and what he had to do tomorrow.

It was all routine stuff – orders to be filled or chased up, letters to this firm or that – and yet, in the face of the disaster with which they were now confronted, it seemed all the more important to maintain some semblance of normality. It was as he was readying himself to leave that he heard footsteps coming along the corridor outside his office. His first thought was that Miss Symonds must have forgotten something, but he knew her step, and this wasn't it. The door opened and before his visitor spoke a whiff of *Je Reviens* told him who it was.

'I've caught you. Good,' said Iris Barnes.

Rowlands smiled. 'To what do I owe this pleasure?' he said.

She didn't reply at once, but sat down in the chair recently vacated by Jean Symonds. 'Can you spare a cigarette?' she said. 'I'm out of mine.'

'Be my guest.' He held out the pack towards her, and she took one. Having lit her cigarette, Rowlands lit one for himself, wondering when his visitor would say what it was that had brought her here. For that it was not a social call, he was certain.

At last she spoke. 'Has it occurred to you,' she said, 'that every agent has a handler?'

'Are you talking about Colquhoun?'

'He'll have been reporting to *someone*, that much is certain,' she said.

'According to Sylvia Pritchard, it was Miss Wingate who was to put him in touch with a contact,' said Rowlands.

'Ah, yes. But I gather *that* particular meeting never actually took place.'

Rowlands rather thought that it had. But he said nothing.

'Yes, what appears to have been the case is that our Mr Colquhoun had been passing information – admittedly of a fairly low quality – for some time,' Miss Barnes went on. 'And yet it's a curious thing, that in all this time, there's been no suggestion from our networks in Germany and elsewhere that intelligence has been leaked. Thanks to the efficiency of our codebreakers at Bletchley, we're able to see exactly what Hitler's crowd do and don't believe about the way the war is going. One thing seems certain: they – the Abwehr – have no idea that their agents in Britain are entirely under our control, and have been since the war started. So you see . . .'

'Whoever it was that Colquhoun was giving the information to, it wasn't the Germans,' said Rowlands. 'But we know he was a communist. So the information must have been fed to the Russians.'

'In a nutshell,' said Iris. She took another deep drag on her cigarette. 'So why, one wonders, if the Russians have been privy to our secrets all this time, have they kept this to themselves? After all, the non-aggression pact between Stalin and Hitler was signed three years ago.'

'Perhaps it didn't include sharing secrets,' said Rowlands.

'Evidently not,' was the reply. 'But it's still going on – the leaking of information, that is. We can't be sure it's coming from Bletchley, but there's a strong possibility.'

'I see,' said Rowlands. 'You're suggesting that whoever Colquhoun was giving the information to is continuing to pass on leaked material in his own right . . . or hers,' he added.

'Something like that,' she agreed.

'One thing I don't understand,' he went on, 'is why you're telling me all this. You surely can't think that *I* can be of any help in finding this individual?'

'I thought you might have a chat with your daughter . . .'

'No.'

'Given that she's on the spot, so to speak.'

'I said no. Margaret's already been too much involved in all this for my liking. Two people have died. I'm not having her put in harm's way, and that's that.'

'Margaret herself might feel differently, of course.'

'You're asking her to spy on her friends.'

'Only to use her ears and eyes, and to let us know if she notices anything untoward. Rather as we've asked you to do, from time to time,' said Iris Barnes, extinguishing her cigarette.

'All right, I'll talk to her,' said Rowlands, with the feeling that he had once more been worsted by this formidable young woman. 'She's got a weekend pass, as it happens, so I'll see her on Saturday.' Of which fact, he felt sure, Miss Barnes was already aware.

But this plan was never to materialise. That night, a German Heinkel bomber, heading back to its country of origin after carrying out a successful mission, dropped what remained of its cargo of high-explosive bombs on West London. Two of them fell on Grove Crescent, the street where the Rowlandses lived in Kingston-upon-Thames – the first reducing the house next door to rubble. A second device fell – but, as they later discovered, did not explode – in the Rowlandses' back garden, a mere twenty feet from the shelter in which Rowlands, his wife, mother-in-law and youngest daughter were spending the night. The impact of this, following close on the first explosion, seemed to shake the very foundations of the corrugated iron shelter in which the family huddled. For Rowlands, who had operated an eighteen-pounder gun during the Great War, such disagreeable sensations were all too familiar. Still, he thought, when the first visceral shock was over, and the air resounded to the crash of falling masonry, they weren't dead yet.

'I'll go and take a look,' he said. 'The rest of you stay here, until I give the all-clear.' But when he stuck his head out of the shelter, it became clear that this wasn't going to be an easy matter.

'Take care, Fred!' cried Edith, who had followed him. 'There's an enormous crater in the middle of the lawn.' Which meant that staying where they were was potentially as risky as getting out.

He took a decision. 'Come on,' he said. 'Let's all hold hands, and make a chain. Edith, you go first . . . then you, Helen. Joanie, you take Granny's hand . . . I'll go last.' In this way, step by cautious step, they edged their way across the now-ruined garden to the relative safety of the street. Here, all was confusion, with the air thick with dust and smoke from the bombed house, and fires raging. A lone ARP warden shouted to people who'd emerged from the houses along the street to get back. From a few streets away, there came the clanging of fire-engine bells.

'Get back, I said! Get back!' shouted the warden, then to Rowlands, 'You can't hang about here, sir. Got to keep the area clear.'

'Do you know if they got out?' said Rowlands, gesturing towards the wrecked house.

'Couldn't say, sir. Now, if you'll just move back . . .'

Realising that there was nothing to be done for the time being, Rowlands turned to his wife. 'Can you see any sign of the Watsons?' he said, referring to their neighbours at what had once been Number 46. He spoke in an undertone, so that Joan wouldn't hear.

'Mary's over there, with June. I can't see Donald, though . . .' Rowlands sent up a silent prayer that his genial neighbour would be found safe and well – although the chances of that, if Watson had been inside the house when it was hit, were next to nil, he knew. Nor could Watson's wife give a very coherent account of what had happened.

'He *said* he was coming back,' she sobbed, as the Rowlandses joined the crowd of onlookers on the far side of the road. 'He was only going to fetch another blanket, because it gets so cold in that shelter. I'd never have let him go if I'd known . . .'

Her tearful protestations were drowned out by the arrival of the fire engines, whose teams at once set to work to extinguish the fire. Only when this was done, and the area made safe, would the rescue party be able to retrieve Watson's body – always supposing he had perished in the catastrophe, thought Rowlands. One *did* hear of people surviving such things . . . he fervently hoped poor Watson would be one of them. Further along Grove Crescent, some of the neighbours had banded together to dispense cups of tea and blankets for those made homeless.

'Come along,' said Rowlands to his wife. 'There's nothing we can do here. You'd better see if there's anything you can do for Mary and the little girl.'

Leaving Edith to look after their distressed neighbour, Rowlands went to the telephone box at the end of the street and made a call. It rang half a dozen times before it was answered.

'Yes? Who is this?' His brother-in-law sounded far from amused. 'Have you any idea what time it is?' When Rowlands had explained, Ralph sounded only a little mollified. 'I suppose you want me to come and get you?'

'If you don't mind. I doubt we'll be allowed back in the house until they've made the area safe.'

Which turned out to be the case. By the time he got back to Number 44, there was a policeman stationed at the gate.

'Sorry, sir, but you can't go in there. Unexploded ordnance. We're cordoning off this whole end of the street.'

Once Edith had returned to say that a bed had been found for the night at a neighbour's house for Mary Watson and her child, there was nothing for it but to wait for Ralph Edwards to turn up. Even though his relations with his brother-in-law had never been of the warmest, Rowlands had to admit that, on this particular occasion, he was heartily glad to see him.

'Bit of a mess, what?' said Ralph as – the women having been safely installed in the back of the Daimler – he stood contemplating the scene of devastation. 'Windows all gone. You're lucky it didn't catch fire, like the one next door.'

'Very lucky,' agreed Rowlands. With the bomb-disposal squad at work in the back garden, and access to the house itself out of the question while this was going on, there was nothing for it but to climb into the car beside Ralph, and return in the morning to assess the damage.

'What'll happen to our things, Daddy?' asked Joan from the back of the car as it set off for Richmond.

'Oh, everything'll be quite safe,' replied Rowlands, although he was far from sure of this. 'There's a policeman to guard them, after all.'

At the Edwardses' house, Diana welcomed them with her customary vim. 'I say! What a frightful business! Being bombed out – what beastly luck! Nobody's safe, these days, are they?' Still talking, she drew them into the sitting room, where a good fire was blazing. 'Come in and get warm. I had the fire lit specially. Now – how about some hot soup? Cook's just heating some up.'

'A brandy wouldn't go amiss, either,' said her husband. 'Just the thing for shock.' He helped himself, and then began handing out glasses of the restorative to those in need of it. 'Go on, Edith. It'll do you good . . . You should've seen it, darling,' he added to his wife. 'Whole street practically blown to smithereens.'

'Not our house,' said Joan stoutly.

'No, thank the Lord,' replied her uncle. 'Yours is still standing – just. Still, unexploded bomb in the garden – *not* what one wants to wake up to! Good job we've got plenty of room here. Put you up for as long as you like, can't we, darling?'

'Rather,' said Diana bravely. '*Bags* of room, with Peter away at school.'

'That's very good of you, Diana,' said her sister-in-law. 'Isn't it, Fred?'

'Yes. We're very grateful.'

'Oh, you're *family*,' was the reply. 'We can't have you sleeping in the street, can we?' Diana laughed merrily. 'Now, Mother' – addressing her mother-in-law – 'I've put you in the blue room. Fred and Edith can have the garden room. And dear Joanie can have Peter's room. He won't mind, as long as you don't break any of his model aircraft.' She gave another hoot of laughter. 'Soup, first, I think, then bed. Goodness! It's one in the morning! Funny to think that the last time we were all together here was on Boxing Day. Seems an age ago, doesn't it? Margaret and that friend of hers – what was her name?'

'Pamela,' said Rowlands, into the silence. 'Pamela Wingate.'

'That's the one. Pretty girl,' said Diana. 'And then those young chaps arrived to carry the girls off, in a *very* dashing sportscar. Bright red, wasn't it? I've always fancied a red sportscar.'

The damage appeared even worse by daylight – not that Rowlands himself could see it, but his brother-in-law's description was enough to convince him that, in spite of the hopes he'd expressed to Edith the night before, about the possibility of their moving back into Number 44 straight away, they wouldn't be doing so any time soon. 'Hmph,' said Ralph. 'It doesn't look good. There's

211

a great crack running the length of the near wall – the one nearest to your neighbour's house, I mean. Structural damage, I shouldn't wonder. The roof's still intact, which is one thing. And the windows can be patched up. But I don't like the look of that wall,' he repeated, with something like relish.

Ralph had dropped Rowlands off a little before nine, on his way to the bank, of which he was the manager. 'Purely an executive role, these days,' he explained, as the chauffeur-driven Daimler purred along the almost empty road from Richmond to Kingston.

'I look in now and then, just to see that things are ticking along. Got a man under me to do the routine work. Name of Harcourt. Assistant manager, you know. Competent chap.' Rowlands, who guessed that Ralph's main 'job' for the past few years had been improving his golf handicap, muttered something in reply, his thoughts preoccupied with what he was going to do about the house in Grove Crescent. 'Pick you up in an hour, shall I?' was his brother-in-law's parting remark.

'That's all right,' said Rowlands. 'I'll make my own way back. I'm sure there's a bus.'

'Suit yourself.' The big car pulled away, leaving Rowlands standing on the pavement outside his house. From what remained of the house next door came the acrid smell of the bomb blast. The ruins had been still smouldering when they'd dug Watson's body out from under the rubble, the night before. Rowlands thought with sadness of his kind neighbour, who'd once done him a service for which he could never have thanked him enough – helping to rescue Anne when she was in mortal danger . . . Now he – Rowlands – would have to do what he could for Watson's own young daughter, and his widow.

As he stood there musing on all this, a car pulled up in front of the house and someone got out.

'I say, Mr Rowlands!' It was Harris, the neighbour from down the road who'd been giving Edith driving lessons. 'Thought it looked as though you could do with a bit of help.'

'That's awfully decent of you.'

'Well, as I always say, it's what neighbours are for,' was the reply. 'How's that girl of yours getting on?' He meant Margaret, in whom he had taken an interest ever since she'd got her place at Cambridge, where his own son was studying engineering.

'She's fine,' said Rowlands guardedly, although he knew that it was highly unlikely that Jeremy Harris – two years younger than Margaret and at a different college – would be aware that she'd left the university.

'Jolly good,' said Harris. 'Clever lass, that.' He had had come prepared, it transpired, with the necessary materials for effecting some immediate repairs: a hammer and nails, and some boards. 'Garden shed fell down,' he explained cheerfully. 'Knew I'd find a use for the wood some day.'

But as Rowlands went to unlock the front door, there came a shout from the street.

'Hi! You can't go in there! It's unstable. Bomb damage.'

'I know,' said Rowlands. 'It's my house. I just want to make it secure.'

'Those are my orders, sir,' said the ARP man officiously. 'On your own head be it if the roof falls in on you.'

'Which it will be, quite literally,' murmured Rowlands. 'We'll be as quick as we can, warden,' he said. Seeing that they weren't to be dissuaded, the man left them to it at last. Inside, Rowlands was struck with the smell of the place, which seemed to have changed overnight into one of desolation. Instead of the homely, familiar aura of furniture polish, fresh flowers and cooking, there was the sour smell of soot and fallen plaster. Strips of wallpaper hung from the sitting-room walls, and there was broken glass all over the floor.

Harris let out a whistle. 'What a mess,' he said. Rowlands was almost glad he couldn't see it, and that Edith wasn't there to lament the devastation wrought in her precious sitting room.

When the glass had been swept up, and the big bay window at the front of the house had been boarded up, he went upstairs to collect some clothes to take back to Richmond. Harris, who'd finished off downstairs, offered to return with some more boards with which to secure the upper windows.

'That's very good of you,' said Rowlands. 'But you've done enough. My brother-in-law and I can come back later.' Harris insisted, however, and so Rowlands accepted his offer with gratitude. It seemed that there were still some good people in the world. It was as he was filling a suitcase with whatever he could find in the way of clothes for himself and his three womenfolk that he heard a step on the stairs. 'Hello,' he called out, thinking perhaps that Harris had returned for some reason. 'I'm in here.'

'Daddy?'

'Hello, Anne. You shouldn't have come in. It might not be safe.'

'*You're* here,' she pointed out.

'Not for much longer. Here, help me with this, will you?' He indicated the open suitcase. 'I've probably packed all the wrong things.'

'You probably have. I'll do it.' She began sorting through clothes in a chest of drawers. 'Where are the others?'

Rowlands explained. 'You'd have been better to have stayed in Oxford,' he said. 'Given that it appears we're now homeless.'

'I realise that.'

'Not that it isn't lovely to see you,' he said. 'It's just I'd rather you were safely elsewhere.'

Anne did not reply, but carried on with what she was doing. 'Just how many days' worth of clothes are we going to need?' she said. 'We'll need more than one suitcase, that's for sure. Thank goodness for the warmer weather. At least we won't need winter coats.' She finished the packing at last, and Rowlands carried the suitcases downstairs.

'Perhaps,' he persisted, 'you ought to think about going back later today.'

'It's too late for that,' said Anne calmly. 'The thing is, Daddy, I've left Oxford for good. I've decided to give up my course and join the WAAFs. I was going to tell you at the weekend, but now's as good a time as any.'

For a moment, Rowlands was speechless. 'But . . .' he started to protest, when there came the cheerful honk of a car horn outside.

'Anybody need a lift?' It was Arthur Harris, returning with another load of boards, as he had promised.

'Thank you,' said Rowlands. 'I'd appreciate a lift. We both would. And I owe you a drink. Several, in fact.'

'I'll hold you to that.' Harris chuckled.

'I had to do *something*, Daddy,' said Anne. 'You must see that.'

'I suppose so,' he said dubiously.

He and his daughter were taking a turn around the Edwardses' garden – which, with its shrubberies and rose garden, ran to two and a half acres, as Ralph was fond of pointing out. 'Getting quite productive, too, since Diana turned the south lawn over to vegetable growing.'

'We've all got to do our bit,' said his wife, with some complacency.

Diana had accepted the addition of another person to the household with equanimity. 'I'm sure Anne's got her ration-book, just as we all have, and so it'll make *practically* no difference at all,' she said. Hadn't Anne herself said that she wasn't planning to stay more than a week? As far as *she* was concerned (said Diana), she wished it could be *twice* as long. It was such *fun* having young people about the place again . . . *Such* a pity Margaret couldn't make it this weekend, after all. Because a letter had come from Margaret, in reply to the telegram Edith had sent her, warning her not to come home. She was sorry to hear what had happened to the house, but glad that none of the family had been hurt. As it turned out, she wouldn't have been coming home, anyway. All leave had been cancelled. She'd write again when she could.

Now Anne returned to this theme. 'I hope to be starting

my training before long. Of course I can't say *where* it'll be, but with any luck it *won't* be the north of Scotland.'

Mildenhall, then, thought Rowlands. Or Duxford. Somewhere not too far from London, at least. 'You must be sorry to give up your painting and drawing,' he said. 'You seemed to be enjoying it so much.'

'I was – and I'm sad not to be going on with it. But I couldn't be the only one not doing war-work. I mean, look at Meg. I know her work's fearfully hush-hush, but she gave up her studies to do it, didn't she?'

He couldn't deny that this was so. 'What made you choose the WAAFs?' he said.

'The uniform,' Anne replied promptly. 'It's much the best of all the women's services. That smart blue-grey colour – heaven! And the fit is far better than that awful mud-coloured ATS uniform. I *was* quite taken with the Wrens,' she went on. 'But flying's always been my first love.'

'Yes,' he said, suppressing a shudder as he recalled the time, ten years before, when Anne's childhood passion for aeroplanes had nearly cost her her life. 'You won't actually be doing any flying, will you?' It was only a few months since the celebrated aviatrix Amy Johnson had been killed, whilst ferrying an aircraft from one military airfield to another. Rowlands had briefly known Miss Johnson when she worked as a secretary for the firm of London solicitors where he had been employed as a switchboard operator. A pleasant young woman, he'd thought her – modest and self-effacing, even after she'd become world-famous. It was another senseless death, to add to the catalogue of deaths.

'No flying for me, worst luck,' he was relieved to hear his daughter reply. 'I'll probably be doing office work. Filing and so on.'

'Nothing the matter with that,' he said.

Chapter Thirteen

On Monday morning, Rowlands got to the office to find Miss Symonds just taking down a message from Major Fraser, asking him to 'step across' to the house, at his convenience. When he'd telephoned on Friday to explain why he wouldn't be in, his employer and long-time friend had told him to take the week off.

'I'm sure Miss Symonds can hold the fort.' But, with nothing more to be done about the house in Grove Crescent until its structural soundness or otherwise could be assessed (which might take months), Rowlands felt he might as well be at work as not. And so, after a brief conversation with Miss Symonds, in which she commiserated with him about the disaster, he joined Fraser in the latter's spacious office. This had once been the drawing room of the Regency mansion, and still retained the elegant aura of its earlier existence.

'Come in, come in,' said the major from his place behind the large oak desk, which, with its telephone, was the only sign of the room's present function. 'Take a pew. How *are* you, Fred?' Rowlands said that he was fine, considering. 'And Edith and the girls? This must have been a terrible shock for them all.'

'Yes,' said Rowlands. 'But they're coping, I think.'

'Splendid. And what's the latest on the house?' During his phone call on Friday, Rowlands had mentioned that Number 44 had not yet been made safe, and that he wasn't sure when he and the family would be able to move back in.

'Much the same as before,' he said, wondering what all this was about.

'So you'll be looking for somewhere to live, until repairs can be carried out?' said Fraser.

'I suppose so. Although my brother-in-law is putting us up for the present.'

'How do you fancy Brighton? Only we – St Dunstan's, that is – have a house in Dorset Gardens, ten minutes' walk from the seafront, which is going begging. It's quite a jolly little place, I'm told. Three bedrooms – but you've only your youngest girl at home, I understand?'

Rowlands agreed that this was so. 'I still don't quite see . . .'

'Why it should be Brighton?' The major laughed. 'I've set about this all the wrong way around. My wife's always scolding me for doing just that. The fact is, I need somebody I can trust to run the Brighton end of things. As you know, the new building at Ovingdean is currently operating as a hospital, but there's still West House.' This was the St Dunstan's centre for the South Coast, Rowlands knew. 'They've exactly the same requirements as our London people,' Fraser went on. 'Orders to be filled and supplies sent out, and so forth. It'd be much the same work that you've been doing up to now. You wouldn't have the estimable Miss Symonds as your secretary, but I'm sure we can find you another. And Dorset Gardens is a fifteen-minute walk from St George's Road.' (This was the location of West House.) 'Nothing to an energetic chap like you, Fred.'

'It sounds an interesting idea,' said Rowlands guardedly. 'But . . .'

'Think about it,' said the major. 'Talk it over with your wife.'

'Brighton?' said Edith that evening, when the two of them had a moment to themselves after dinner. The advantage of the Edwardses' large house, Rowlands thought, was the opportunity it afforded for getting away from people – a necessity, where he and his in-laws were concerned. 'Why would I want to live in Brighton?'

'It's a nice place,' said her husband. 'And I've been offered a job there.'

'But it's so far from London, and everyone we know.'

'It's not that far. An hour on the train. And you know very well that most of our London friends have already left, to escape the bombing. With Anne joining up, we'll only have Joanie at home . . . and your mother, of course.'

'Mother won't want to move,' said Edith. 'Not at her age.'

Although as it turned out, Mrs Edwards was rather taken with the idea. 'Always liked Brighton,' she said, when the news of their imminent move was broken to her. 'Used to go there as a gel. Seaside holidays, you know. Donkey rides and Pierrot shows on the pier. Great fun.'

Anne, informed that her parents would be moving, said it was all the same to her, since she'd be starting her training in a few days' time. 'Although I'll come down as soon as I get leave.'

It was thirteen-year-old Joan who proved resistant to the idea. 'What about school?' she protested. 'I'm supposed to be going into the top set next term. And I'll miss my friends.'

'You'll make new friends,' said her mother, but on this occasion, the usually phlegmatic Joan would not be consoled.

'It's not fair,' she said mutinously. 'I don't *want* to go to the seaside. I *hate* the seaside.'

It was Diana, surprisingly, who came to the rescue. 'Why doesn't Joanie stay here, with us? We've plenty of room. Then she needn't change schools. We're as close to St Winifred's here as you were in Kingston.'

So it was settled. The furniture from Grove Crescent was packed up and put into store, with only what the three adults needed in the way of clothes and personal effects to accompany them down to Brighton. The end of the month saw them ready to depart. Rowlands went into the Regent's Park offices for the last time, to hand over the reins to Miss Symonds. Although even she would not be staying long.

'The boy I'm engaged to is being posted abroad,' she said. 'He can't say where of course, but I thought I'd like to do my bit too. I've said to the major that as soon as he can get a replacement for me, I'm joining the services. I'd like it to be the Wrens, because Leslie – that's my fiancé – is in the navy, but I'll take anything really.'

Although it might have been said to be out of the epicentre of the bombing, Brighton had suffered its share of raids during the past two and a half years, usually as a result of home-going German bombers dropping their remaining loads on the coastal town as they returned from bombing missions inland. Only a few months before, Kemptown, where the Rowlandses would now be living, had suffered over fifty casualties, several of them children, when a bomb had fallen on a cinema. That these civilian deaths were the result of accident rather than design didn't make them any easier to bear for those who'd lost loved ones. The town had the atmosphere of a garrison, thought Rowlands, with the beaches off-limits due to the landmines with which they were seeded, and heavy concrete blocks, tangles of barbed wire and anti-tank defences cordoning off all but a narrow strip of the seafront. Military vehicles – jeeps and lorries – roared up and down all day, and both the West Pier and Brighton Pier itself had been partially dismantled to render them inaccessible to landing craft. Mrs Edwards's Pierrot shows were decidedly a thing of the past.

'Really, we're no safer here than we were in London,' said Edith. 'In some ways, the war seems more obvious here than it was in Kingston.' She was pleased with the house, however. The previous tenant, a retired naval officer who had gone to live with his sister in Torquay, had left it as ship-shape as one might have expected from one of his profession.

'He's even left us a supply of coals,' said Edith, coming up from the cellar. 'And the kitchen is spick and span.' There was a small park opposite. 'Perhaps we should get a dog?' said Edith – something she had hitherto resisted. While she and her mother busied themselves with unpacking, and setting the place to rights ('Although thanks to Captain Ormerod, there's very little to be done'), Rowlands accustomed himself to his new routine.

West House was a once-grand Regency house, one of a row of similar houses, in a street a few minutes' walk from Dorset Gardens. The first couple of mornings Rowlands had walked there with Edith, to memorise the route; soon, it would become as familiar to him as the walk from Marylebone Underground to Regent's Park. The ground floor was given over to recreation rooms for the permanent residents – although most of these had been moved to other annexes at the beginning of the war, at St Leonards, Cheltenham, North Berwick and Church Stretton.

Only a handful of men, too ill or disabled to stand the move, remained. One of these was George Fairfield, who had been caught up in the explosions at La Boisselle in July 1916. He'd been buried for two days, and when they dug him out at last, he was deaf and blind. Now he was one of the fixtures of West House – often to be found in his favourite armchair in a corner of the lounge, with a Braille volume open on his lap (it was currently *David Copperfield*). When told that he'd have to leave, he'd smiled and shaken his head.

'I'm too old to move again,' he'd said. 'In any case, what more can the Germans do to me? I've been blown up and left for dead, I'm blind and deaf – but I still enjoy my walks along the seafront.' So George was permitted to stay, along with the few other St Dunstaners who preferred risking the bombs to leaving their beloved Brighton.

Rowlands's office, a spacious, high-ceilinged room on the first floor, was, if anything, an improvement on the rather poky quarters he'd occupied in the stable block at St John's Lodge. As befitted his new role – which was essentially running the show – he'd been given two secretaries instead of one. The first of these, a pleasant young woman by the name of Mavis Bates, was responsible for all the typing – a not-inconsiderable task – and with helping Rowlands deal with the daily flood of letters requesting supplies, or demanding payment for the same.

The other secretary was Mrs Dacres – the widow of a rear admiral, as she was quick to inform him. She did no typing, nor would she stoop to any of the other office work, but she condescended to answer the telephone, in an affected drawl that got on Rowlands's nerves after a day or two. She had a son at Cambridge – the apple of her eye, it transpired. He – Rupert was his name – was reading English.

'But his *real* love is art history. His tutor – such a charming man – said to me, "Mrs Dacres, your boy has a true *feeling* for the subject."' The widow gave a deprecating laugh. 'I said to him, "Oh, Dr Blake, I'm sure you say that to *all* the mothers." Although Rupert's always been very *artistic*, even as a little boy . . . But *he* said, "My dear Mrs Dacres, I must assure you – I only select the very *best* undergraduates for my little *coterie* . . . The more *impressionable* ones, with a *sensitivity* for the subject."' She would have gone on, extolling the merits of her darling, if one thing in all this verbiage had not caught Rowlands's attention.

'Blake?' he said. 'Would that be Aubrey Blake?'

'That's right.' She seemed taken aback to find that he knew of the distinguished art historian.

'Thought so,' said Rowlands, without disclosing how it was he'd come to hear of the man.

'Which was naughty of you, Fred,' said Edith, when he told her this story.

'Why? I've no intention of letting her know I've a daughter at Cambridge. The woman's enough of a pest as it is.' Even so, he found that Mrs Dacres's manner towards him was marginally less condescending than before, as if she'd initially misjudged him.

During the second week of May, Margaret wrote to say she'd been granted a weekend's leave, and that she'd be down to see the new house. She seemed taken with the place, particularly with the room in which she was to sleep – an attic eyrie, with views over the park and, if one squinted a bit, the sea.

'It's like being in a crow's nest on a sailing ship,' she said to her father – an unusually fanciful turn of phrase for his down-to-earth daughter. 'I think Brighton's an awfully jolly place – if one could ignore the barbed wire on the beach, and the Bofors guns along the seafront.' She and her father were taking a stroll along Madeira Drive on Sunday, after lunch. Both had lit cigarettes, and stopped for a moment to savour the taste of these. It was a beautiful spring day, and the coconut smell of gorse blossoms drifted on the warm breeze. From far below the clifftop on which they were walking came the lazy, swishing sound of waves breaking against the pebbled shore.

'So how are things?' said Rowlands, after a silence.

'Fine,' was the reply. 'Busy, you know.'

'Of course.' They walked on a bit further.

'Gosh, this is glorious!' cried Margaret. 'One might almost forget there's a war on.'

'One might indeed.' But even as he said it, he sensed the tension in the slim young figure at his side as she stood contemplating the view.

'Yes, it's good to get some fresh air in one's lungs, after weeks of being cooped up in that stuffy hut.' There was a tremor in her voice as she spoke, and it struck him that it was an effort for her to keep up the appearance of cheerfulness.

'If there's anything you want to talk to me about,' he said quietly, 'I'm listening.'

For a long moment, she said nothing. Then she let out a sigh. 'It's been so awful,' she said. 'Since Pamela . . . well, you know.'

'I know.'

'And then with Jock disappearing . . .' Rowlands realised as she spoke that she hadn't yet learnt the truth about what had happened to Colquhoun. 'And Sylvia leaving . . .' She broke off, and took a deep drag on her cigarette. 'Well, it's made for a very bad atmosphere, that's all.'

227

'I can imagine.'

'But that's not the worst of it,' said Margaret in a low voice. 'I . . . the fact is, I haven't been quite straight with you. I . . . I meant it for the best, but . . . Oh, Daddy, I feel so dreadful . . .' He started to say that she mustn't blame herself for what had happened, when she cut across him. 'No. You don't understand. There's something I haven't told you.' She took his arm. 'Let's walk on a bit, shall we? It helps me to think.' They did so, and after a moment, Margaret went on. 'You know that Pam and I shared a room for all those months . . . She and I . . . well, we weren't exactly close friends, but we got on all right, you know?' Rowlands had the sense to say nothing, but to let her talk. 'I mean . . . She'd tell me things . . . about her life . . . although of course it seems now as if she made some of it up . . . and I'd tell her things, too. Nothing important, really.' She hesitated a moment. 'There's a boy I like. His name's Frank. Frank Dawson. He's in the navy . . . on a Destroyer. I'm not supposed to say where . . . He writes to me.' Rowlands remembered the framed photograph he'd found by Margaret's bed in her lodgings. So it hadn't been Jonathan Simkins, after all. 'Pam was awfully sweet about it . . . listening to me going on about Frank, that is.'

'It's what friends are for.'

'Yes. And I listened to her, of course . . . about all the parties she went to, and . . . and the people she met.' Again, she paused, as if considering what she'd said. 'I . . . I don't think she made *that* part of it up, although she might have laid it on a bit thick, sometimes . . . I didn't mind, though. She could be awfully good fun . . .' There was a wistful note in her voice, and Rowlands thought how little of the kind of glamour and excitement Pamela Wingate had offered there had been in his daughter's life, up to now. She'd gone from being a diligent scholarship girl to being a dedicated research student, and from thence to working round the clock doing whatever it was she did at Bletchley Park. No wonder Pamela's tales of London high life had seemed so beguiling. 'The thing is . . . I don't think she was happy,' said Margaret. 'Not really.'

'What makes you say that?'

'Oh . . . just a feeling,' she said. 'It was towards the end . . . I mean, before she went away . . . I got the impression she was holding something back.'

'What sort of thing?'

'It's hard to say, really. It's just . . . well, she was excited about getting engaged to Hugh, of course. Talked a lot about the swanky engagement party they were going to give, and whether he'd be able to get leave for a spring wedding . . .' Rowlands held his breath, conscious that he mustn't interrupt her train of thought. An army truck full of soldiers roared along Madeira Drive, leaving in its wake the sound of raucous laughter at somebody's off-colour joke, and the stink of exhaust fumes. 'But underneath it all, I think Pam was worried about something,' Margaret went on. 'Once or twice, in those last weeks, she'd have these fits of crying – coming out of nowhere, seemingly. She'd be laughing and talking about some party she'd been to, and all the handsome men she'd danced with, when suddenly she'd burst into tears, saying her life was rotten, and that she hated it.'

'Maybe her conscience was troubling her? She *was* planning to commit treason.'

'I don't believe she'd have gone through with it,' said Margaret earnestly. 'Pam wasn't bad, really – just a bit wild. I think she'd have found it all a bit of a joke . . . all that cloak and dagger stuff.'

Rowlands wasn't entirely convinced by this, but he let it pass, knowing his daughter's reluctance to speak ill of anybody. 'So maybe she'd had a falling-out with the boyfriend?' he suggested.

'Maybe. But somehow I don't think it was that. She was thrilled about the engagement to Hugh, of course – what girl wouldn't have been?' said Margaret, with the wistful note in her voice once more. 'Hugh was . . . is . . . so handsome, and, well, from such a good family and all that . . .' She broke off, as if something had just occurred to her. 'I mean, she *must* have loved him, or she wouldn't have agreed to marry him, would she?'

'I suppose not.' He sensed there was more to come.

'That was what was so strange,' said Margaret, after a moment. 'Pam *should* have been on top of the world. Yet she wasn't happy – I just *know* it! It was as if . . . I don't know . . . she'd got cold feet about it all . . . getting married, I mean. She stopped talking about Hugh all the time – the way she had when they first met. She seemed almost irritated if I mentioned his name. Then, in those last few days . . .' She drew a breath. 'I think she had something on her mind. Or some*one*. I think,' she added in a small voice, 'she was seeing somebody else.'

They walked on for a while longer in silence, before Margaret said that perhaps they should be turning back if she was to catch the ten past five train and still have time for tea.

'Yes, of course,' said her father. 'Your mother will be most upset if you don't have tea before you go.' Then, following on from what she'd said earlier, 'Have you told anybody else about Pamela? I mean . . . what she was like in those last few days?'

'No. Why? Do you think I should?'

'I don't know. It might be important – if she was seeing another man, I mean. He . . . whoever he is . . . might be able to cast some light on her movements in the days leading up to when she was killed.'

'Or he might have been the one who killed her,' said Margaret flatly. 'Isn't that what you're thinking?'

'It's a possibility.'

'Oh God, I never thought . . . I was just trying to protect her from . . . well, the kind of insinuations some people were making . . . about the kind of girl she was. Some of that crowd – the Bletchley lot – were saying she'd brought it on herself, going about with men the way she did. I . . . I didn't want to give them any more ammunition, I suppose . . .' She broke off suddenly. 'Oh, Daddy,' she said, in an appalled whisper, 'you don't think it might have made a difference to the investigation if I *had* said something?'

'I'm sure the police will have looked at every eventuality,' he said, wishing there was more he could say to comfort her. 'They'll have talked to some of her other friends. It's more than likely that they know about this man.'

'Yes, but they might not,' she said. 'You will tell them, won't you, Daddy? It could be important.'

'Well . . .' he began. 'I think it might be better coming from you. After all, you were the one she confided in.'

'Oh, but Daddy . . .'

'There's another thing,' he said, ignoring her protests. 'You'll need a bit more than just a vague suspicion that Pamela was seeing another man, if you're to convince the police. I mean . . . what exactly was it that she said or did that gave you that impression?'

Margaret was silent a moment. 'She asked me to cover for her,' she said at last. 'About staying out overnight, I mean. It . . . it happened a couple of times. She . . . she was going to London for a party, she said, and it wouldn't finish until very late, so a . . . a *friend* would put her up. But I wasn't to say anything to Hugh. He was away at the time, on his ship. I thought . . . the first time, at least . . . that she meant she'd be spending the night with a girlfriend, in town. But . . .' She hesitated a moment. 'Something she said afterwards made me realise that that wasn't the case.'

'What was it?'

'It was the second time it happened – a few days before she . . . went away. She'd been out all night, and got back very early one morning. I was just getting ready to leave the house, to start my shift. Pam was supposed to be at work, too, but she said she had a bad headache and wouldn't be in until later. She'd been "out on the tiles", she said. I remember she was laughing as she said it. "Oh, Maggie," she said. "You'll never guess what I've gone and done . . . and you're *far* too good and pure to guess . . ." When I told her she was being an ass, she said, "You must promise on your *life* not to tell anyone what I've been up to . . . especially not dear, sweet, stupid Hugh – who'd never forgive me . . . Although I sometimes wonder if I wouldn't *like* him to find out that his precious fiancée's a bit of a tart . . . *There!* I've shocked you, you dear, good thing! I know *you'd* never betray your darling Frank . . ." Then I had to go,' said Margaret. 'So I never got to ask who it was she was talking about. But you do see,' she went on earnestly, 'there really *was* somebody else, wasn't there?'

'It sounds very likely,' said Rowlands grimly, thinking it was no good reproaching her for having kept this information to herself all this time. That it made a difference, he was not in doubt. Nor were Rowlands's misgivings resolved by the time his daughter came to catch her train, even though there was a further opportunity to discuss the matter on the twenty-minute walk to the railway station.

But Margaret seemed reluctant to revive the topic, talking instead of inconsequential things – the beauty of the weather, and how steep the climb was to the railway station from the town centre. It was as if, having betrayed (as she saw it) her friend's secret at last, she could hardly bear to admit as much to herself.

'I promised her I wouldn't tell,' was all she said when her father made an allusion to their earlier conversation. 'And now I've told. I don't feel very proud of myself, I can tell you.'

It was in vain for Rowlands to point out that it could hardly matter now if the fact that Pamela Wingate had had a clandestine affair were known, and that the knowledge might help the police to discover the identity of her killer.

'I can't go to the police, Daddy – not after all this time. They'll think me such a liar. Withholding evidence is a crime, isn't it?'

'You were trying to protect her good name,' he said, aware of how hollow an excuse it sounded. And something else troubled him as he took his leave of his daughter on the station platform – the fact that her guilty knowledge might put her in danger. 'What's happened to WPC Briggs?' he asked, as he lifted Margaret's suitcase onto the rack. 'I thought she was supposed to be looking after you. Doesn't that extend to weekend leaves?'

'She's been returned to general duties,' was the reply. 'They can't afford to waste police resources these days, you know.' Margaret gave a rather forced laugh. 'Don't worry, Daddy – if anyone was going to bump me off, they'd have done it by now.' Of which Rowlands was not in the least convinced. It was with a heavy heart that he waved his daughter off, waiting on the platform until he was sure she would no longer be able to see him from the train. It was hard to conceal his low mood from Edith, who knew him too well to be fobbed off with the pretext that he had a headache.

'You're not usually this down-in-the-dumps when one of the girls has been for a visit,' she remarked as they sat drinking their tea after supper. 'I know it'll be a while before Margaret can get leave again, but Anne'll be here next weekend, so you'll have that to look forward to.'

'I worry about Meg, that's all.'

'I worry about her, too – and all our girls,' said his wife. But I try to tell myself that there's no sense in worrying. We're all in the same boat, after all. Why,

234

a bomb could drop on us tomorrow . . . almost did, a month ago. You can't live in fear of what *might* happen.' With all of which he agreed. It didn't stop him from lying awake that night, thinking about what Margaret had told him, and wondering what to do about it.

Chapter Fourteen

These dark thoughts accompanied Rowlands to work on Monday morning, and overshadowed the business of that day. It was lucky for him that Miss Bates was capable of getting on with her work unsupervised, since he found himself continually distracted from even the simplest task. Mrs Dacres was no earthly use, of course. As if she sensed his unease, she was especially irritating that day – answering the telephone in an affected manner that set his teeth on edge, and complaining about the coffee the 'girl' had made.

'Really, this stuff is *quite* undrinkable . . .'

'Perhaps you should make it yourself,' said Rowlands, in as sharp a tone as he had ever used towards a member of his staff.

'Well, *really*,' said Mrs Dacres.

It was perhaps fortunate that at that moment an exclamation from Mavis Bates drew their attention. 'Ooh, Mr Rowlands, there's ever such a big motor car pulled up outside, and a lady getting out of it. I *do* like her hat. *Very* smart, with that turned-up brim . . . I wonder if she's coming in here?' A moment later, a brisk step on the stairs announced the arrival of their visitor, whose identity Rowlands had already guessed, from Mavis's thrilled description.

'Good afternoon, Mr Rowlands,' said Iris Barnes. 'I hope I'm not interrupting? But I was in the vicinity, and wondered if you could spare me a few minutes? What charming offices,' she remarked.

'Yes, they're not so bad,' he replied, reaching for his hat. 'Miss Bates, could you hold the fort for an hour? Mrs Dacres, perhaps you'd be good enough to answer the telephone?'

'Who was that sour-faced female?' said Iris as, settled into the back of the chauffeur-driven Rolls, they drove off in the direction of the seafront. 'If looks could kill, I'd be stretched out on the floor of your office by now.'

'On the contrary,' said Rowlands. 'I'm the one she wants to kill. She'd have thought *you* were perfectly splendid.' He explained about Mrs Dacres, to Iris's amusement.

'What a pity I don't use my title,' she said carelessly. '*That'd* put you in her good books – being on calling terms with an Hon . . . Speaking of which,' she went on, 'there've been some developments regarding the Montfitchet boy.'

'Have there?' said Rowlands, guiltily aware of 'developments' in another part of the story. 'What kind of developments?'

'It appears he was lying about the time he left his flat

on the night of the Wingate girl's murder,' she said. 'He says he left Mount Street at seven-thirty – but he was seen by a witness coming out of the building nearer to half past eight – when he claims to have been already waiting for the girl at the Café de Paris.'

'So he could have killed her,' said Rowlands.

'Exactly. And his car was seen in the vicinity of Bletchley Park on the day of Colquhoun's death. Either piece of information would look pretty black for him,' said Miss Barnes. 'Together, they add up to some pretty damning evidence.' She tapped on the glass separating them from the driver. 'Pull over here, would you, Johnson?' Then, to Rowlands, 'Let's walk for a bit, shall we? If we go down these steps, there's a quiet stretch of promenade where we won't be disturbed.' She took his arm as they descended the steep flight, and kept hold of it while they strolled along the esplanade that lay directly below the cliff. Here, shrubs made a screen along the seaward side, while climbing plants tumbled down the cliff wall, giving the effect, as Miss Barnes put it, of a 'green tunnel', secluded from the noise and bustle of the town.

'Why has it taken the witness – or witnesses – so long to come forward?' said Rowlands, when they had been walking for a few minutes. 'It's been two and a half months.'

'The man who saw Montfitchet leave his flat has been away with his unit for most of that time,' said Iris. 'He was posted abroad two days later, and didn't hear about the murder until his return to London a week ago. Even then, he mightn't have put two and two together, if the police hadn't been following up on the interviews they did at the time. This man – name of Harbison – lives in the same building as Montfitchet. Knows him by sight, though not to speak to. Anyway, some bright spark at Scotland Yard was going through the file and realised that Harbison had still been in residence at the time of the murder, but had been missed in the first round of interviews.'

'*He'll* be due for a promotion, whoever he is,' said Rowlands.

'I should say so,' was the reply.

'What about the car?' he asked, more because he had the feeling she expected it than out of any real interest. A flat depression overwhelmed him. To think that, after all, it had been that silly, impetuous boy who'd choked the life out of Pamela Wingate . . . and then coolly lied about it. It must be so, he supposed – and yet his every instinct revolted against it.

'The car? Oh, that was your friend the chief inspector's doing. He had the idea of getting one of his men to show a photograph of Montfitchet's car at all the stations along the line where Colquhoun's body was found. The station master at Bletchley recognised the vehicle at once. It's a distinctive make, apparently.'

'An Alvis,' said Rowlands.

'That's the one,' she agreed. 'Bright red, too. You couldn't miss it, the man said.' It was quiet on the ledge on which they stood, surrounded by the smell of tamarisk and pine, while the gentle sounds of the waves offered a sweeter music than seemed fitted to this talk of death and deception.

'Has he confessed?' said Rowlands, after an interval.

'Not yet. But he will. The evidence is too conclusive.'

'So he must have been the one passing on secrets all along – the contact in London Pamela wanted Colquhoun to meet?'

Iris Barnes did not at first reply, but instead lit a cigarette, and drew deeply on it.

'Here,' she said, placing it between his lips, and lighting another for herself. 'That's just the funny thing,' she said. 'I don't see how he – Montfitchet – could have been the source of the leak at Bletchley. The dates don't match, for one thing. We know that Montfitchet was away on his ship for all of January and the first part of February, which is when we first noticed the leak. So Colquhoun must have had another handler to whom he was passing information. We know he stole those documents and hid them in Margaret's locker . . . How *is* Margaret, by the way?' she added, in a tone that sounded casual but wasn't.

'She's fine,' he said, feeling a guilty flush steal across his face. 'If he wasn't the source of the leaks, then . . .'

He broke off, as a dreadful thought struck him. If Montfitchet wasn't the traitor, then who was? More than this, what was Montfitchet's motive for killing Pamela, if it wasn't to silence her about his treachery? Perhaps he'd had another motive entirely – one unconnected to the passing of secrets to the enemy, but which had to do with an all-too common reason for a man to murder his fiancée . . . What if he'd discovered that she'd been unfaithful to him?

'I think,' said Rowlands miserably, 'there's something I ought to tell you.'

* * *

'Police work,' said Chief Inspector Douglas, in a satisfied tone. 'All down to good, old-fashioned police work.'

'You've arrested Montfitchet, then?'

'Got him in custody, as we speak.' Douglas puffed contentedly on his pipe. 'Course, it's still early days, but I think we'll get a confession from him before too long.'

'Isn't the evidence rather . . . well, *circumstantial*?' said Rowlands. They were sitting in the chief inspector's office at Scotland Yard, a little after 6 p.m. the next day. Rowlands had had some loose ends to tie up at St John's Lodge, and had spent a busy afternoon signing correspondence, and going through his files, with Miss Symonds. He had taken the opportunity of being in London to drop in on his old friend, in order to pass on the information Margaret had given him, concerning the Wingate affair. He'd already made up his mind to do so before his conversation with Iris Barnes. Now Douglas emitted one of his characteristic grunts of disbelief at what Rowlands had said.

'Circumstantial?' he echoed, his Edinburgh burr more pronounced than usual. 'If you mean, did we actually catch him in the act of strangling the puir wee lassie, the answer's "no".' He took the pipe from his mouth and poked at it. 'Drat the thing!' he muttered. 'It was drawing fine until a minute ago. What you're *really* saying,' he went on, in a disgruntled tone, 'is that the evidence isn't strong enough.'

'I only meant—'

'I grant you,' said Douglas, ignoring this intervention, 'that our witness – Captain Harbison – isn't certain that it was Montfitchet he saw. All he'll swear to is that it was a man of about Montfitchet's height, dressed in naval uniform, whom he saw coming out of Montfitchet's flat.'

'Then that suggests—'

'Nor is the station master at Bletchley – a Mr Grindley – certain that it was Montfitchet behind the wheel of the car he saw driving at speed along the London Road, but there's a strong possibility it *was* him. Which, together with the information you've just given me about what young Pamela was up to, gives our man a very good motive for murder. O' course, I'll have to have it from the horse's mouth,' he added, puffing once more at his pipe. 'Luckily, I have to visit Bletchley on another matter, or I might have found myself getting aw'fy cross with that girl o' yours for keeping this to herself all this time.' There was not much that Rowlands could say to this, other than to hope that Douglas wouldn't be too hard on Margaret, when they met.

'Miss Barnes didn't seem to think that Montfitchet was responsible for leaking that information to the enemy,' he said. 'Which means he doesn't have a motive for killing Colquhoun.'

'Unless Colquhoun was the man with whom Miss Pamela had been having her little fling,' replied Douglas. '*That* would have given him a motive, all right.'

'I suppose so,' said Rowlands dubiously. He recalled Marjorie Milward's remark when it was suggested to her that Miss Wingate might have been involved with one of her fellow cryptographers: 'She'd set her sights higher than some Bletchley boffin in a baggy tweed jacket and flannels . . .' He hadn't been able to corroborate this unappealing description for himself, but he was willing

242

to bet that it applied to Jock Colquhoun, as much as to the others in his circle of Bletchley cryptographers.

'Anyway, we're not re-opening the Colquhoun case,' said Douglas. 'As you're aware, my superiors want it tied up with ribbon and put on the shelf with a label saying "Accident/Suicide". It's the Wingate murder we're concentrating our efforts on. And, "circumstantial" or not, it looks like we've got the evidence to solve it.'

'What if it *wasn't* Colquhoun she was seeing?' said Rowlands. 'It could have been another man entirely. Isn't it possible that he – whoever he is – is the man we should be looking for?'

'Anything's possible,' admitted Douglas grudgingly. 'But the likelihood is that it *was* Montfitchet who killed her. You can't escape the facts, Fred. He was seen leaving his flat at around the time the girl was murdered.'

'But you said the witness couldn't *positively* identify him,' said Rowlands.

'It's as good an identification as we're likely to get,' snapped the other. 'A man of Montfitchet's appearance and wearing his uniform was seen leaving Montfitchet's flat at the time in question. What more do you want?'

'I don't know.'

'I must say, you seem awf'y keen to defend the lad.'

'Not really,' said Rowlands. 'I just think there's room for reasonable doubt.'

'As Montfitchet's lawyers will doubtless be at pains to point out, when the case comes to trial,' groaned the policeman. 'You're not making my job any easier, Fred. But dinna fret yersel'. I'll make sure to look into this matter of the other man in Miss Pamela's life. No doubt he'll be able to cast some light on those missing two days.'

The thought had also occurred to Rowlands. 'Do you think she was with him during that time – our mystery man, I mean?'

'Seems likely, doesn't it? Although why the devil she turned up at Montfitchet's flat that night, if she'd been cohabiting with lover boy, remains to be seen,' said Douglas. 'I must say,' he went on. 'I don't like this case at all. Sending a young man who's been serving his country to the gallows, because he's killed his girl in a fit of jealousy . . . Well, I'd rather not have to do it, that's all.'

'Pamela Wingate didn't deserve to be murdered,' said Rowlands. 'Whatever she may or may not have done.'

'I thought you were on Montfitchet's side?'

'I'm not on the side of anyone who commits murder, any more than you are.'

'Whsst! No need to take offence, man. I think we're both on edge. The bombing was bad again last night. I was on duty here until midnight, and it looked as if the Thames was on fire, with all the burning buildings.'

Rowlands was silent for a moment, picturing this. 'You're right. It's been a difficult few months,' he said.

'It has. I suppose you're out of it, where you are?' said Douglas.

'Not exactly,' replied the other. 'We still have our share of Heinkels going over – but the bombing's not as relentless as it is here.' Rowlands got up to leave, and the two men shook hands.

'Good to see you, Fred,' said the chief inspector. 'Give my regards to that wife o' yours, won't you?'

'I will. And Alasdair . . . don't be too hard on Margaret, when you see her. She was only trying to protect the other girl's good name.'

'Don't worry, I won't bite her head off. As it happens, what she's told us makes little difference to the case. It's Harbison's evidence that will put the boy in the dock.'

'I expect you're right,' said Rowlands. 'There was one other thing . . . Margaret tells me that WPC Briggs has been returned to general duties. Does this mean that you think there's no further risk?'

'We've got the fellow in custody, haven't we?'

'If he *is* the "fellow" who did this,' said Rowlands.

'Hmph. You're hard to please,' said his friend, who had risen from his desk to accompany Rowlands to the door. 'All right, Fred. I'll see what I can do. I know your Margaret and Betty Briggs hit it off quite well. I'll see if young Betty would care to return to Bletchley Park for a few more days.'

Reassured by the thought that Margaret would once more be under the protection of her female bodyguard, presumably suitably disguised as a Bletchley cryptographer, Rowlands returned to Brighton. Back at West House, he was caught up in the usual round of administrative work, which occupied his time for the next few days. But on Friday of that week, having telephoned in advance, he waited at the bus stop for the shuttle that would take him along the coast to Ovingdean, and the recently completed St Dunstan's building, now converted to a hospital for newly blinded servicemen. It had been Major Fraser who'd suggested the visit, when Rowlands had called in at St John's Lodge on the Monday. 'Been around the new building yet?' he'd asked, having enquired how Rowlands was settling in at West House; then, when the latter admitted that he'd only visited the place once, on the occasion of its inauguration three years before, he said, 'No time like the present. It'll give you some idea of the work we're doing with the new intake – all young chaps, as you might suppose. Talking to someone like yourself, who's been through what they're going through now, will be a tonic for them.'

Rowlands said he wasn't so sure about *that*, but his friend insisted. 'Go on with you, Fred! You know it made a difference, when you were first admitted to St Dunstan's, to know that other men were managing to build their lives again. It'll do you good, too, I shouldn't wonder. Take your mind off things.' Because even though he'd said nothing about it, Rowlands must have conveyed some of the anxiety he'd been feeling on Margaret's behalf.

So it had been arranged. The bus dropped him off at the bottom of the drive, and he followed the path, with its convenient handrail, all the way to the top, drawing in deep breaths of the bracing marine air as he did so. He knew, from having had it described to him on his first visit, that the building resembled a great aeroplane, resting on top of the Downs, and that it boasted magnificent views of the sea. Which might have struck some people as strange, given that most of the inmates (with the exception of the nursing staff) would have been oblivious to the view. Yet as Rowlands knew from his own experience, the mind has its own vistas – drawn from memory or from imagination, it mattered not. Being within the sound of the sea, and smelling the salt-tasting air, would conjure up for many of his fellow St Dunstaners, as it did for him, the memory of what it looked like, also. And the architect who had designed this striking edifice, with its 'wings' stretched on either side of a glass 'cockpit', had made it as light and airy as possible. The blind needed light and air as much as the sighted – if not more, thought Rowlands, as he reached the entrance of the building, where the matron – a Mrs Goodley – was waiting for him.

'Welcome,' she said. 'Is this your first visit?'

Rowlands explained. 'Although we didn't get to see much of the place on inauguration day,' he said. 'So I'd very much like to take a closer look, if someone wouldn't mind showing me around.'

Mrs Goodley said she'd be happy to do the honours. 'I hope,' she added, 'that you'll stay to tea afterwards? Some of our new boys are just settling in, so it'll be a treat for them.' Rowlands wondered if that was how the 'boys' themselves would look at it, but said he'd be delighted.

Before the tour proper began, the matron invited Rowlands to examine the scale model of the building, which stood in the entrance hall.

'You'll observe that we're very symmetrical,' she said, as he ran his hands over the structure, familiarising himself with the layout of the corridors. 'All straight lines, you see – and rounded corners. It's one of the few buildings purpose-built for the blind.' On the ground floor were the public rooms, just as at Regent's Park and West House, although these were on an altogether grander scale. In the main lounge, chairs were arranged in straight lines, for ease of movement. The dining hall, whose chairs and tables were numbered, with rubber strips to mark the aisles between, could seat up to a hundred and thirty-four, said Mrs Goodley. She pointed out that the edge of each door was cushioned with rubber, to prevent injury when colliding with the same (an all-too frequent accident for the newly blinded).

'We've kept several of the workshops open, as part of our rehabilitation programme,' went on Rowlands's companion. 'Although we've had to convert some of them to operating theatres – and of course the dormitories are being used as wards. We've a hundred and twenty beds, but there's room for expansion, when the time comes.'

At Rowlands's request, they eschewed the lifts, and climbed the stairs. He ran his hand up the long sweeping curve of the banister, enjoying the warmth of the afternoon sun coming in through the glass walls of the 'cockpit', and the feeling of spaciousness overhead. At the top of the first flight, his hand encountered a steel stud, about the size of an overcoat button.

'Ah, that's to tell you which floor you're on,' said the matron, when he commented upon it. 'You'll see it's the same on the next floor – and on all the remaining floors, of which there are six in all. The floors are identical, so it matters, knowing which one you're on.' Rowlands murmured that he saw that it did. 'Yes, if it weren't for those Braille markings, I confess I'd get confused, sometimes,' she said. 'With exactly the same layout on each floor, it's very easy to get lost.'

Unless you're blind, thought Rowlands, in which case it's very easy to find your way.

* * *

In the lounge, a group of young men was waiting for tea to be brought. 'This is Mr Rowlands,' said the matron, as she and her visitor joined them. 'He's in charge of West House, where some of you will have been for dances and the like. Mr Rowlands, these are some of our recent intake . . . perhaps it's best if you introduce yourselves, gentlemen.'

'I'll go first,' said one; he sounded young, thought Rowlands – but then they were all young, he reminded himself. 'Anstey's the name. Number 12 (Bomber) Squadron's my outfit. Or it *was* before I had my prang. Crate was a write-off, and so was I . . . almost.'

'Good to know you,' said Rowlands, shaking hands.

'Jackson,' said another. 'Royal Fusiliers. Nothing so glamorous as our Brylcreem boy here. Landmine went off, rather too close for comfort.'

'Bad luck,' said Rowlands. 'Glad you're on the mend.'

'McGinty,' said a voice with a distinctive Canadian twang. 'You can probably guess *my* outfit. We'd just been posted to France when I had my smash-up. Truck hit a crater in the road and overturned.'

'Pleased to meet you, Mr McGinty. I made some good friends from your country during the last war.'

'And my name's Joliffe,' said a fourth man. 'Can't leave the senior service out of things. I was on HMS *Calypso* when she got torpedoed. Damn lucky to be here, I can tell you.'

'I should think you must be.'

All the while the others had been talking, Rowlands was conscious that there was fifth member of the little group who had not yet spoken. He'd only become aware of this man's presence because of the latter's nervous habit of drumming his fingers on the arm of the chair. Now he burst out, irritably, 'I suppose you'll want to know my name, too? It's Harvey. And before you ask, I didn't lose my sight in some heroic fashion, like the rest of these chaps. It couldn't have happened in a stupider way, in fact. I was leading an exercise during training – with the East Lancashires, as it happens. Some fool pointed his rifle at me and a blank cartridge went off in my face. So I never even got within *sight* of the enemy. Now I'm fit for nothing.'

'Come, Mr Harvey, that's not the sort of talk we like to hear,' said Matron, before Rowlands could respond to this outburst. 'Everyone's fit for *something*, isn't that so, Mr Rowlands?'

'Well, yes,' began Rowlands; but just then a nurse arrived with tea, and the next few minutes passed in the business of handing it round, and in general conversation, all of which displayed a determined effort on the part of Harvey's fellow patients to drown out the sour note he'd introduced. But the bitterness in the young man's voice reminded Rowlands of the way he himself had felt, in those first terrible weeks of blindness. How useless he'd thought himself, and how angry he'd been at the world for what had seemed a uniquely cruel and unfair affliction. Why, if you'd asked him to describe himself, in those dark days, he'd have said he was 'fit for nothing', as this poor lad had done.

On his way out, Rowlands had a word with each of the young men in turn, wishing them well in their rehabilitation. 'It does get easier,' he said. 'Take it from

250

me. The first year is the hardest. After that, it's just like anything else. You get used to it – and you start to enjoy life again.' He guessed it would sound like so much bromide to them, but it was true, nonetheless. They would all, he hoped, find it out for themselves, in time. When he came to Harvey, who was skulking near the door, he said none of this, guessing that the young man would close his mind to even these mildly encouraging words. Instead he said, 'If you're ever in Brighton, look in at West House, won't you, Mr Harvey? There's someone it might interest you to meet.'

Chapter Fifteen

Things settled into a routine, not so very different from the one Rowlands had established, over the years, in London: he got up, went to work, came home, had dinner and got on with whatever pursuits he beguiled his leisure hours. Hitherto, these had included rowing, gardening and walking. Now, in the absence of a river on which to pursue his favourite sport, and the fact that the 'garden' at his present home was a paved courtyard, scarcely large enough to swing the proverbial cat, he contented himself with the last of these blameless activities. On this particular May evening, he was returning from a walk along the cliffs at Kemptown, swinging his stick and enjoying the mild spring air. Really, the move to Brighton hadn't turned out badly, all things considered. The job was certainly all right, and the house better than expected. Once Joanie was home for the holidays, they'd feel like a family again. He wondered if, after all, he might take up Edith's suggestion and get a dog – Joan could help to train it. Something steady, he thought. A Labrador, perhaps? Quite a few of the other St Dunstan's men had them. Some swore it that it made getting about as easy as it had been in the days before one was blind.

Still turning this interesting idea over in his mind, he turned along Madeira Place and into Dorset Gardens. He reached Number 6 and climbed the short flight of steps to the front door, found it on the latch and pushed it open.

'Hello,' he called. 'I'm home.' But nobody returned his greeting. From behind the sitting-room door came the murmur of voices. Visitors, then? He opened the door.

'Thank goodness you're back, Fred,' said his wife. 'Miss Briggs . . . I mean, WPC Briggs . . . is here.'

'Hello, Mr Rowlands,' said the young police officer. She sounded nervous – as well she might – about what she had to tell him. 'I came straight away . . . I thought Maggie might be here. I haven't seen her since lunchtime and . . .'

He was instantly alarmed. 'What do you mean, you haven't seen her?' he demanded. 'You were supposed to be looking after her.'

'I was . . . and I am . . . but . . .'

'But what?'

'Don't *bark* at the poor girl, Fred,' said Edith. 'She's doing her best to tell us what happened. Go on, my dear.'

'I was so *certain* she must have come home,' said Betty Briggs. 'I thought at first she was playing a trick on me. We've often joked about it . . . her giving me the slip, I mean.' Her voice quavered slightly. 'Now you tell me she isn't here.'

'You'd better start from the beginning,' said Rowlands.

'I'll make us all a nice cup of tea, shall I?' This was Mrs

Edwards, who had been knitting placidly in her corner. 'And what about something to eat?'

'Thank you. I had a sandwich at the railway station,' said WPC Briggs. 'But tea would be lovely.'

So the story unfolded: Betty Briggs had called for Margaret at her lodgings that morning, as she did every day. They had bicycled to Bletchley Park, where both women had gone as usual to Hut 6 – Margaret getting on with decrypting the latest intercepts that had come in the night before, and Betty doing some routine collating work.

'It's quite boring, really,' she said. 'But I suppose it must be of *some* use . . .' At midday, they had walked across to the canteen, where both had ordered their usual soup and sandwich lunch. While they'd been eating, one of the Wrens had brought a note for Margaret. She'd read it, and then she'd said, 'Bother. Something's come up.' Then, as Betty had started to get to her feet, 'No, finish your lunch. I won't be a tick.'

'And that,' said Betty Briggs, 'was the last I saw of her. When I realised she wasn't coming back, I searched all over for her. I thought at first she must have decided to go straight back to Hut 6. But she wasn't there, and no one I asked had seen her. I wasted a bit of time looking around the grounds – thinking she might have gone for a walk, you know – and then I went to look for the Wren who'd brought the note, but *she* wasn't to be found either.'

'Would you know her again, do you think?' said Rowlands.

'I think so,' was the reply. 'She was tall, with red hair. Well, *then* I thought of checking whether Maggie's bicycle was where she'd left it. It wasn't, and so I got my own bike and cycled to Maggie's lodgings, to see if she'd turned up there. *That* was no-go, and so I cycled down to the railway station – it was about half past three by this time. Maggie's bike was in the rack outside the station, so I asked at the ticket office, but nobody could remember whether a fair-haired girl wearing a fawn mackintosh had caught a train after midday. I'm not in uniform – we decided when I took this post that it's better if I try and blend in with everyone else – so the station master wasn't keen to go through all the tickets that had been sold that afternoon, besides which, it would have wasted more time. So I took a guess that the message might have been to ring home, and that on the strength of it, Maggie had decided to come straight here. I knew the name of the street, but not the number – only as it happens Maggie had shown me a photograph of the house, which she took when she was in Brighton a couple of weeks ago. So here I am,' she said dolefully. 'I expect you think I've let you down.'

'We don't think that, do we, Fred?'

'No,' said Rowlands. 'You acted very promptly. But I think I'm going to have to go back with you to Bletchley. How late do the trains run?'

This time, neither his wife nor mother-in-law made any attempt to stop Rowlands carrying out this plan, even though it was already past eight o'clock, and they were unlikely to reach Bletchley before eleven.

'Do you really think Margaret's in some kind of danger?' said Edith, as Rowlands was putting on his coat.

'I don't know. But I'll find her, don't worry,' he said, sounding more confident than he felt. The train was packed with servicemen and women returning to their bases, and not a few Bletchley people, Rowlands supposed, since the line was a direct one. From all around where he sat, opposite the young policewoman, came the murmur of talk and the smoke from numerous cigarettes. He lit one himself, having offered the pack to WPC Briggs.

'Thanks,' she said, accepting one. 'Look, I'm awfully sorry about this . . .'

'Don't mention it,' he said. From the next bank of seats came the mildly flirtatious exchanges between a group of RAF men and some girls, who might or might not have been on their way back to 'BP'. A thought occurred to Rowlands. 'This letter,' he said. 'How did Margaret react when she read it? I mean, did she seem pleased or excited?'

'Not particularly. Why?'

'Oh, just an idea.' Because it had struck him that perhaps this chap Margaret liked – Lieutenant Dawson, wasn't it? – had sent the letter, in which case her disappearance might have a less sinister explanation than the one Rowlands feared. But he dismissed the idea almost at once. Margaret would never act in such an irresponsible way as to go off for a romantic assignation without asking leave. No, whoever it was who'd sent that letter, it wasn't her naval officer sweetheart.

They were at the gates of Bletchley Park by a quarter past eleven. This time, Rowlands was determined to be let in, with or without a pass.

'Just ring up Commander Murchison's office, will you?' he told the guard. 'He'll want to talk to me.' Perhaps it was the fierce note in Rowlands's voice, combined with the police identification proffered by WPC Briggs, that convinced the man he was in earnest, for no more than ten minutes later, Rowlands and Betty Briggs were in Murchison's office. The commander listened in silence as Rowlands told him why they had come.

'I must say, this is all damnably perplexing,' he said at last. 'Have you any idea where your daughter might have gone – assuming our friends in the secret service haven't spirited her away again?'

'I was hoping that you might be able to help me with that, Commander.' Briefly, Rowlands explained about the Wren who'd delivered the letter. 'WPC Briggs here was unable to track her down. Perhaps you could?'

'You want me to get all my Wrens on parade, on the off-chance that this young woman will recognise one of 'em?' demanded Murchison, sounding dangerously close to one of the outbursts for which he was famous.

'Just the ones who were on duty earlier in the day,' replied Rowlands calmly.

'Hmph.' Murchison sounded as if he was controlling his temper with difficulty. 'Very well. I'll see what I can do.' He picked up the receiver from the telephone on his desk and barked an order into it. A moment later, Petty Officer Smedley put her head around the door.

'Sir?'

'Can you find out which of our women officers and ratings were on duty at oh-twelve-hundred hours, and get them in here, PDQ?'

'Yes, sir.'

'So you think something's happened to your girl?'

said Murchison, as the three of them waited for the petty officer's return.

'I'm afraid so,' was the reply. 'It isn't like her to go off without a word.'

'In which case, shouldn't you be involving the police?' said the commander. 'Specifically, your friend the chief inspector? I should've thought missing persons was more his beat than mine.'

'Well . . .' began Rowlands, but before he could say any more, Betty Briggs piped up, 'Permission to speak, sir. It's my fault that Maggie . . . Miss Rowlands . . . has been lost. I was detailed to look after her. When the chief inspector hears about this, he'll want my resignation. I . . . I'd hoped to put things right before he got to hear about it, but . . .' Her voice shook slightly. 'If anyone should bear the blame, it ought to be me.'

'I'm sure Chief Inspector Douglas will feel as I do, that you did your best in trying circumstances,' said Rowlands. 'If Margaret turns up in the next few hours, then there's no reason why he should hear of it. Now, if it's all right with you, Commander,' he went on, 'perhaps WPC Briggs could see if she can pick out our Wren?' Because it was evident from the murmur of voices in the corridor that Petty Officer Smedley had carried out her orders. There had been eight Wrens on duty at the time specified; one by one they filed into the office. Several, still hastily buttoning their uniforms, had evidently just got out of bed, and had to face a reprimand for appearing 'incorrectly dressed'. When seven of the eight had presented themselves, and been rejected, there came the sound of hurried footsteps in the corridor, and a young woman came rushing in.

'You're late, Wren Potts,' said Murchison severely.

'Yes, sir. Sorry, sir.'

'And put that cap straight.'

'Yes, sir.'

'No excuse for sloppiness.'

'No, sir.'

'It's her,' whispered Betty Briggs to Rowlands.

'May I ask a question of the officer?' he said.

'Go ahead.'

'You delivered a letter to my daughter, Miss Margaret Rowlands, at lunchtime today, in the staff canteen, didn't you?'

'Yes, sir,' replied Wren Potts, sounding more than a little apprehensive, after the rocket she'd just received from her commanding officer.

'Can you tell me who gave you the letter?'

'It was Professor Box, sir. I often carry messages from the Cottage . . . that is, from Professor Box's section.'

'That's quite in order, Wren Potts,' said Murchison, in a more conciliatory tone than he had used hitherto. 'Is that all you want to know, Mr Rowlands?'

'Yes. Thank you. I don't think I need keep your officer any longer.'

'All right. Dismiss,' said Murchison to the Wren. 'Will that be all for tonight?' he added to Rowlands.

'Not quite. I know it's late' – it was gone midnight – 'but I wondered if I might have a word with Professor Box?'

They found Mostyn Box in his office. With him was another man, with whom he was discussing Greek poetry. 'So these whatyoumacallits you've been working on . . .'

'*Papyri.*'

'You're telling me most of this stuff is obscene?'

'Oh yes,' replied Box happily. 'Utterly *filthy*, I'm afraid.'

'Do tell.'

'Well, in the fragment I've just been translating, a pimp complains that his favourite whore has been stolen from the brothel . . . I say, may I help you?'

'Good evening, Professor,' said Rowlands. 'We met a few weeks ago.'

'Did we?' The other must have taken a closer look, for he said, 'So we did. I remember now. You were with that policeman. Wanted to know about poor little Pamela. Afraid I wasn't much help. Ever catch the fellow who did it?'

'Not so far. But it isn't about that I've come.' Rowlands hesitated, conscious of the other man, to whom he had not yet been introduced, hovering on the edge of things. Since he, whoever he was, didn't seem to feel himself *de trop*, Rowlands went on, 'Earlier today, you sent a letter, via one of the WRNS officers, addressed to my daughter.'

'I?' Box sounded bemused. 'A letter? When was this, exactly?'

'It was midday – isn't that right, WPC Briggs?'

'Ah, so you're a policewoman, are you?' said Box. 'I must say, you don't look like one.'

'No, sir,' said Betty Briggs. 'But I was there when the Wren brought the note. She's quite sure it was you who gave it to her.'

'Too thrilling,' murmured the other man. 'Sending *billets-doux* to young ladies. You *are* a dark horse, Molly.'

'*Billets* fiddlesticks,' was the tart reply. 'I remember

now. It came to me as an enclosure in another letter. Marked "For the attention of Miss M. Rowlands". That your girl?'

'It is.'

'Cambridge alumna, isn't she? Mathematics.'

'That's right, sir.'

'Curiouser and curiouser,' said the unknown man.

'Oh, *do* pipe down, Wilcox!' So *that* was who it was, thought Rowlands. The writer whose sartorial choices the chief inspector had so disliked. 'I'm trying to think. Yes,' went on Box, 'I've got it now. As I said, it was an enclosure, in a letter addressed to myself. Naturally I didn't read it. A Wren happened to be passing, so I gave it to her and told her to find Miss Rowlands – which you tell me she did.'

'Indeed,' said Rowlands, sensing that they were getting somewhere at last. 'You say it was sent in a covering letter – can you tell me who sent *that*?'

Mostyn Box considered a moment. 'I don't mind telling you,' he said at last. 'It was one of my former students, as a matter of fact. Brilliant chap. He's teaching at the university himself now, of course. Although he's gone in for the *modern*, rather than the *ancient* languages.'

'Where is it that he teaches?'

'Didn't I say? Trinity, of course. My own alma mater, as it happens.'

'I was at the other place,' murmured Wilcox. 'I can't say it did me much good.'

'So the letter was posted from Cambridge?'

'Haven't I just said so? Yes, it was just a short note, asking me to some lunch or other. I can't go, of course. Too much going on here. But nice of him to ask me. We keep in touch, you know.'

'And the letter addressed to my daughter – did your correspondent give any explanation about that?'

'What do you mean, my dear chap?'

'It's just that it seems a little surprising that someone Margaret's never met should send her a letter . . .'

'Oh, but they *have* met,' said Box. 'At least, I assume so. She'll have attended some of his lectures, no doubt. They're very popular, I gather. Art history's his specialism, although, as I say, he studied modern languages.'

Rowlands felt his mouth go dry. 'What's this man's name?' he asked, although he thought he knew already.

'Blake,' was the reply. 'Aubrey Blake. He's making quite a name for himself these days.'

They had missed the last train to Cambridge, and so there was no alternative but to stay overnight and catch an early train next day. It was a fast service, and so they could be in the town soon after it was light, should they wish it – although, as Molly Box pointed out, it wouldn't do them much good. 'Blake never sees visitors before breakfast.'

'He'll see me,' said Rowlands grimly, but he accepted Box's offer of his sofa for the night.

'I often camp out here myself,' said the latter. 'Saves a long drive, late at night, and it means I'm in the office bright and early.'

Betty Briggs said she was happy to bicycle back to her lodgings. 'We often finish quite late . . . I mean, when Maggie's on the night shift.'

'I'll walk with you as far as the gate,' said Rowlands.

Bletchley Park at night was a very different place from its daytime incarnation. Instead of the cheerful bustle Rowlands recalled from his earlier visits, a hushed atmosphere prevailed, suggestive of urgency and intense concentration. No sound came from the huts, although at one point someone – perhaps a messenger – came dashing out of one of them, heading in the direction of another. They would be working particularly hard just now, thought Rowlands, remembering that the German codes changed at midnight. It was work all the more vital because, if the U-boat attacks on convoys bringing food from abroad could not be thwarted, then the country would soon starve; nor would there be oil enough for war production to continue.

Reaching the gate at last, they found themselves challenged by the sentry – evidently unauthorised personnel were as much the object of suspicion on this side of the gate as on the other. Both produced their identity cards, and confirmed their bona fides. Having arranged to meet at the station after breakfast, they said their goodnights, and WPC Briggs pedalled off into the night. Preoccupied with all that he had learnt in the past few hours, Rowlands wasn't paying as much attention to his surroundings as he might have been, trusting to the fact that the paths along which he and Betty Briggs had been walking were deserted at this hour. So he was unprepared for the sudden emergence of a figure from one of the huts, who nearly collided with him.

'Hi! Look where you're going!' He knew the voice at once.

'Good evening, Dr Twining.'

'Oh, it's you.' Twining didn't sound especially surprised to see him. 'Can't see a thing in this dark. Which way are you going?'

Rowlands told him.

'I'll walk that way myself. Need a breath of air.' The two men fell into step, and for a few minutes there was no sound but the crunching of their footsteps on the gravel, and the sleepy calling of a waterfowl from the lake. 'Yes, we're starting to achieve some satisfactory results,' said Twining abruptly, resuming their conversation of three months ago as if hours, not months, had elapsed. 'Once we get some more machines working, it'll increase our chances of a breakthrough.' Rowlands made a sound indicative of comprehension and the other went on, 'Of course, I've had to contend with some pig-headedness in certain quarters. People who think they should be running things *their* way. But they'll have to see reason, eventually. Tell me, how do you know which direction to take, without being able to see your way?' Because they had come to a junction. One path led towards the stable block and the Cottage, the other, by way of the park, to the mansion.

'Do you mean now, or in general?'

'Both.'

'I rely on memory, a good deal – as well as my other senses,' said Rowlands. 'At this moment, for example, I've the fact that I've walked this path on several previous occasions to help me. So I know that it's fairly even, without any obstacles to trip me up. I can hear the wind in those trees over there, and the splash of a fish jumping in the lake, which gives me a sense of the lie of the land. Because it's night-time, there are fewer people around – but if there *were* others approaching, I'd be able to hear them – and smell them, too, if any of them happened to be smoking. I'd be able to tell, from shaking hands, something about a person's age, build and character. How they speak, of course, is another very revealing thing.'

'Yes,' said Twining. 'It's what I thought. You use your intelligence. Many people don't.'

They reached the door of the Cottage and said goodnight. Twining continued his walk. It struck Rowlands that, in spite of his occasional outbursts of irascibility, usually provoked by what he saw as the stupidity of others, Twining was rather a shy man. For himself, he rather liked him. In the little sitting room of the Cottage, he found his host had left a pile of blankets and a pillow on the sofa, with which to make up his bed. He accordingly did so, and settled down to what proved to be a surprisingly sound night's sleep.

They were in Cambridge before nine the next morning. The journey was just over an hour on the Varsity Line that ran between Bletchley, Oxford and Cambridge. A bus took them to the town centre, where WPC Briggs, for whom it was a first visit, was full of admiration for the charm and antiquity of the colleges, and for Trinity in particular. 'D'you mean to tell me that the students have all this to themselves?' she asked, as they crossed the wide expanse of Great Court.

'Not entirely,' said Rowlands. 'But I think quite a few of the undergraduates live here.'

'Lucky them,' said Betty Briggs. 'Although I'm not sure I'd feel comfortable living in a place like this. Makes me think of churches. Or the Inns of Court.'

The porter having directed them to the right staircase, they found themselves within a few minutes in front of Dr Blake's door. The 'oak' was sported, but Rowlands knew from the porter that Blake was in. He knocked, and there came a faintly querulous voice from within.

'Yes, yes. All right . . .' A moment later the outer door opened, and a man Rowlands guessed to be Aubrey Blake stood there. 'Oh!' It was evident from his startled tone that he'd expected somebody else.

'Dr Blake?' said Rowlands. 'I wonder if you can spare us a few moments?'

'I . . . Just what is this about? If you've an enquiry about the college, then the porters' lodge is the place to take it. I'm a member of the teaching staff. I don't deal with the general public.'

'What I've got to say won't take long,' said Rowlands firmly. 'Perhaps we could come in for a minute?' Ignoring the other's gasp of outrage, he pushed past him into the room, with WPC Briggs following in his wake. 'You . . . you can't just *burst* in here!' cried the academic. 'These are my private rooms . . . Who *are* you, anyway?'

'The name's Rowlands. I gather you sent a letter to my daughter.'

'What a preposterous suggestion! I don't *know* your daughter, whoever she is. And I'm certainly not in the habit of writing to *women* . . . You must have got me mixed up with somebody else.'

'The letter was enclosed in one you wrote to Professor Box. It was delivered to my daughter, Margaret Rowlands, yesterday. This young lady's a witness.'

'But . . . but . . . I fail to see what all this has to do

with me,' protested the other. 'Letters . . . enclosures . . .
It's like something out of Sexton Blake! No relation,' he
added with a whinnying laugh. 'Are you *sure* you've got
the right man?'

'Oh yes,' said Rowlands. 'Professor Box was quite clear
that it was you the letter was from.'

'Was he really? Dear old Molly! He *is* getting on a bit,
you know. Probably got me confused with another of his
former acolytes . . . Now, if you've quite finished, Mr,
er . . . I do have a supervision starting in five minutes.'

'I believe my daughter Margaret arrived in Cambridge
yesterday afternoon,' persisted Rowlands. 'Did she by any
chance come to see you, Dr Blake?'

Again came the high-pitched laugh. 'My dear man,
what are you insinuating? First you accuse me of sending
her letters, next you imply that we're having some kind
of clandestine *affaire* . . .' He gave the word a French
intonation. 'I can promise you, my inclinations lie in an
entirely different direction.' Abruptly, his manner changed.
'I haven't seen your daughter,' he said coldly. 'And there's
an end of it.'

'Then I'm wasting your time,' said Rowlands, deciding
that he'd get nothing more out of the man. 'If she does
contact you, perhaps you'd be good enough to let me
know?' He handed Blake one of his cards, which had the
St Dunstan's telephone number on it. 'Or you can contact
me through St Gertrude's College.'

'Oh, she's one of the *Gertie* females, is she?' murmured
Blake. 'Well, well. Afraid I haven't been of much help,
Mr, er . . .' He consulted the card. 'Rowlands. It can't
be easy, trying to track down an errant daughter, when

one's *blind*,' he went on in an amused tone. 'I wish you luck, Mr Rowlands – and your charming companion, too. Ah,' he added, as the thunder of footsteps on the stairs announced the arrival of his student. 'Here's my ten o'clock, now. Good day to you.'

Chapter Sixteen

'He's lying,' said Betty Briggs as they emerged once more into Great Court.

'Yes, I rather think he is,' agreed Rowlands.

'I was watching him all the time you were asking him about Maggie, and he looked thoroughly shifty,' said the policewoman. 'You get to recognise the signs, when somebody's hiding something.'

'I'm sure you do,' said Rowlands, who was familiar with at least some of those signs. Forced laughter – conveying not amusement, but anger and fear. The tendency to 'protest too much' . . . Blake had betrayed himself in both these ways, he thought. As they crossed the vast space, their footsteps ringing on the paving-stones that surrounded the grass – on which none but the fellows were permitted to walk – Rowlands thought of his long-dead commanding officer, who had frequented these hallowed courts as an undergraduate. Gerald Willoughby had not died during the war in which both men had fought, but he had been, to Rowlands's mind, as much a casualty of it as if he had fallen in battle. Preoccupied with these sombre reflections, he was paying less attention to his surroundings than he usually did, and so it came as something of a shock when, on the point of exiting through the great gate onto Trinity Street, he found his way blocked by a solid form.

'An' just where are ye going, may I ask?' said a voice he knew, in tones of mock severity.

'Chief Inspector. I might ask what brings *you* here?'

'As if ye didn't know!' boomed his friend, tapping Rowlands on the chest, with heavy playfulness. 'As for *you*, WPC Briggs, I'd like to know why you didn't think it worth your while to inform me what you were up to.'

'I'm sorry, sir,' began Briggs, but then Rowlands intervened.

'WPC Briggs has been helping me to find my daughter—'

'Whom she should never have let out of her sight!' thundered Douglas.

'I know, sir,' said the policewoman. 'It was remiss of me.'

'Save it for the inquiry,' growled the chief inspector; then, to Rowlands, 'But you still haven't told me why you're here, Fred. I hope,' he added darkly, 'you haven't been queering the pitch?'

'WPC Briggs and I have just been to see Dr Blake.'

'Just what I was afraid you might have done,' muttered Douglas. 'Ah, there you are, Sergeant!' This to his officer, who had just joined them under the capacious arch of the gateway. 'What took you so long?'

'Sorry, sir. Couldn't find a parking place. The streets here are that narrow.'

'Yes, yes,' replied the chief inspector impatiently. 'Well, now you're here, we can proceed with the business. Wait outside, until I give you the signal. You, too, WPC Briggs.' Drawing Rowlands along with him, Douglas entered the porters' lodge. 'So I gather you're here on account of Miss Margaret?'

'Yes,' said Rowlands. 'According to WPC Briggs, Margaret received a letter yesterday, enclosed in one sent by Dr Blake to Professor Box. He – Blake – denies knowing anything about it, however.'

'Well, he would,' said Douglas, 'if what Margaret told me is correct . . . Now where's that porter?' He pressed a bell on the counter.

But something he'd just said stopped Rowlands in his tracks. 'You've *spoken* to Margaret?'

'I have. It's why I'm here.'

'When was this?'

'She telephoned my office last night. Told me she'd been to see Blake about a certain matter . . . I can't discuss it now . . . Ah, good day to you,' he went on, addressing the porter, who had appeared from his cubbyhole at the summons.

'Good day,' replied the latter. 'What can I do for you gentlemen?'

'Chief Inspector to you,' said Douglas, producing his identification. 'I want to speak to Dr Aubrey Blake.'

'But he's occupied with a student at present.'

'Never mind that. This is police business. You'd better direct me to his room.'

271

'I can show you where it is,' said Rowlands quickly. 'Follow me.' It seemed to him that speed was of the essence. Pursued by the faint protests of the porter, the two men exited the lodge, collecting the others as they did so. 'How did she sound? Margaret, I mean.'

'She sounded fine,' said Douglas, as their little party, with Douglas's sergeant and Betty Briggs bringing up the rear, walked rapidly in the direction from which Rowlands and the WPC had lately come. 'She was telephoning from her college. I imagine she's there now.' *Of course*, thought Rowlands – he should have realised that Margaret would take refuge at St Gertrude's. 'Grand sort o' place this,' remarked Douglas, seeming to become aware of his surroundings at that moment. 'Rather a step up from Hendon police college.'

They had reached the intersection of the path that ran at right-angles to the one that led directly from the porters' lodge, and that formed one side of a square, at the centre of which stood the great stone fountain. Blake's rooms were on the first floor, directly opposite this.

'It's that staircase straight ahead of us,' said Rowlands, pointing it out.

'All right,' said the chief inspector. 'I think it best if you and WPC Briggs wait here, Fred. We don't want to give the man any more warning than we have to.'

He was approaching the door Rowlands had indicated, when there came the sharp click of high heels approaching along the path. Someone – a woman, evidently – was walking briskly towards them.

'I don't believe it,' muttered Douglas, under his breath. 'What's *she* doing here?'

'Good morning, Chief Inspector,' said Iris Barnes. 'Doing a bit of sight-seeing, are we? It *is* a beautiful day.' Before Douglas could marshal a suitably withering response, she went on, 'It's good to see you too, Mr Rowlands. But I must warn you – and you, Chief Inspector – that you're not to go a step further.'

Douglas found his voice at last. 'I've a warrant for this man's arrest on charges of high treason,' he said. 'You're surely not going to stop me carrying out my duty?'

'Indeed I am,' she said. 'And I'd be grateful, Chief Inspector, if you and your officers – and Mr Rowlands here – would return with me to the porters' lodge with as little commotion as possible. I'll explain everything when we get there.'

In a thunderous silence, Douglas turned on his heel, and, followed by his two officers, marched back in the direction from which they had come. Rowlands turned to follow suit, when Miss Barnes slipped her arm through his. 'I'm told you paid a visit to our celebrated art historian earlier today,' she said. 'I wish I'd been in time to stop you, but we must hope that no damage has been done.'

'I had to ask him about Margaret,' said Rowlands.

'I see. And did he tell you anything?'

'No. He denied ever having seen her.'

'He would,' she said, as they reached the porters' lodge. 'Let's go inside, shall we?' she said, addressing Douglas, but including Rowlands in this invitation, he assumed. The chief inspector made no demur, but instructed his officers, as before, to remain outside. Nor was the porter anywhere to be seen. 'I've asked that we shouldn't be disturbed,' said Miss Barnes. 'Now,' she went on, addressing her remarks to them both. 'I expect you'd like to know why I stopped you from what you were about to do?'

'I'd appreciate it,' said Douglas bitterly.

'Very well,' she said. 'The facts are these. We've known for some time that the man you were going to arrest . . . no names, I think . . . has been working for the enemy. The Russians, that is. Put bluntly, he's been recruiting likely candidates to the cause – young men, mostly, but he was prepared to make an exception to the rule when your Margaret went to see him yesterday. With her first-class brain, and a job in military intelligence, she'd have suited our man's purpose admirably.'

'It's what she telephoned to tell me,' put in the exasperated Douglas. 'He's behind the whole conspiracy to sell secrets. And you stopped me from taking him up.'

'As I said, we've been watching him for some time,' said Miss Barnes calmly. 'We could have picked him up on any one of a dozen occasions, but it suits us to leave him in place.' She let the implications of this sink in, then continued. 'Just as long as our man doesn't know that we're on to him, he provides a very useful guide to the strength or otherwise of enemy networks in this country. We can keep an eye on the agents he's recruited over the years, and pull them in if any of them show signs of becoming a nuisance to us . . . such as the agent our man was able to infiltrate at Bletchley Park. That is,' she added, 'we *would* have pulled him in, if someone else hadn't got to him first.'

'Are you referring to Jock Colquhoun?'

'We said no names,' replied Iris Barnes. 'But that is the individual I meant. I believe our art historian friend was looking for a replacement, and decided to make an approach to Margaret. Thankfully, she proved resistant to his blandishments—'

'Of course she did!' said Rowlands indignantly. 'More than that, it sounds as if she put herself at considerable risk to do so. I just hope she isn't too upset by all this, that's all.'

'Do you mean to tell me you don't know where Margaret is, at present?' For the first time, there was a note of uncertainty in the secret agent's voice.

'No, I don't. The chief inspector tells me that she telephoned from St Gertrude's College last night. So I suppose—' He was interrupted by the sound of raised voices from outside; a moment later, the door was flung open.

'No, ma'am, you can't go in there,' cried Sergeant Jones. 'It's private.'

'We'll see about that,' said Maud Rickards. '*There* you are, Fred! I thought I might find you here. Where's Margaret? Isn't she with you?'

'No. I thought she must be with you.'

'Oh dear! When she wasn't in her room this morning, I was sure she must have come back here.' Miss Rickards sounded quite distressed. 'What on earth's happened to her?'

'Chief Inspector,' said Rowlands, making an effort to keep calm, but unable to quell a rising sense of panic. 'It appears my daughter's gone missing.' He turned to Iris Barnes. 'I don't care what you say, I want Blake's rooms searched at once. He may be detaining her against her will.'

'I can assure you,' she said, 'I've been having him watched. No one's gone into his rooms apart from one of his students, half an hour ago – and you and WPC Briggs, ten minutes before that.'

'But—'

'Excuse me, sir,' said Sergeant Jones, who had been hovering in the doorway, since his unsuccessful attempt to stop Miss Rickards from entering the lodge.

'What is it, Sergeant?'

'If it's the young lady that Betty . . . I mean WPC Briggs . . . has been looking after, then I saw her not twenty minutes ago, down by the river,' said the young policeman.

'*What?* Why didn't you say so before, man?'

'I didn't realise the young lady was lost,' was the faintly aggrieved reply. 'She was with a young gentleman at the time. They were taking a punt out on the river. I was just parking the car – you don't half have to search for parking places in this town,' he added. 'Not a bit like London.'

'Yes, yes, we don't need your thoughts on parking problems,' said his senior officer. 'But are you sure it *was* Miss Rowlands, Sergeant?'

'Oh yes, sir. I recall the young lady well. Very pleasant young lady. But it was the car that drew my attention first.'

'The car?' said Rowlands sharply. 'What make of car?'

'Alvis, sir. Newest model, I'd say. Bright red.'

'Chief Inspector,' said Rowlands. 'You've got to get after them. Margaret may be in serious danger.'

'I don't get it,' said Douglas. 'That's Montfitchet's car, unless I'm much mistaken. What's it doing here? The fellow's in custody.'

'But his friend Gilbert Burton isn't,' said Rowlands.

'So you think it's Burton who's with her?' Douglas sounded unconvinced.

'Yes.' Rowlands didn't have time to go into why he was sure of this. 'You say they were hiring a punt, Sergeant?' he went on. 'Can you tell me whether they were going upriver or down?'

'I . . . I'm not sure, sir. They were below the weir, when I saw 'em.'

'Downriver,' said Rowlands.

'All right.' This was Douglas to his sergeant. 'You'd better fetch the car. If we take the riverbank road, we'll catch up with them before too long.'

But Rowlands had a better idea. 'I need to borrow a punt,' he said to Maud Rickards.

She seemed unperturbed by this request. 'Nothing easier. Trinity has several, moored along the stretch of river beside the library. I'll show you the way.'

'I'll need somebody to steer,' said Rowlands. 'Betty, will you?'

'Try and stop me,' said the WPC.

Maud took his arm, and the three of them hurried back across Great Court, up the steps and through the passageway that led past the dining hall into Neville Court.

'I did some nursing here, during the last war,' panted Miss Rickards as she guided Rowlands down the broad semicircular flight of steps on the other side. 'I was seconded from First London General around the time

Edith started at St Dunstan's.' This was where Rowlands had met his wife, during her time as a VAD. 'They had the beds out, under the colonnade there, with awnings to screen the men from the sun. It was a very hot summer, as I recall.'

Walking rapidly, they reached the far side of the court and entered the undercroft of the Wren Library, which Rowlands recalled from having seen it from the river, on a long-ago pre-war visit. He'd gone punting that time, too – a hired punt, taken out to entertain a girl called Elsie, who'd been his companion that day. Now, as he hurried across the lawn that sloped down to the river, he tried to remember all he had learnt then about the art of punting. Surely it was something you never forgot, like riding a bicycle? Given the choice, he'd have preferred a skiff or a rowing boat, both of which type of craft he'd handled many times since he'd lost his sight. St Dunstan's had a well-respected rowing team, of which he had been a member, competing in championship races along the Thames. But the heavy flat-bottomed craft was all that was available, and so he must make the best of it.

'There's a punt tied up just here,' said Maud. 'I was hoping there would be.' She took his hand and helped him into the punt. Betty Briggs climbed in afterwards, having first untied the mooring rope, and Rowlands took up his station on the platform at one end of the craft.

'Hand me the punt pole, will you?' he said. She did so, and then took her seat at the other end, facing him. 'All set.' Balancing the pole as expertly as he could, Rowlands shoved off from the bank, from which Maud called encouragement.

'That's the way! Don't dig too deep, or you'll have yourself in the river!'

He nodded and smiled, to show he'd understood, but really, it wasn't too difficult after all. He braced his feet on the deck, and drew the pole upwards between his palms, before dropping it down again into the water. There was a rhythm to it, he now recalled. The craft glided swiftly across the smooth surface of the river, which was here contained between shallow grass banks, but which would later narrow still further, between the walls of the colleges.

'Bridge coming up,' sang out Betty.

'Thanks. And let me know if you see any other punts approaching.'

'Will do.'

The beautiful weather would of course attract a crowd to the river, Rowlands knew – although it would doubtless be somewhat depleted by present conditions, with many of those who might once have sported blazers and white flannels now wearing uniform, and flying planes or driving tanks in remote regions, instead of messing about in boats on the Cam. Having successfully navigated the first bridge, they were almost immediately faced with another – a fact Rowlands recalled from that earlier visit, even as Betty drew his attention to it. 'Bridge ahead. Quite a fancy-looking one, too.'

'It's the Bridge of Sighs.'

'Like something out of a fairy tale, this place, isn't it?'

Rowlands agreed that it was. With the part of his mind that was not occupied with what he was doing, he was thinking about Margaret and how she might be feeling at that moment. If he was right in his supposition that the man she was with was Gilbert Burton, then things looked very bad for her. He was convinced now that Burton had killed both Pamela Wingate and Jock Colquhoun. That he wouldn't stop at killing Margaret was all too likely.

'Punt approaching,' said Betty Briggs, although Rowlands had already heard the shouts and laughter, as a party of youths made a performance of getting past Magdalene Bridge. 'RAF boys, by the look of them,' said Betty. 'Making rather a mess of things . . . I say, look out!' she shouted, as the other punt shot past. 'You nearly hit us then.'

'Awf'lly sorry!' came the reply. 'Not used to flying this kind of crate.'

From Magdalene Bridge it was a straight run as far as Jesus Lock, Rowlands remembered – glad to have left the narrowest part of the river behind. He calculated that it had taken them no more than ten minutes, since pushing off from Trinity. Surely they must catch up with the other punt soon? It would have to turn around before it reached the weir in any case.

'Can you see them yet?' he said.

'I'm not sure,' was the reply. 'There are some punts moored by the bank, but nothing else on the river that I can see . . .' Then, as they drew nearer to the lock, she gave a gasp. 'Oh no! There's a weir up ahead . . . and a punt, stuck right on the edge of it.' She stood up, causing their own punt to rock wildly from side to side. 'There's someone lying in it,' she said. 'I think it's Maggie. She isn't moving. I think she must be unconscious.'

It was what he had feared. 'Sit down,' he said. 'Or

you'll have us in the river. Now tell me exactly what you can see.'

'There's a punt, as I said . . . It's caught on the edge of the weir.'

'Caught on what?' It seemed important to know how precarious or otherwise the situation was.

'It's a bit of wall, sticking out into the river, next to the lock gates,' said Betty.

'The flank wall of the pier,' he said. That it was a substantial structure offered at least some hope. 'Is the chain across the top of the weir broken, then?'

'I can't really see . . . It looks as if part of it's missing.'

So Burton must have unhooked the chain, then guided the punt towards the danger zone, before scrambling to safety, thought Rowlands, with a surge of anger. If he'd needed convincing that murder had been intended, then this was the proof. Now, as they approached the weir, the sound of roaring water grew louder, so that he had to shout to make himself heard.

'Listen, Betty. I'm going to aim for that bit of wall, too – or as near as I can get without dislodging the other punt. If you want to get off now, I'll take you in towards the bank.'

'I'm not getting off,' she shouted back. 'You'll need someone to guide you.' Which was certainly true. The current here was strong, and it was as much as Rowlands could do to control the punt. Reaching the place where the chain had been removed, he guided the heavy craft forward, foot by foot.

'I'm going to try and bring the punt in behind the other one,' he shouted, although he wasn't sure if she could hear him or not. 'Then I'll be able to climb across and reach her.'

His plan was to try to steer the punt in which Margaret was lying away from that dreadful drop into the lower reaches of the river. Failing that, he'd try to drag her to safety. 'Hold tight,' he said. A few more strokes, and the punt bumped against the nearside pier, so that it was directly behind the one in which Margaret was lying. He dug down with the punt pole, but the river was too deep at this spot for it to have any effect. It would be no good trying to manoeuvre the other punt to safety – that could risk moving it further towards the edge of the weir. He'd just have to try to get Margaret out as best he could.

Just then, above the roar of water, there was the sound of a car pulling up on Chesterton Lane. A moment later came a shout. 'There she is!' and the sound of running footsteps on the footbridge overhead. 'Hold on, sir! I'll be right there!' shouted someone – it was Sergeant Jones – but Rowlands hadn't time to waste. Lying flat on his stomach, he had already started to crawl from one punt to the other, straining with all his might to reach the still figure that lay there. Where was she? Ah, he'd found her. His fingers encountered soft hair, and a lolling head. He touched her throat. Was there a faint pulse there? Gently, he grasped her under the shoulders, and began to drag her into the other punt.

'Give her to me, sir.' It was Jones, who'd lowered himself over the railings of the bridge, and now knelt beside Rowlands in the punt. His arms and back aching with the effort of supporting his unconscious daughter, Rowlands allowed the younger man to take the strain.

Together, they pulled Margaret to safety. Only when she was safely lowered into the bottom of the punt did he allow himself to breathe. Was she alive still? He didn't dare to hope.

'Looks like she's been drugged, sir,' said Jones. 'Got any smelling salts, Bet?' WPC Briggs duly produced these, and applied them, while Rowlands rubbed Margaret's hands and wrists.

For a moment, nothing happened; then, 'She's opening her eyes,' said Betty.

'Daddy,' said Margaret faintly.

He felt the tears start to his eyes. 'Don't try to talk,' he said. 'You're safe now.'

How close they had come to disaster became apparent as, a few moments later, Sergeant Jones began to lever their craft away from its temporary resting place, using the punt pole to do so. His efforts dislodged the first punt.

'Look out! She's going over!' cried the young policeman, as the craft slipped over the edge, where it had been precariously balanced, and into the turbulent waters below.

On the Jesus Green bank waited the chief inspector, with Miss Rickards, who had brought a rug from the car, which she placed around Margaret's shoulders. She also produced a flask from her handbag. 'Brandy,' she said. 'Go on, it'll do you good.' Margaret coughed and spluttered as the fiery spirit went down, but seemed to revive a little.

'Would the young lady like to come in and rest awhile?' It was a woman – the lock-keeper's wife, it transpired – who made the suggestion. 'It's only two steps to the door.'

'Thank you,' said Margaret. 'But I'm all right now.' It was plain to her father that she wanted to get away from the scene of the near catastrophe as quickly as possible.

'Did you see what happened?' he asked the woman as, helped by Betty Briggs, Margaret got shakily to her feet.

'No, sir,' was the reply. 'I was hanging out washing, back of the house . . .' This was the lock-keeper's cottage, he surmised. 'Didn't see nothing. And what with my Bert being called away . . .'

'What's that?' said the chief inspector sharply. 'You mean to say your husband wasn't at his post?'

'No, sir. It isn't like him at all, to leave the lock during working hours. But he had a telephone call . . . 'bout an hour ago it was . . . to say that somebody'd opened the sluice gates at the Mill Pond, and to come and take over while they closed 'em.' So *that* was why the river had seemed higher than usual, thought Rowlands. 'Prob'ly one o' the undergraduates having a joke,' said the woman. 'They don't realise what a lot of extra work it makes.'

Rowlands had his own ideas about who must have opened the sluices – and he didn't think it had been a student prank.

'So I suppose that means your husband wasn't here to notice that the chain across the weir had been removed?' he said, guessing the answer already. In planning Margaret's murder, the perpetrator had left nothing to chance. But then, that had been the case all along, Rowlands thought.

Once Margaret felt able to walk, the six of them made their way back over the footbridge to where the Wolseley was parked. Only then did Rowlands notice that Iris Barnes wasn't with them. No doubt she'd gone in pursuit of the man she now knew to be the spy at the centre of the Bletchley Park affair, he thought. Just at that moment, he didn't care one way or the other. All that mattered was that Margaret was safe. Revenge could come later.

Chapter Seventeen

In Maud Rickards's rooms at St Gertrude's College, Miss Rickards brewed a pot of her excellent coffee, as Margaret, now recovered from her ordeal, filled in some of the gaps in the story.

'Well, you know most of it already,' she said. 'I had a letter . . . or rather, a note, because it wasn't signed. You were there when I received it, Betty.'

'Do you still have it?' interjected the chief inspector.

'I'm afraid not. It said I was to destroy it.'

'What else did it say?' said Rowlands. Margaret thought for a moment. 'It said . . . as far as I can remember . . . "If you want to save H.M. from the gallows" – I assumed it meant Hugh Montfitchet – "meet me in Dr Blake's rooms at Trinity today at 4 p.m. Don't tell anyone where you're going and burn this as soon as you've read it." Then I gave you the slip,' she added to Betty Briggs. 'Sorry about that.'

'So you'd no idea who'd written the note?' said Rowlands.

'Not then,' replied Margaret. 'Actually, I thought it might have been Dr Blake himself. Hugh was a former student of his. But he said he hadn't written it.'

'You *did* see him, then?'

'Of course. I wanted to ask him what it meant – about saving Hugh. But he didn't seem very interested in that. He started talking about how important it was that what he called "enlightened people" should come together to put an end to this terrible war. He thought I might be one of them – the enlightened people, I mean. He said that idealistic young people like myself were tired of all the lies the politicians had spun, which had dragged us into a war no one had wanted. Fortunately, certain far-sighted individuals – he liked to think he himself was one of them – had taken matters into their own hands . . .' Margaret paused for a moment. 'It was then that I started to realise where I'd heard this kind of thing before. It was exactly the kind of stuff that Jock used to come out with – only with him, it was usually mixed up in some tirade about the workers, and how they'd been stitched up by the rotten system. I don't know if any of this is making sense.'

'Och, it makes sense all right,' said Douglas gloomily. 'These blasted Reds get in everywhere.'

'Being a communist isn't a crime, Chief Inspector,' Maud Rickards reminded him tartly. 'In fact, I'd say that a good number of people in this university hold very similar views, and are none the worse for them.'

'Aye, but we have to hope that most of 'em aren't selling out their country to the Russians,' was the reply.

'Go on, Meg,' said Rowlands, feeling that this

ideological dispute had gone far enough. 'That is, if you're feeling up to it.' Even though she seemed to have recovered well enough, he was still concerned that his daughter's strength shouldn't be overtaxed. And with the principal suspect having got away, and an embargo on arresting the man who'd presumably set him on, it surely made little difference if they heard the full story now or in a few hours' time.

But Margaret said she wanted to continue. 'After he – Dr Blake – had been going on like this for some time,' she resumed, taking a sip of her coffee and refusing a second slice of the seed cake Miss Rickards had produced, as if by magic, from her store cupboard, 'I asked him what all this had to do with saving the life of Hugh Montfitchet, because if he wasn't going to do anything about *that* then I'd better be getting back to Bletchley before I was missed. I thought he was going to lose his temper when I said that, but he only laughed, and said, "My dear young lady, you really mustn't take such a *narrow* view of things! What's *one* life, when set against the lives of so many? Don't you care at all about those millions who are dying because of this war?" Then I said that of course I did, but that surely individual lives were important, too? Dr Blake just smiled, and said, "You might very well think that, but when it comes to the greater good, individual lives are of no consequence." It was then,' she went on, 'that he asked me if I would be prepared to act in the interests of "the greater good" and help bring the war to a swift end, saving thousands, if not millions of lives.'

She was silent a moment; then she went on, 'I said of course, and that anyone would. Then Dr Blake said that, in which case, there was something very straightforward I could do. All he'd ask would be for me to telephone a certain number he would give me, and use a certain code-word – it would be different each time. There would be an answering code-word, which would be the signal for me to pass on the date and time of the next convoy sailing, each week. "That's all that would be required of you," he said. "Not a very arduous task, is it?" It was at that point that I realised what he was asking me to do.'

'Commit treason,' said Douglas. 'And that wouldn't have been the last of it, you can be sure.'

'Yes,' said Margaret. 'I . . . I didn't know how to reply, so I said something about having to think about it, and that I would let him know . . . and he said of course, but not to leave it too long, because lives were at stake. I think he saw from my expression that his proposal hadn't gone down well, because he suddenly remembered he'd got a supervision to do, and almost pushed me out of the room. It all happened so quickly that I wasn't even sure I'd heard him say what in fact he'd said. Then I left, and was on my way to catch my train, when I ran into you, Miss Rickards.' It occurred to Rowlands to wonder whether, had this fortuitous meeting not occurred, his daughter would have made it back to Bletchley alive.

'Well, you know the next part,' said Margaret to the chief inspector. 'After I'd telephoned you, it was getting too late to go back to Bletchley, and so I took up Miss Rickards's suggestion, and stayed the night in college. I knew I'd be in hot water when I got back to BP for having taken unauthorised leave, but I thought the circumstances would explain it all. I'd wait until you arrived, Chief

Inspector, and give my statement to the police, and then catch my train back.' She gave a rueful laugh. 'Only it didn't turn out quite like that.'

'Yes, why on earth did you agree to go off with that man?' demanded Maud Rickards. 'It's not a bit like you to be so reckless, Margaret.'

'He was very clever,' was the reply. 'I'm afraid he took me in completely, at first. When I got down to breakfast, there was a note for me by my plate. It was from Gil. Signed, this time. It said he'd discovered that Blake was a traitor, and that I should meet him outside the college gates, and he'd show me some proof. When I got there, he was waiting in his car . . . or rather, Hugh's car. He told me to get in, and said he'd take me to a man who'd got proof that Blake had been a Russian spy for years, and that I could blow the gaff on him and on the whole operation. I asked him why, if that was the case, he didn't expose Blake himself. Then he gave me some flannel about needing to stay undercover, so that he could track down the other agents in the network. Something about it didn't ring true. He must have realised that I didn't believe him, because when I tried to get out of the car, he pulled a gun on me.'

She was silent a moment. 'I suppose I should have known all along that Gil was too good to be true,' she went on, at last. 'Unlike poor Pam. She was really taken in by his charm. Of course that was what it was all about . . . getting me to come to Cambridge, and setting up the meeting with Aubrey Blake. It was nothing but a blind for what he really intended – which was to get rid of me. Gil guessed that Pam had told me about their affair. He knew that sooner or later I'd put two and two together, and work out who the man she'd been seeing was . . . Of course, if I'd taken the bait, and agreed to take Pamela's place at Bletchley, and carry on their dirty work for them, it would have been a bonus for them. But I think that, even so, Gil knew he couldn't allow me to go on living. I was a danger to him, knowing what I knew. And once he'd heard from Blake that I wasn't going to play their game, he knew he'd have to do for me – the way he did for Pam.'

'Did he admit to killing Miss Wingate?' asked the chief inspector.

'Not in so many words,' was the reply. 'He wanted to know how much Pamela had told me about her meetings with him. When I tried to pretend I didn't know what he meant, he said he didn't believe me. "Women always talk," he said. "It's why you can never trust them. *She* talked . . . and look where it got her."' She shivered suddenly. 'I don't think he likes women very much.'

'What about Colquhoun?' said Douglas. 'Did he say anything about that?'

'He didn't mention Jock at all. Do you mean it *wasn't* an accident, what happened to Jock? But that's horrible!'

'It looks as if Colquhoun may have been another of your Dr Blake's recruits,' said Douglas. 'Perhaps he got cold feet about what he was asked to do.'

'I . . . I don't believe Jock was a traitor, any more than Pamela was,' said Margaret. 'He believed in a fairer system, that's all.' This wasn't exactly the case, but Rowlands was in no hurry to disillusion his daughter about a man she'd regarded as a friend, but whose political beliefs had led him to betray his country.

'Well, he's beyond caring about it now,' was all he said. 'And you're out of danger, thank Heaven.' He reached for his daughter's hand and squeezed it. 'You've had a very narrow escape.'

'Don't I know it! If it hadn't been for you and Betty . . . and Sergeant Jones, of course . . . By the way, where *is* Sergeant Jones?'

'I've sent him to the railway station, to see if anyone answering to Burton's description was seen leaving by that route. He abandoned the car, so he'll likely be on foot . . . Unless, o' course, he arranged for somebody to pick him up.'

'It was lucky for you that Sergeant Jones was so quick-witted,' said Rowlands. 'If he hadn't spotted the car – with you in it – when he did, this might have turned out to be a very different story.'

'I'll say!' cried Margaret. 'He ought to get a medal. He *will* get a medal, or commendation, or something, won't he, Chief Inspector?'

'Hmph,' said Douglas. 'We'll see about that. But since you've got to that part of the story, perhaps you could say what happened *after* Sergeant Jones saw you?'

'There's not a lot more to say, really. By the time we got to the Mill Pond, I knew it'd be touch and go whether or not I got out of it alive,' said Margaret calmly. 'When Gil said we were taking out a punt, I guessed he had something nasty in mind – although I was surprised when we didn't go upriver, towards Grantchester. It's quieter that way, with not many people about. You could drown somebody quite easily, without anybody seeing. So when I realised we'd be heading *down*river, past the colleges, I thought I'd have a better chance. I could shout for help – because I knew he wouldn't be able to handle the punt pole *and* fire a gun – or I could try and push him off balance into the river. But he must have guessed that I'd try something, because that's when he stuck me with that needle. I don't know what it was he injected me with, but it certainly knocked me out. After that, I don't remember anything more until you dragged me out of that punt, Daddy, and Betty stuck those beastly smelling-salts under my nose. I'm awfully glad,' she said fervently, 'that you happened to come along when you did, or I'd have been a goner, for sure.'

'Yes, it was a clever – diabolically clever – plan,' said her father. 'And like Burton's previous plans, it was rigged to look like something other than it was. Once the punt, with you in it, had been swept over the weir, it might have been days before the body or bodies were recovered. Burton would have taken care to get himself noticed when he booked the punt, and to leave evidence that there were two people in it, when it went over. He'll have made sure to give himself an alibi for the time of the so-called "accident". The police weren't likely to connect Montfitchet's car with a drowning accident downriver, and so he could quietly abandon the vehicle, and find his way back to London. Perhaps he arranged a lift with an obliging friend, as you suggested, Chief Inspector.'

'If he did, we'll find out,' said Douglas. 'He won't get away with it this time.'

'Yes, he's been good at getting away with things,' said

Rowlands. 'In the case of Pamela Wingate, he arranged things to make it seem as if her death was the result of a lovers' quarrel. When he met Pamela – through his friend Hugh Montfitchet – he immediately saw her as an opportunity to obtain information about the workings of Bletchley Park. At first, it was probably fairly minor stuff – the real intelligence was being supplied by Colquhoun, who had no idea of the name of the man to whom he was supplying it. But then Pamela, who was no doubt keen to impress Burton, with whom she fancied herself in love, saw Colquhoun leaving Hut 8 with the stolen documents. She told him she knew a man who was "well-connected in Whitehall", and who would pass on the documents to the Russians on Colquhoun's behalf. When she mentioned his name, Colquhoun realised that he knew Burton, because they'd been at Cambridge together. It was when Burton found out that she'd given him away that he knew he'd have to kill her – and Colquhoun too. He must have persuaded her to accompany him to Montfitchet's flat. Perhaps he told her they were going to make a clean breast of things . . . confess that they'd fallen in love, or some such. We'll never know – unless we catch him.'

'We'll catch him,' said the chief inspector. 'Never fear.'

'Anyway, he killed Pamela at Montfitchet's flat, and then left, wearing Montfitchet's spare uniform, and making sure he was spotted by at least one witness. That part of the plan went a bit awry when the witness, Captain Harbison, was posted abroad two days later. But otherwise it all went like clockwork. Burton took the next available opportunity to return the uniform he'd borrowed to Montfitchet's flat (he had a key, of course) and took up his role as Montfitchet's loyal friend, offering moral support when Pamela's body was discovered. Without Harbison's testimony, however, there wasn't enough evidence to convict Montfitchet, but Burton knew from the information he was getting from Colquhoun that MI6 suspected a naval man as the source of the Bletchley Park leaks, so Montfitchet remained a suspect. He'd already learnt from Pamela that she'd told Colquhoun who he was, and so Burton knew he'd have to act quickly. Once again, he faked the murder to look like something it wasn't – in this case, suicide – by choosing a method of killing that might easily have been interpreted that way . . .' At this point in Rowlands' recital, the chief inspector gave an embarrassed cough. 'And making sure the police found a note Colquhoun had written to Sylvia Pritchard, which also pointed to that conclusion.'

'How did you tumble to him, Fred?' said Douglas. 'You seemed to get there quicker than the rest of us.'

'Oh, there wasn't anything I could put my finger on, at first,' said Rowlands. 'I just kept coming up against the evidence against Montfitchet. It was all too neat, somehow, too "pat". First there was the matter of the witness, Harbison, happening along just at the precise moment a man he *thought* was Montfitchet was leaving Montfitchet's flat . . . It occurred to me that it might have been the other way around . . . I mean that whoever it was he saw, dressed in Montfitchet's uniform, waited until he – the witness – came along, before showing himself. Then there was the fact that Montfitchet's car – a very conspicuous one – was seen in the vicinity of the railway station around the time Colquhoun was killed. I couldn't see the logic in it – I mean, why use a car that was instantly recognisable as belonging to a certain individual, unless your plan was to incriminate that person? As soon as I saw *that*, it all fell into place. Burton and Montfitchet were the same age – and, I gather, around the same height, build and general appearance. They'd been to the same school and university. It seemed to me that this was a case of similarity being mistaken for identity – a confusion deliberately fostered, in this instance. It's something one learns to look out for, as a blind man,' he added, half-apologetically. 'Otherwise it's very easy to mistake one thing for another.'

'Well, whatever the reasoning behind it, you were proved right again, Fred,' said the chief inspector. 'But if I'm to get on with catching Burton, I'd better go and see whether my sergeant has had any luck at the railway station.'

'If I might make a suggestion?'

'Yes, Fred?'

'I think you should call off the search for Burton . . . at least for now.'

The chief inspector, who had risen to his feet, sat down again. 'All right,' he said. 'I'm listening.'

'It strikes me,' said Rowlands, 'that just at present we've got an advantage over Gilbert Burton, in that we know something he doesn't – which is that Margaret is alive. As soon as he discovers that's not the case, we lose our advantage, and Meg is put at risk.'

'We'll see to it that she comes to no harm *this* time – won't we, WPC Briggs?'

'Yes, sir.'

'I've no doubt of it,' said Rowlands. 'But that isn't the point. For as long as Burton believes himself safe, he'll be much more likely to play into our hands.'

'And how are we going to get him to do that?' said Alasdair Douglas warily.

'Well,' said Rowlands. 'Here's my idea . . .'

Chapter Eighteen

Next day, a small item appeared in the early edition of the *Cambridge Evening News*: TWO MISSING, FEARED DROWNED, IN PUNT TRAGEDY. A brief paragraph followed:

A young woman and her male companion, both as yet unidentified, are believed drowned, after their hired punt was thought to have gone over the weir at Jesus Lock, at around 11 a.m. yesterday. The bodies of the couple, described by Mr William Flanagan, prop. of Scudamore Punt Hire, as 'young and well-spoken', have yet to be recovered, and may have been swept downriver by the unusually heavy flow of water brought about by the accidental opening of the Mill Pond sluice gates. 'I don't know how it happened,' said lock-keeper Albert Gotobed. 'With the rain we had earlier in the month, the river was higher than usual for the time of year, so the gates ought to have been kept shut.' A punt, containing a hamper and an empty bottle of champagne, was found drifting along past Stourbridge Common. Police have asked for witnesses who saw the young couple to come forward . . .

'Which is stretching the truth as far as it will go,' remarked the chief inspector, in a disgruntled tone. 'I don't like it, Fred, I never have – playing fast and loose with the facts. I had to call in a number of favours to get my man at the *Evening News* to publish the piece. And I don't see what good it'll do. If, as we think, Burton has gone back to London, then he won't even see the piece.'

'No, but Aubrey Blake will,' said Rowlands. 'And you can bet *he'll* let Burton know that his plan's succeeded. The main thing is to lull him – Burton, that is – into a false sense of security. If he thinks he's got rid of Margaret, and that no one suspects his hand in it, he's more likely to make a mistake.'

'I hope you're right,' said the other gloomily. 'I had the assistant commissioner on the phone earlier, wanting to know what progress we'd made with the Bletchley affair. These security breaches look bad for the country, he says. We're fighting a war, he says. We can't afford this kind of slip-up, he says . . .'

'Did he agree to write the note?' said Rowlands, who hadn't been paying attention to this tirade. They were once more in Douglas's office at Scotland Yard.

'I assume you're not referring to the assistant commissioner?' replied his friend with heavy sarcasm.

'Aye, he agreed. Wanted to know what it was all about, naturally.'

'You didn't tell him, I hope?'

'O' course I didnae tell him – or at least not the reason we wanted him to write that note. He was understandably curious about why we wanted Burton to go to the flat. I fobbed him off by saying it was a matter of confirming an identification. He seemed to accept that.'

'Good,' said Rowlands. 'What did the note say?'

'I told him to write what you'd said to write: "Could you bring me Pamela's photograph from the flat? I want to have it with me." He's still stuck on the girl, evidently, so it'll make sense to Burton, I imagine. And since Burton only lives two streets away, it'll be no bother for him to pop in.'

'He's got a key,' said Rowlands. 'Did the note say it was urgent?'

'Aye, I told Montfitchet to make that very clear. "Don't delay. I haven't much time." That should do the trick.'

Rowlands hoped he was right about that. Montfitchet's Mount Street flat was being watched around the clock – as was Burton's flat in Bruton Street. His office at the Admiralty was also under constant surveillance. He'd attended a reception there on the night of the supposed drowning, during which – according to Douglas's watchers – Burton had made himself as conspicuous as he had been at the American Embassy, on the night Rowlands had been a guest there. 'Wanted to make sure he was noticed,' said Douglas. He'd been spotted having lunch at his club earlier the same day – no more than a couple of hours after Margaret had been saved from a watery grave. 'He must have got hold of a fast car to do it in under two hours.'

'Either that, or whoever picked him up on the Chesterton Road was a fast driver,' agreed Rowlands.

'Well, he'll need a very fast car indeed to escape what's coming to him,' was the chief inspector's laconic reply. Because an examination of the abandoned Alvis, which had been towed from its parking place at the Mill Pond, had revealed some incriminating evidence. 'This'll put the noose around his neck good and proper,' Douglas had said, in what for him was a tone of high glee. 'They always make one mistake, the clever ones.' Now he and Rowlands sat, in an atmosphere of barely suppressed tension. The anticipation of action was always the hardest thing, thought Rowlands. It was like waiting to go 'over the top' or for a bombardment to start. The chief inspector fiddled with his pipe. 'Blessed thing's never been the same since I dropped it, during that last bad air raid,' he muttered. 'How's that girl of yours, by the way? Recovered from her nasty experience, I hope?'

'She's fine. Her mother's pleased to have her at home, of course. But she's impatient to get back to work. I've told her she's got to lie low for a little while longer.'

'Aye, she mustn't appear before this affair is over. We don't want our man to get wind of what's in store.'

The telephone rang: a short, shrill burst, which Douglas answered on the second ring.

'Yes?' He listened to what was said, then replied curtly, 'All right. We're on our way.' He replaced the receiver. 'He's left the office,' he said to Rowlands, who was already on his feet. 'I think we're in business.'

* * *

301

The Wolseley was waiting outside, with the engine running. They got in, Douglas barked an order, and they set off at speed, hurtling across the corner of Trafalgar Square and down Pall Mall, then sharp right into St James's Street and across Piccadilly, dodging a phalanx of approaching traffic, Rowlands surmised, from the blare of car horns. Then they were into Old Bond Street, and turning left into Bruton Street, and across the north end of Berkeley Square, to finish up outside the Mount Street building where Montfitchet's flat was to be found, in under ten minutes. Which was still cutting it pretty fine, said the chief inspector.

'Are you sure you want to go through with this, Fred?'

'Of course.'

'It's likely he'll be armed.'

'I know.'

'Well, don't take any unnecessary risks. Now where's that man got to? Anyone seen Prewett?'

A constable came panting up. 'Here, sir.'

'Have you carried out my orders?'

'Yes, sir. Door on the latch, blackout curtains drawn, sir.'

'All right,' said Douglas. 'Now make yourselves scarce, you men. And get that car moved. We don't want our quarry to take fright.' He handed certain items to Rowlands. 'Don't forget these. And sing out if he tries anything. Remember – we'll be close by.'

'Taxi approaching, sir,' called the officer who'd been designated as lookout. It was the signal for Rowlands to enter the building.

Eschewing the lift, he took the stairs to the first floor,

two at a time. As arranged, the door to Montfitchet's flat was on the latch; he slipped inside and released the catch, locking the door behind him. Moving as quietly as he could, he crossed the room, and took his seat in an armchair facing the door, beside which, he knew from Douglas's description, a lamp stood on a low table. A photograph of Pamela Wingate in a silver frame stood beside it, Douglas had said.

'So he'll likely make for that first,' the chief inspector had added.

Breathing slowly and evenly to calm the rapid beating of his heart, Rowlands had no sooner settled himself in the appointed place than he heard the groan of the lift ascending and, a moment or two later, the scratch of a key in the door. Seconds later, the door opened, and he braced himself for discovery, and for the confrontation that would follow, when the light was switched on. Instead, to his surprise, the new arrival seemed as intent on concealment as he was: stealthy sounds indicated that the former was moving around in the dark, feeling his way with the help of the furniture, but with no very great expertise – once knocking into a chair that was in his path, and swearing under his breath as he caught his foot on the edge of a mat.

His destination, it became apparent, was Montfitchet's bedroom, or dressing room, because a moment later, Rowlands heard the creak of a wardrobe being opened, followed by the sound of coat hangers being roughly shoved along a rail, as if the intruder were searching for something in the pockets of the clothes that hung there. The search must have proved unsuccessful, for after a few minutes, he came back into the room where Rowlands was waiting for him.

'Are these what you're looking for?'

Rowlands's voice, coming out of the darkness in which the flat was shrouded, seemed, momentarily, to paralyse the other, for there was a shocked silence before he spoke.

'What the hell?' said Gilbert Burton. In the same moment, Rowlands switched on the lamp that stood beside him, and held up the gloves – an expensive pigskin pair – that had been left in the glove compartment of the Alvis, two days before.

'I suppose you recognise these?' Rowlands went on. 'Driving gloves – rather good ones, with a smart monogram: "G.B." Can you explain how they came to be in Hugh Montfitchet's car?'

'Easily.' In the intervening seconds since he had first become aware of Rowlands's presence, Burton had recovered his sangfroid. 'I lent them to him. Least I could do. Hugh was always lending *me* things.'

'His car,' agreed Rowlands. 'His uniform. Even his girl. Although I don't suppose you asked his permission in *that* instance.'

'I didn't need his "permission",' said the other contemptuously. 'Silly little tart practically threw herself at me.'

'You killed her.'

'What if I did? She was getting to be a nuisance. Always on at me about wanting to get married – to me, not Hugh. Not the most loyal *fiancée*, our Pam. If you ask me, old Hugh's well out of *that* little affair.'

'You framed him for Pamela's murder,' said Rowlands.

'Rather clever, wasn't it?' Burton giggled suddenly – a sound that made the hairs stand up on the back of the other's neck. 'Yes, I pretended to be him for an evening. It wasn't difficult. Persuaded the chit that we had to "talk it over" with her intended. Got her round here, on the night Hughie was expected back on leave, slipped her the dope in a glass of Scotch and . . . she never felt a thing. Then all I had to do was don Hugh's uniform – he does look so handsome in it! – and wait for that ass Harbison to come out of his flat . . . I'd heard the gramophone earlier, so I knew he was in there. Really,' he said, with another giggle, 'I impress *myself* sometimes.'

'You killed Colquhoun,' said Rowlands, ignoring this burst of self-congratulation, 'when you found out that Pamela had given away who you were. You knew that you couldn't afford for it to become known that a senior civil servant with a job in the War Office was in the pay of Russia.'

'It's true that I killed Colquhoun,' said the spy. 'He would have betrayed me – and the cause. He was already starting to have second thoughts about what he'd been ordered to do. Even if that stupid girl hadn't given me away, I'd have had to put an end to him, eventually. But you're wrong if you think I did what I did for money. I don't expect you, with your narrow little ideas about *patriotism*, to understand, but I serve a higher power. One that has to do with the greater good.'

'I've heard that kind of claptrap before,' said Rowlands. 'Serving the "greater good" usually means having no respect for individual lives.'

'There you *are*, you see!' cried Burton. 'You've just

proved my point. You sentimental fools, with your gush about "individual lives", haven't the least idea of the new age that is upon us. An age when the "individual" will be swept away by the tides of history . . . when the world will be free from the profiteering class wars that have deformed society. An age—'

'However you like to dress it up,' said Rowlands quietly, 'you sold your country to the enemy.'

'There you go again!' This time there was no laughter in Burton's voice. 'Trotting out your hand-me-down platitudes about the "enemy", when all the time the real enemies are all around us. Look at the city!' he almost screamed. 'Look at the silk-hatted boards of directors, making money off the backs of the proletariat.'

'Was it for the sake of the proletariat that you murdered an innocent girl?' said Rowlands, suddenly sick of this posturing.

'You're referring to your daughter, I imagine – since the lovely Wingate was anything *but* "innocent",' said Gil Burton. 'Yes, I'm sorry about that. But she – your Margaret – got in the way. I simply couldn't afford to let her live. You do see that, don't you? Or perhaps you don't,' he added, as Rowlands started to reply. 'No matter. I'd love to stay here chatting,' he went on. 'But I need to get on, if I'm to be . . . well, where I'm going, tonight.'

'Somewhere neutral, I suppose,' said Rowlands. 'Ireland, perhaps – where you can lie low until the fuss dies down. And then, ultimately, Moscow.'

'How very astute you are!' said Gil Burton. 'And what a pleasure it's been, talking to you. But I'll have to bring our little chat to an end.' There was the sound of a safety-catch being released. 'I wish I could have made you understand how unimportant individual lives are, in the scheme of things. Alas, there's no time, so you'll have to take my word for it.'

The door opened. 'Drop the gun,' said Chief Inspector Douglas.

In that instant, two things happened: the gun went off, with a report loud enough to bring plaster down from the ceiling. Rowlands supposed that the bullet had missed him, since he wasn't dead – or not yet. Because, his first attempt having failed, Burton must have leapt across the room like a cat, for the next sensation of which Rowlands was conscious was that of a gun barrel being held to his head.

'Don't think I wouldn't shoot,' said Burton, his breath sounding ragged. 'You'd better let me go, or it'll be the worse for your blind friend.'

'Drop the gun,' said Douglas again. 'You're only making things worse for yourself, Burton.'

At which Gilbert Burton gave a crow of laughter. 'What difference does it make, if I kill him, or not?' he said. 'You'll still hang me. This way, I've got a chance . . . Come on.' He jerked Rowlands to his feet, still holding the gun to the latter's temple. 'Now we're going to walk *slowly* towards the door,' he said. 'You' – to the chief inspector – 'stand aside. And call off your men. You know I won't hesitate to pull the trigger, if anyone tries any funny business.'

'Don't listen to him,' said Rowlands, but Douglas hesitated.

'All right, get back,' he ordered the officers who'd accompanied him. 'Let him pass.' And so Rowlands had no choice but to start descending the stairs, his arm gripped by his captor, who seemed determined to allow as little space between them as possible. Painfully, step by step, they reached the door that led onto the street.

'Open it,' said Burton to the policeman who stood there.

'Do as he says,' called Douglas from the stairs. Then they were outside.

'Keep walking,' said Burton, letting go of Rowlands's arm, but keeping the gun pressed against the small of his back. Rowlands did as he was told, conscious that any sudden move might be his last. Across the street, a car's engine started up. At the sound, Burton quickened his pace, pushing Rowlands ahead of him as he hurried towards it.

What happened next, Rowlands wasn't entirely sure. As he reached the kerb, a few paces ahead of Burton, another car came along the street at speed, from the direction of Berkeley Square. It struck Burton with some force; Rowlands heard the impact, and the cry that followed it. He himself had only avoided being hit by a whisker, it seemed to him afterwards. Nor did the car slow down, but sped away along the street. Shocked by what had happened, Rowlands turned back to see if there was anything he could do for the injured man. As he bent over Burton, who was lying in the middle of the road, the first car – the one towards which, it had seemed to Rowlands, the spy had been eagerly hurrying – drove away. At the same moment, Douglas came running over, followed by two of his men.

'All right, Burton,' he said. 'You can give me the gun, now.' He took it from the man's unresisting grasp. 'Call an ambulance,' he said to one of the officers. 'And get this street cordoned off.'

But that it was too late for Burton must have been evident to both the senior policeman and the dying man himself. 'Sorry . . . to disappoint you . . . Chief Inspector,' he gasped, between laboured breaths. 'But . . . you'll . . . never . . . see me . . . in court . . .'

'Don't talk,' said Douglas. 'The ambulance is on its way.'

'Too . . . late,' said Burton. After which, he said nothing more.

'Yes, we'd had a tip-off from one of our sources that the traitor had to be somebody with access to naval intelligence,' said Iris Barnes. 'Somebody working at the Admiralty – which of course Burton was – or with connections to somebody there.'

'So you suspected Hugh Montfitchet?'

'Montfitchet was never a suspect until that business with the Wingate girl,' was the reply. 'It was then that we traced the leak back to Bletchley Park, and things started to look a lot more complicated.'

'That's one way of putting it,' said Rowlands. A day or two had passed since events had come to such a shocking conclusion in that Mayfair street, and they were once more comfortably ensconced in the library of Miss Barnes's club in St James's. The sun being over the yard-arm, as she put it, they were drinking whisky and soda. 'Yes, for a while it did seem as if Montfitchet might be our man,' she said. 'We never really thought of Burton – although, with hindsight, he was the more obvious candidate. But with the collapse of Montfitchet's alibi for the murder of Pamela Wingate . . .'

'Thanks to the efforts of Gil Burton,' put in Rowlands.

'Indeed. Well, it certainly *looked* as if he was the traitor. Whereas in fact . . .'

'In fact it was Burton who betrayed not only his country, but his friend, by setting him up as the "fall guy",' said Rowlands, taking a sip of his drink. 'It was cleverly done, the way he made sure he'd be seen leaving Montfitchet's flat, at precisely the time he knew Montfitchet would be most open to suspicion.'

'Yes, and he cultivated Pamela, whom he met through Montfitchet, as a second string to his bow,' said Miss Barnes. 'He was already running Colquhoun as an agent, although Colquhoun wasn't aware who his "handler" was, until Pamela mentioned his name. She thought it'd be a coup for her, to have captured Colquhoun, and to persuade him to hand over the stolen documents to her lover. What she didn't realise was that in blowing Burton's cover, she was signing Colquhoun's death warrant – and her own. Colquhoun was an idealist, like so many who've signed up to the communist cause. He thought he could help to shorten the war by leaking naval and military secrets to the Russians. When he realised that this had resulted in an increase of attacks on convoys by German U-boats, he was horrified. He let his handler, Burton, know that he wouldn't be a part of it any more, and Burton killed him.'

'Then used Montfitchet's car to make his getaway from the murder scene,' said Rowlands. 'The station master noticed the car, but not the man driving it.'

'He was clever,' said Iris. 'A pity he used that cleverness

in the service of the wrong cause. Although there's a certain irony in that,' she added. 'Given that . . .' She broke off, as if she had said more than she meant to.

'Given what?'

His companion took a sip of her drink. 'Nothing like it, after a hard day, is there?' she said; then, when he remained silent, 'Given that, if he'd waited a few months, he'd have found that we were on the same side. Oh yes,' she went on. 'I have it on good authority that, as of the middle of next month, the Russians will be our new best friends. Comrade Stalin will make a good ally, for as long as it suits him to remain one. He'll be granted *official* access to British military intelligence, instead of having to steal it. Fortunes of war, I suppose.' She took another sip.

'Then why . . . ?' It was his turn to break off.

'Why what?'

'Nothing.'

'Now you're being mysterious.' Although it seemed to Rowlands that she had been expecting this question.

'All right. Why was Burton killed, if the people he was working for knew that Britain and Russia would soon be allies?'

'It *is* a bit of a puzzle, isn't it?' said Iris Barnes. 'Another Scotch?'

'No, thanks.'

'Go on. You've earnt it.' She touched a bell. 'I'd imagine,' she went on, 'that having one of their top men put on trial for murder might have been rather an embarrassment at a critical stage in negotiations . . . Two more whiskies, please,' she said to the waiter.

'Yes, I can see that it might have been embarrassing, as

you say,' said Rowlands, when the man had gone to carry out this order. Embarrassing for both sides, he thought, but did not say. Because of course there had been *two* cars that night in Mount Street, hadn't there? The first, which had been waiting outside Montfitchet's flat, and towards which Burton had rushed so eagerly, must have been the one delegated by his spymasters to take him to the Pembrokeshire coast, and from thence to neutral Ireland. If that surmise were correct, then who had been driving the *second* car, which had come out of nowhere, it seemed, to destroy him, and all his grandiose dreams? The more Rowlands thought about it, the less he liked the question. One thing was certain: he wouldn't get a straight answer from the woman sitting opposite him.

Their whiskies arrived. 'Well,' said Miss Barnes. 'Here's luck.' They clinked glasses. 'I expect you'll be glad to be getting back to normal life, now it's all over.'

'Oh yes,' he replied. 'Very glad.' But he wondered if life would ever seem entirely normal again.

The three o'clock bus from Ovingdean stopped at the end of the esplanade, and a few people got off. There were two couples, arguing between themselves about which programme to see at the local picture house, and a family group, discussing which of the various tea-shops along the front might still be open for custom.

'I already told you, Ma. Snow's closed last week. There's that fish and chip place in the Lanes. They do a nice pot o' tea there.'

One man was on his own. Rowlands waited until the others had gone by and then, drawing his companion along with him, stepped forward. 'Mr Harvey?'

'Yes. That is . . . do call me John. I've got used to first names, these past few weeks.'

'Glad you could make it, John. This is George Fairfield, whom I spoke of when we last met. George is a veteran of the last war, as all we older men are.'

'How do you do?' said Harvey.

'I should mention that George can't hear you, so the best way of communicating with him is by spelling out the letters of what you want to say one by one on the palm of his hand. Since that's rather a laborious process, it might be better to wait until we're sitting down, having tea. In the meantime, I suggest we all go for a walk along the front. George is a grand walker.'

'Do you mean to say he can't see either?' said John Harvey, as if the implications of this had only just struck him.

'That's right. But he knows you're here, don't you, George?'

Rowlands tapped the older man on the wrist, and at once he said, 'Hello, young feller! Mr Rowlands here tells me you're new to this game.'

'Yes . . . I . . . Can you tell him I'm pleased to meet him?' said Harvey as the three men fell into step.

'He knows that already, because you're here,' said Rowlands. 'Why don't you take his other arm? That way, we can all keep pace with one another.'

They began walking, three abreast, along the broad esplanade. It was an occasion when Rowlands was glad of his white stick, and the fact that Fairfield wore dark glasses – if only to signal to oncoming pedestrians the reason why their party was taking up so much of the available space.

'Like the sea, do you, young feller?' said Fairfield, after they had been walking for a while. His voice had the curiously flat timbre of the deaf. 'I never saw it till I went to France. Country boy, see? *Now* I never miss a day, if I can help it.' He laughed. 'Can't see it or hear it, but I can *smell* it. Nothing like the smell of sea air. Feel the breeze in my face, too. Lovely warm breeze, ain't it?'

When they had walked the length of the front, skirting the gun emplacements and the groups of soldiers on leave, some with their girlfriends, Rowlands suggested that they should all return to West House for tea.

'If we're lucky, we'll be in time for some of Mrs Clarke's carrot cake,' he said. 'And George can show you his latest model ship. He's made some beauties over the years. Very delicate work. You'd think he'd grown up in a coastal town like this one, instead of in rural Shropshire.' Harvey murmured a reply, but his thoughts were elsewhere, Rowlands guessed. 'Do you think,' he went on, taking a chance that the lad might be in a more receptive mood than he had been at their previous meeting, 'you might get to like living here, John? It's not so bad when you get used to it – lots of good sea air, as George says, and there's plenty to do for young people. Why, my two elder daughters say they don't even miss London, when they're home on leave – which says something, considering that they were born and bred there.'

'You're married, then?'

'Well, yes. At least, so my wife tells me.' Rowlands laughed.

'Sorry. Of course you are,' said Harvey. 'I only meant . . .'

'A good number of us older men are married, with families,' said Rowlands, knowing this was what the young man needed to hear. 'I got married just after the last war, as a matter of fact. I was young, then, like you, with my life ahead of me. Being blind didn't alter that – for me, or for any of the other St Dunstan's men. It just made us more determined to make a decent life for ourselves.'

'Thank you,' said Harvey. His tone was thoughtful. 'I've enjoyed our walk . . . and meeting Mr Fairfield.'

'Oh, George likes company,' said Rowlands. 'He gets plenty of visitors, too. You don't often meet a man with such a capacity for enjoying life.'

'No,' said John Harvey. 'You don't.'

As if he sensed they were talking about him, Fairfield came to a stop in the middle of the path, drew a deep breath, and let it out again.

'There,' he said. 'Didn't I say? Nothing to beat the air in Brighton. Like wine, it is. That's what I say. Like wine.'

Acknowledgements

With thanks to Julie Kavanagh and Vic Blickem, for a memorable day at Bletchley Park, which was the starting point for this book. Attentive readers will have noticed the similarity between some of the characters in this section and that of historical figures associated with Bletchley. 'Anthony Twining' owes something to Alan Turing, just as 'Mostyn Box' bears some relation to Dillwyn Knox, 'Angus Murchison' to Alasdair Denniston, 'Jock Colquhoun' to John Cairncross, 'Aubrey Blake' to Anthony Blunt and 'Gil Burton' to Guy Burgess. These are, however fictional characters, and so any anomalies must be seen in this light.

CHRISTINA KONING has worked as a journalist, reviewing fiction for *The Times*, and has taught Creative Writing at the University of Oxford and Birkbeck, University of London. From 2013 to 2015, she was Royal Literary Fund Fellow at Newnham College, Cambridge. She won the Encore Prize in 1999 and was longlisted for the Orange Prize in the same year.

@christina.koning
christinakoning.com